Praise for the Retired Witches Mysteries

"Fun and highly entertaining . . . you will instantly love these charming characters."   —Moonlight Rendezvous

"To say I was totally engaged would be an understatement. This story had me spellbound. Kudos to Joyce and Jim, they had me completely captivated!"
—Escape with Dolly Cas Into A Good Book

"A witch's brew of mystery, paranormal, and fun. Positively magical! . . . The story was well plotted and filled with incredible detail . . . The writing so fantastic that I felt like I was much more than a mere reader, but indeed a quiet observer hiding in the shadows of each scene."
—Lisa Ks Book Reviews

"A fun read . . . I enjoyed this story that boasted great conversations, a small town magical feel and a supporting cast that envelops our main protagonists."
—Dru's Book Musings

"A delightful premise, a couple of enchanting protagonists, and cats as essential familiars . . . It is a promising series for urban fantasy and paranormal mystery readers."
—*Library Journal*

PUTTING ON THE WITCH

Joyce and Jim Lavene

BERKLEY PRIME CRIME
New York

BERKLEY PRIME CRIME
Published by Berkley
An imprint of Penguin Random House LLC
375 Hudson Street, New York, New York 10014

ISBN: 9780425268278

First Edition: October 2016

Printed in the United States of America
1   3   5   7   9   10   8   6   4   2

Cover art by Mary Ann Lasher
Cover design by Katie Anderson and Lesley Worrell
Book design by Laura K. Corless

I'd like to dedicate this book to Joyce Lavene, who passed on October 20, 2015. My loving wife and partner in writing. We were married for 44 years and wrote together for 20 years. It was a wonderful time and she will be missed dearly.

CHAPTER 1

Olivia's jaw dropped. "Drago? Is that really you?"

It was hard to say which of us was more startled to see him there at our witches' paraphernalia shop, Smuggler's Arcane. Dorothy took a step back. Brian took her hand. Elsie's eyes narrowed. And I stared. I couldn't help it.

So this was Dorothy's infamous father. He looked like a pirate, dressed in tight leather pants and a leather vest over his white cotton shirt. He had a slash of a smile on his lean, tan face, as though he were laughing at us. Tall and thin, his hair was white and cut close to his well-shaped head. His eyes were a shade of brilliant blue.

"I've come to see you, Dorothy," he said. "I think it's about time that we met, don't you?"

As he advanced toward Dorothy, Olivia put her ghostly form between them.

"Oh no. I've worked too hard all these years to keep you away from her. You can't have her, Drago. If you knew what

I had to go through to keep her a secret—you'd know you can't just barge in here and take her away."

Drago put his hand right through Olivia to take Dorothy's. "You are so lovely. So like your mother." He glanced at Olivia when she tried to keep herself between them. "At least as lovely as she was when you were born."

"I'm warning you!"

He was a powerful witch. There wasn't much we could do about him being there if he wanted to stay. I was disappointed that our protection spells hadn't held up better. That would have to be the subject of another time.

Drago laughed, puffed out his cheeks and directed a breath of air at Olivia. She was thrown out of the way as surely as if a hurricane had come into the room.

Olivia Dunst was Dorothy's mother. She'd only been dead a short time and was having trouble using her ghost powers to their best effect. She still looked like her old self, if you were looking at her through a glass of water. Fine blond hair framed spritely features that she'd carefully maintained until the day she'd died in her late fifties. Her gray eyes were less well defined since she'd come back as a ghost, but her voice was never in question.

"You stop that right now, Drago Rasmun!" Olivia came back at him without hesitation from the side of the shop that held clothes. "Leave my little girl alone."

The little girl in question was Dorothy Lane, full-time librarian, and now full-time witch as she followed in her parents' footsteps. She'd become a member of our coven last year while we were looking for three witches to replace us, as we were three witches who were ready for retirement in Boca.

That would be me—Molly Renard—Elsie Langston and Olivia at the time. She'd still been alive back then. We'd wanted to give our coven and our spell book to three other witches who would continue the tradition in our hometown of Wilmington, North Carolina. There had been witches from our coven for hundreds of years. It was as important to the area as the Cape Fear River and the Atlantic Ocean. Not something to mess around with!

But that was before Olivia was killed and our spell book was stolen. It seemed like such a long time ago. The last year had been a difficult one for us.

And now Dorothy's evil witch father was here. Could anything else go wrong?

"Why don't we let Dorothy decide if she wants to spend time with me?" Drago suggested.

Dorothy, in her twenties, tall like her father and a little plain with her short brown hair and matching eyes, looked a trifle starstruck.

Up until last year, Dorothy had thought she was an orphan. Olivia had given her up at birth to keep her father from finding her. It was a huge sacrifice but one Olivia was willing to make so her little girl wouldn't be ruined by her father, who'd been designated an "outsider" by the Grand Council of Witches. Elsie and I knew nothing about Dorothy. If you knew Olivia, you'd know what a major feat this was for her not to tell us, her best friends.

Olivia had located Dorothy as an adult, and we'd recruited her for our coven. Besides learning the beginning magic most young boys and girls learned when they were starting to walk and talk, Dorothy had also learned about her father. All she'd ever heard about him were stories about his powerful yet evil lineage and magic.

I wasn't privy to the discussion between mother and daughter about how Olivia had allowed herself to be seduced by an evil witch, but I was certain it was interesting.

"I think—" Dorothy paused and shot a glance at Brian, her new boyfriend. "I think I'd like a cup of tea. Really strong tea."

Brian Fuller was a powerful young witch in his own right. He was her exact opposite in that his family was not only magically powerful but also politically so. His grandfather was on the Grand Council and held great sway among witches. Brian was wealthy and careless, and he knew magic that he'd cobbled together since his family had taken almost no interest in him.

Elsie and I were trying to convince him that he should join our coven. He had power but had never learned control. Having Dorothy with us was turning out to be a strong incentive.

He stepped up and took Dorothy's free hand in his and gave it a squeeze before he smiled provocatively at her father. Brian was handsome and sure of himself in a way that comes from too much money and not enough common sense. "Good to meet you, sir. Dorothy and I have been spending a lot of time together. You might know my grandfather—Abdon Fuller—he's on the Grand Council of Witches. And my parents are Schadt and Yuriza Fuller. Fuller is a respected name in the witch community."

Drago's expression was less than welcoming and definitely not impressed. He looked as though he wanted to blow Brian away as he had Olivia. He didn't release Dorothy's other hand, nor did he offer his hand to Brian. "Nice to meet you, Mr. Fuller. I'm afraid I don't know your parents, although your grandfather, Abdon, and I have crossed swords from time to time. I think the last time was during the French Revolution."

Brian would have had to be a moron not to hear the hostility in Drago's voice. Thankfully Brian, with his thick brown hair and lovely blue eyes, was neither a fool nor a moron. He also didn't plan to let Drago take away his girlfriend.

"Maybe it would be better if you left, Drago." His tone was hard on the name. "What's that about anyway? Related to the dragon?"

"Yes." Drago was quick to claim his heritage. "Perhaps

it would be better if you left, Mr. Fuller. What's that about—too much in the gut?"

"Why don't we have some tea?" Elsie suggested with a toss of her fading curly red hair. "I think we could all use a cup or two and certainly a time-out. I'll get some water started."

I was relieved when she gestured to the kettle and murmured a spell for hot water. The kettle filled and the hot plate turned red. In short, everything went exactly as it should.

We'd had some problems with our magic the last few years. What had once been simple tasks for our magic had become uncertain mountains of anxiety. Would the magic work or wouldn't it?

Elsie's magic had begun to fade first. She was about twelve years older than Olivia and me. As our magic had begun to fade from simple nonuse, Elsie's magic became even more unpredictable. We were never quite sure what would happen when she muttered a spell.

This was a tricky situation in which not to be absolutely sure about our magic.

Obviously Drago was more powerful than all of us—probably combined. No doubt that was one reason the council had banned him. They tended to be afraid of anything or anyone they couldn't control, just like people without magic.

He could take Dorothy and we couldn't stop him. Even given time to prepare, I wasn't sure if the three of us could fend him off. And I wasn't sure if Dorothy would help us or not. After all, he was her father. For all the stories she'd heard from Olivia about him being evil, there also were the stories of how much Olivia had loved him. It had to be confusing.

Brian released his hold on her hand to allow her to go with her father. He followed behind them with an angry, protective expression on his handsome young face.

And despite all the nightmare stories we'd heard about Drago and his brand of outsider magic, he finally nodded and led Dorothy to the table set in the middle of Smuggler's Arcane. He sat beside her and talked to her in low tones. She giggled a few times.

Olivia seemed ready to burst seeing them together, knowing there was nothing she could do to get rid of him. She'd done everything she could while she was alive, but parents' influence changes once a child becomes an adult.

I was going through the same thing with my son, Mike, who was in college. It wasn't easy to see children grow and begin making their own, sometimes bad decisions.

"Chamomile or green tea?" Elsie asked as I hurried behind the counter to help her.

"Whatever you have on hand is fine," Drago said. "I've come a long way and waited a long time for this moment. It was worth every second."

He turned away to study his daughter again and take her hand. His eyes said she was the most wonderful thing he'd ever seen as he asked about her life and magic. Dorothy being Dorothy, she quickly spilled everything about herself. She was even worse than her mother about keeping secrets.

But I loved that ingenuous quality to her.

"Do you think we should send some kind of terrible curse at him while he's not looking?" Elsie asked me.

I admit that I was holding my mother's amulet as she spoke. I didn't think it would put a curse on Drago, but I might use it for protection against him. We all knew why he was here. There wasn't one of us who wouldn't lay down our life to keep Dorothy safe.

"I doubt if we could," I finally answered, though I knew she was only joking. "He's so much stronger than us. Let's hope he doesn't try anything. Maybe he really is just here for a friendly visit."

Elsie made a *humphing* sound in the back of her throat.

"And I'm the queen of Sheba. But I suppose you're right. We shouldn't attack him willy-nilly. We need to be together on this. I don't know about Dorothy, but take a look at Brian's face. He'd be willing to banish Drago to the underworld."

She was right, of course. But what young man was comfortable around his girlfriend's father? We had no real sense of Drago at all—only what the council and Olivia had said about him.

"We should wait and see what happens."

"Wait and see what happens?" Olivia came behind the counter with us as we put cups of tea on a tray to take to the table. "This is the Alamo, ladies. We need to strike hard and fast if we don't want to end up dead."

"He knew we were coming," I reminded her as I added sugar and milk to the tray. "He was already here, and could have struck us down as we walked into the shop. Our wards weren't strong enough to keep him out. I think we should give him the benefit of the doubt."

"I don't see where we have much choice anyway." Elsie added a small bowl of lemon slices.

"That's easy for the two of you to say! You don't know Drago and the things he's capable of," Olivia said. "And that's not your daughter he's threatening. What if it was Mike or Aleese?"

Dorothy laughed. She seemed to be enjoying her father's company. Given that she didn't know him either, he seemed to be pleasant enough. He was very handsome and charming, probably the traits that had led Olivia to take up with him in the first place. If he decided to take Dorothy with him, I wasn't sure we could discourage her from going. What a life he could offer her.

And being on the good side of the Council of Witches wasn't exactly enough to tip the scales. Dorothy had already run into them and seen what they were like—including Brian's grandfather.

"Ah, tea!" Drago sat back as we put the tray on the table. "The old-fashioned way. Ladies, you've made a splendid home for yourselves here. Am I to assume Dorothy is part of your coven?"

"Yes." Brian leaned forward and glared at him. "So am I."

Without a sign of anger or hostility, Drago helped himself to Olivia's cup and ignored him. "That's wonderful. It's important for young witches to have support. I was with a coven for most of my formative years. The things I learned while there have stood the test of time." He kissed Dorothy's hand. "And for me, that's a lot of time!"

Dorothy stared at him as though he was about to sprout wings and fly away. The stunned look in her eyes said it all. How could anyone compete with a thousand-year-old super witch?

Olivia quietly pouted. "He took my cup, Molly."

"Hush. You can't drink out of it anyway. No theatrics right now. We need to concentrate."

She backed down. I knew she was terrified, having dreaded this moment for so many years. But it was upon us now. We needed to be very careful what we did and said next. Attacking Drago didn't seem like the best course of action to me. It wasn't completely my decision, but I hoped even Brian would see that Drago's magic was beyond us. This needed a diplomatic solution.

Elsie and I sat at the small table with Dorothy and Drago. Olivia hovered above us. Brian sat just behind Drago and Dorothy as though it was a strategic choice for him. I doubted it was, but it did keep him from glaring at them.

In the old days, before Olivia's death, and before Dorothy joined us, it was just the three of us. We'd sat at this table in Smuggler's Arcane surrounded by books of magic, herbs, candles and other witch's tools. We'd worked on our spells and discussed the world across tea, and the occasional chocolate cake.

Time passed and we held our magic in check, not going beyond the small acts of daily life—repairing flat tires and broken dishes. Elsie and I had married men without magic and each had a child with no magic. We were women, mothers and wives more often than we were witches. That distinction, and our choices, had left our magic weak and fading.

But things had changed.

"What brings you here?" Dorothy asked her father. "I mean, I know you didn't just come to see me, right? It's been a long time between visits."

We all stopped speaking, surprised that she'd asked the question. She'd seemed so enthralled with him. The question, and the tone, might be saying otherwise.

Drago smiled and took a careful sip of his tea. "Surely a man might come to meet his only child who was kept secret from him for so many years."

His strangely iridescent blue-eyed gaze locked with hers across the table. Brian covered Dorothy's hand, and Olivia moved in closer with a sigh that whispered through the shop.

"You've never come before," she said. "I know how powerful you are, or at least are said to be. You could've found me if you'd really wanted. I never even knew I had living parents until last year." She shrugged. "Well, at least one of you is still alive."

"I'm very sorry." Drago's words sounded sincere. His face appeared to be earnest. "Believe me, if your birth hadn't been hidden from me by your mother, I would've been here long ago to claim you as my daughter and heir to my magic. Nothing could have kept me away."

His glance toward Olivia was both angry and unflattering. "It was wrong for you to keep her a secret, Olivia," he said. "I did nothing but show you kindness. You believed the things the council says about me without giving me an opportunity to prove that I am not the man they say I am."

"Isn't this excellent tea?" Elsie nervously laughed. "I'm thinking about a second cup. Anyone else?"

But everyone else was involved in a staring contest as we all waited to see if Drago could or would try to take Dorothy away.

Father's and daughter's gazes finally broke free. Dorothy's uncertain brown eyes went to Brian for support. Drago saw where her attentions were riveted and looked down to study the tea in his cup.

"I can see I make you unhappy," Drago said. "I assure you, my intentions are honorable. I don't want to disrupt your life, Dorothy. I just wanted to see you for myself. I'd like to be part of what you do from here on. I know it will take some time to get used to me. But I have as much time as you need."

He slowly got to his feet as we all watched him carefully—and held our breaths.

"But I won't force myself on you, no matter what anyone has told you about me. Your mother did a remarkable job of hiding you. I truly didn't know you existed until yesterday." He smoothed a hand down her sleek hair. "You are the only child I have ever conceived, my only heir. That means something to me. I'll be close by, my dear, if you decide you'd like to talk." He leaned down and kissed her cheek. "Let's have lunch. I'm sure your protectors wouldn't object. Shall I give you a call? Or you could call me when you're ready."

"I don't have your cell phone number," Dorothy calmly replied.

He smiled. "I don't need one, darling. Speak my name and I shall be there."

He vanished, and the rest of us let go the breaths we'd been holding.

CHAPTER 2

"Never mind the tea. I think this calls for a drop of whiskey."
Elsie got up to rummage around behind the counter.

"There is no whiskey. You don't even drink whiskey,"
Olivia snapped at her. "You'd better stop keeping company
with that werewolf. He's teaching you bad habits."

Elsie had been dating Larry Tyler, a local werewolf who
lived on a houseboat so he could escape to the sea when it
came time for his monthly change. All of us liked Larry—
we'd known him as a shop customer for years. He was fun,
vegetarian and a great friend. But Olivia was right. Dating
Larry had changed Elsie. For the better, as far as I was concerned. She was a lot more like her old self that I recalled
from our younger days. She was stronger and healthier. Even
her magic had come up a notch or two. I was excited for her,
though her daughter, Aleese, wasn't.

Olivia and Elsie just liked to give each other a hard time.
It was friendly, the kind of joking that could be done with
someone you've known all your life.

"I'm with Elsie." Brian dumped out his cold tea and took a flask from his pocket. He poured whiskey into his cup and held it out. "Anyone else?"

Elsie took some with a scornful glance at Olivia, but Dorothy and I abstained.

"I wish I could have a drop or two," Olivia said.

"Are you dating a werewolf too?" Elsie asked with a laugh. "Oh no. You're a ghost. I almost forgot. Ghosts don't date, do they?"

"Why are you always so mean about me being dead?" Olivia demanded. "It's not like it was my fault. I don't like being dead, you know."

"I think we should all go home and get some rest," I recommended. "It's been a long day and we're all on edge. We'll meet back here tomorrow to resume training."

"Sounds like a good idea." Brian put his arm around Dorothy's shoulders. "How about dinner, beautiful?"

"I think Molly's right," Dorothy said, surprisingly stern about it. "I think we should each go home and get some rest. I'm exhausted. I'll see you tomorrow."

"Okay." His smile vanished. "I'll be here. Just don't take off with your dad without telling me, okay?"

"What do you mean?" Olivia asked. "Dorothy's not going anywhere with Drago. I've told her what he's really like. She knows better. She wouldn't do anything like that after all I went through to keep her safe."

"Don't take this the wrong way," he replied, "but I know what it's like to have relatives who are uber powerful and want to lead you astray. It can be very seductive."

He and Olivia stared at Dorothy as though she was a specimen they were about to dissect.

"I'm not going anywhere with Drago," she denied. "I mean, sure he was captivating and knows everything after being alive so long. No telling what he could teach me and the wonders of the world that he could show me." She took a deep breath. "But I'm not interested."

Brian appeared unconvinced. Olivia looked tearful and uncertain.

"Really," Dorothy continued, "I'm not interested—at least not enough to run away with him. Maybe to have lunch with him. Or drinks. Or something. What? He's my father. I can't just ignore him even if he is evil."

Dorothy said good night and picked up her mother's staff so that Olivia's ghost would accompany her. It was the only thing that tethered Olivia to her earthly form. Olivia had collected runes for it—she was an air witch—for many years. Dorothy, an earth witch, was only able to wield her mother's staff because they were blood relatives. Dorothy's own tool was a piece of emerald cull.

As soon as they were out the door, Brian turned to me and Elsie.

"I'm not gonna get a wink of sleep worrying about her. I might as well hang around their house until we find out what's going on. I wish I wouldn't have found an apartment already. I could still be living with them. You two want to take shifts on this or what?"

"I really think this is Dorothy's decision," Elsie said. "Like you said, many witches have powerful, seductive friends and relatives who could lead them astray. She has to figure this out for herself."

"But she doesn't have the background for it," he argued. "I grew up in the Fuller family with the Grand Council breathing down my neck and my parents trying to tell me what I should do. Dorothy doesn't have that experience. And she trusts everyone." Brian, an air witch, took out his wand.

"I think Elsie's right," I agreed with her. "We can't actively interfere, as much as we might like to. But the three of us could put a locator spell on her so that if he does manage to convince her to leave, we could find her. It would give us the chance to talk some sense into her."

"Okay." He nodded. "Let's do that. I'm not giving her up without a fight."

"That's the spirit." Elsie patted him on the back. "You have to fight for what you want. Look at me and Larry. We couldn't even be together if it was up to other witches and the council."

Elsie was a fire witch. She took out her sword and repeated an incantation for power.

I was a water witch—the most powerful among us as far as elements went. Wilmington was in a strong position for water magic, sandwiched between the coast and the river. I had always used a small cauldron as my symbol of magic until last year when I'd rediscovered the amulet passed down to me from my mother. Now I used that strong charm that held a bit of the sea in it—a gift to an ancestor from an ancient sea god. I could feel its strength flow through me.

The three of us held hands and whispered a locator spell that would keep Dorothy in our sights. It was her decision to make, but I was too fond of her to take it for granted that she would ignore her father's charm. At least we could offer help and guidance if she needed it.

Creating the spell was much simpler now than it had been last year. Elsie and I were more focused and in tune with our magic. Brian, of course, not only had youth and focus on his side, he had passion and fear motivating him. He loved Dorothy. I didn't believe that he would let her go so easily.

Elsie, Brian and I set stronger protection spells on the shop before we left. I wasn't sure there was a spell we could conjure that would keep Drago out, but we all felt the need to try. I locked up and followed Brian and Elsie into the parking lot. Brian left in his bright red corvette with the WCHYMAN license plate, a gift from his family.

"What do you think, Molly?" Elsie asked as we got in my car. "If Drago was here to hurt Dorothy or take her away, he was certainly nice and polite about it, wasn't he? Not like the water witch trying to take Brian! I'm sure he could've done whatever he wanted and we couldn't have stopped him. Maybe Olivia has exaggerated how evil he was so we'd be on her side in all this."

"Maybe he really only wants to connect with her." I started the car. "Although I really believe Olivia felt that there was a threat or she wouldn't have gone off on her own to have Dorothy in the first place. I can't imagine she wanted to leave Drago, as exciting and fascinating as everyone seems to feel he is. But if he's telling the truth, and she's his only child, that could make someone different. Or maybe he's not as evil as Olivia thought he was."

"Or he's mellowed," she said. "Either way, it's not like she ever said he wasn't charming."

"That's true. But all we can do is keep an eye on Dorothy and see what happens. She's an adult, and all this was started a long time ago. Olivia made her choice when she and Drago made a child."

"And now those roosters have come home to roost."

I dropped Elsie off at her home. She waved as I pulled away. Traffic was light in Wilmington. Storms were moving in from the Atlantic. I'd felt them coming a few days before the weatherman mentioned it, and so did Elsie, Brian and Dorothy—as well as every other witch. They'd been coming to Smuggler's Arcane for protection candles and other storm-related magic paraphernalia. We were as ready for what was coming as possible.

My son, Mike, was home on a break from East Carolina University, which meant a ton of laundry and other problems that had come up while he'd been gone. His cell phone had died, and my husband, Joe, had taken him to get another. Mike had slept the whole first day he'd been back and then had eaten two pizzas by himself. In between he'd talked about a girl he was dating at school—nothing serious, he assured us, just wanted us to know.

Joe and Mike were still out. I didn't mind. It would be good to have some time to myself to decompress. Life had been crazy the last week or two. I decided to take a nice pomegranate bath and lie back with a cucumber face mask on for a while. I needed a little tinting on my brown hair. Maybe some blond highlights? Those would look good with my dark blue eyes. I was no beauty, but I tried to keep up with my appearance.

My key was barely in the lock when my familiar, Isabelle, let me know that we weren't alone. She was a large, gray long-haired cat who held the spirit of a witch who'd been burned at the stake in the 1300s. She was very protective, waiting at the door for me as I opened it.

"What's wrong?" I could feel her distress as I put my handbag on the counter. "Who's here?"

Before Isabelle could answer, my niece, Sunshine Merryweather, stepped forward. Her visit was a surprise, since I'd just seen her in Norfolk, Virginia, before I went to pick up Mike from school.

"Sorry to drop in on you this way, Aunt Molly," she apologized. "But some things have happened at home that I need your help with."

CHAPTER 3

I saw the terrible mark on her pretty face. "What in the world happened to you?"

Sunshine was a powerful young witch. She was a great deal more powerful and independent than myself, or her mother, my sister, Abby. She'd moved away from the area almost as soon as she'd reached adulthood and rarely came to visit. We were a little too tame for Sunshine. She had grand plans for her life and didn't hesitate to go after them.

"I was hoping Mom was home, but she's off somewhere and I can't reach her," Sunshine said. "I guess you can see I've been injured, and I brought someone with me who needs healing worse than I do."

She gestured to a woman on the sofa who was as yet unmoving.

"How did this happen?" I glanced at Sunshine's injury, but the other woman's condition was much worse. I carefully checked her, guessing it was a magical injury and not something she could have healed at the hospital. "She's near death. I hope I can help her, since I'm assuming you can't."

Sunshine tapped her purple fingernail on the counter. She was plump with a ripeness of life that showed in her bright blue eyes and pink cheeks. She had a mass of strawberry blond hair that never stayed where she put it when she tried to clasp or pull it back. It truly had a life of its own.

"You know how it is, Aunt Molly. I've never been a strong healer."

"It's true. You need patience for that. Never your strong suit."

"Can you help her? I'm not worried about me. This thing on my face won't heal, but it's not going to kill me."

"Of course. I can help both of you. But I'd like to hear how this happened. What caused these marks? They look like more than scratches. Was poison involved?"

I took out a glass bottle of water I'd blessed with moonlight. Other ways could have worked, but being a water witch, I needed my element. Sunshine gave me a quick rundown of what had been happening at her detective agency since I'd been there. I felt sure she was holding something back, but I didn't mention it. She needed my help, not my curiosity.

Closing my eyes, I sprinkled some of the purified water onto the woman's wounds. Sunshine and I had moved her to my bedroom, where we could work without being interrupted. I invoked the strongest healing spell I knew as I smoothed the water on the woman's shoulders, back and chest. It was as though something with claws had grabbed and ripped at her.

With the water and the spell put to good use, I turned to Sunshine. "Now you."

"You don't have to do this, Aunt Molly. I'll be fine." She shook her head. "Besides, I might have to come back again before this is over if you heal me now. Just take care of Malto, please."

"All right. But don't wait too long. I don't like the way that looks. I know you don't want your mother to see it."

"You're definitely right about that!"

I knew my sister didn't approve of Sunshine's life as a private detective taking care of problems that involved werewolves, witches and other creatures. Abby felt like her daughter should get married and settle down. She wanted her to move back to Wilmington to be part of her coven. My sister was a true conservative witch who felt strongly about witches staying with their own kind. She'd almost hit the roof when she'd found out that Sunshine had been dating a werewolf last year.

I checked the woman on the bed. Her wounds were starting to fade, and color was coming back into her face. Sunshine and I concentrated our magic and healing energies on her friend. I carefully directed some of those energies toward my niece too. She seemed more stressed than usual and less happy. Whatever was going on in her life wasn't good.

Joe got back and came in to see what was going on. His thick dark hair had a few more strands of silver every year, and his lean face had a few more wrinkles. But I seemed to love him better too. "Molly?" He waved to Sunshine and stared at the woman on the bed. "What's up in here?"

"You probably don't want to know." I avoided his question. Joe had only recently learned about magic. It was difficult for him to grasp most of it. I'd finally found a way to protect him from the Council of Witches' ever-present watchfulness—my amulet—so he could safely know anything about witches. The council didn't like non–magic users to know about us. The penalties were harsh.

"Hi, Uncle Joe." Sunshine waved back to him. "How are you? I understand you know all about witches now."

Joe turned his head toward Sunshine. "Are you—?" And then looked at me. "Is she—?"

"A witch," I filled in for him. "Yes. Abby is a witch too."

His dark eyes were full of questions. "And Danver? Is he a witch too?"

"No." Sunshine laughed, the painful mark on her face causing her to put her hand to it. "Dad's not a witch, but he's not protected like you either. Please don't tell him what you know."

"Wait a minute." Joe walked closer to the bed, his eyes narrowed. "I know this woman. We were on a joint task force together a couple of years ago. Detective Sharon Malto from Norfolk. Why is she here?"

"It's a long story, Uncle Joe," Sunshine said. "But she's gonna be fine, right, Aunt Molly?"

I checked Detective Malto's wounds. "Yes. I'd say she's going to be just fine."

"What happened? I mean, why didn't she go to the hospital in Norfolk?"

"Healing is best done by family members where possible." I tucked my arm through his to get him out of the bedroom as I explained. "The detective isn't part of our family, but she's a friend of Sunshine's. How has your day been so far? Did you get the cell phone replaced?"

Joe stopped walking and kissed my cheek. "In other words, leave it alone because I don't understand. Okay. I get it. I am a detective, you know."

"I know." I smoothed back a strand of his hair.

"We caught a homicide this morning. It's down by the docks." He shrugged. "Reminds me of Olivia's death. Anything going on in your community that I should know about?"

We'd never had talks like this before in the more than thirty years we'd been married. I had protected Joe and Mike by not telling them about magic until something had come up that could have endangered Joe's life if I hadn't told him. Mike still didn't know. I didn't plan to tell him either, even though he was also protected from the council.

"No. Everything is quiet except for the storm coming toward us," I told him.

"Check the weather again, Molly. They say it's going to pass us by this time."

"It won't pass, not without some high winds and flooding."

"You know that for sure, huh?" His voice was still husky even though he'd given up smoking years before.

"Yes. All the witches are stocking up for it. Are you going to eat lunch, since you're home?"

"I have some time. How about if you and me get some lunch out? It's kind of crowded here. Or do you have to stay with Sunshine and Malto?"

"No. They should both be fine. What did you have in mind?"

I said good-bye to Sunshine and wished her well, quietly adding a protection spell to shore up her own defenses as we hugged. She promised to come back as soon as she could to get her face healed. I was worried about her, but there wasn't much I could do until she was ready to allow herself to be taken care of.

Joe and I went to lunch at one of our favorite places, a small Italian restaurant that was in an older building. We'd both always loved this place and came here for anniversaries and other special occasions that didn't include Mike. It wasn't a good place to bring a child, and we'd just never included him as he got older, thinking of it as "our place."

"I've been thinking about the whole retirement thing again." Joe took my hand in his across the white linen table-cloth. We each had a large glass of water while we were waiting for lunch. Joe was technically still on duty.

"Still thinking about giving up the job?"

"Yeah. Things have gotten a lot worse here in the past few years with drugs and gangs. Now there's magic too. I don't just have to watch out for guns and knives. Now I have to wonder who's a witch and who isn't. I can't even explain that to Suzanne. Sometimes I think she wonders if I'm crazy the way I approach a case."

Suzanne Renard was Joe's ex-wife who'd moved back here from Savannah after they'd worked a case in Wilmington together last year. If I was one sliver less certain of my relationship with my husband, I'd insist that he had to have another partner. They worked long hours together, sometimes gone all night. But I trusted Joe and had even come to like Suzanne, almost despite myself. After all, their marriage had only lasted a short time, more than thirty years ago. I couldn't allow myself to be that insecure.

"I understand. I could help with a protection spell."

He kissed my hand. "I think if I'm too nervous to work without that, I should retire. Have you given any more thought to what you want to do? You said something about selling the shop to Dorothy when we were ready to go. Is that still happening?"

I had mentioned that to him when we had first recruited Dorothy to be one of the three witches who would take our places and our spell book when Olivia, Elsie and I "retired." Not that a witch ever truly stopped practicing witchcraft.

All that had changed with Olivia's death. Dorothy still needed a good deal of training, since she hadn't been raised to be a witch. Brian was part of the coven now too but still needed guidance. Things were different now, at least for me.

And the amulet had made my magic stronger, more vibrant. I wasn't sure I wanted to cut back on something I had only just begun to explore. Elsie seemed to be feeling the same way since her relationship with Larry the werewolf had blossomed. We didn't make as many mistakes, and we were evolving into different witches than we had been. I knew Elsie wouldn't want to move to Boca without Larry, and it seemed unlikely to me that he would leave his escape route that protected him from people during his "monthly."

"I don't know." I tried to think of some way to explain all that to Joe. Not being a witch, how could he relate? "It's complicated. Dorothy could certainly afford to buy Smuggler's Arcane, since she inherited Olivia's house and money. Brian only makes our second witch to keep our coven going though, and we have no spell book to pass down, since it was stolen."

"I see." He said it like he didn't see at all and drank some water. "I guess we have to put off retirement then."

"You could still retire. They offered you that job teaching at the community college. That wouldn't be as dangerous."

"Nah. You're the teacher in the family." He grinned. "I don't think I'm cut out to teach a bunch of rookies how not to get killed. I guess we'll just keep going the way we have been. It's not like I'm at mandatory retirement age or anything yet."

Lunch arrived, but I could see the discussion was far from over. I knew Joe had dreams of packing up and traveling around the country in an RV. It was what he'd always wanted—me too, but mostly because he wanted it. We were still young enough to do it, but for my commitment to my friends and my magic.

The new magic I'd found in my amulet was too difficult to explain to him. We ate baked ziti and homemade garlic bread in silence as we both contemplated the future. They seemed to be two different futures for the first time in our lives. I didn't like the way that felt.

As usual—particularly during romantic moments, birthdays, Christmas—Joe got a call about the homicide he was working, and we had to pack up the last of our food and take it with us. He dropped me off at the house with a grin and a kiss.

"Don't worry about it, Molly," he said. "We'll figure it out. We always do, right? I'll see you later. Don't wait up."

I put my arms around him and hugged him as best I could through the open window of the SUV. "I love you, Joe. We can't let this come between us. We've gone through worse, haven't we?"

"We have," he agreed, but his smile didn't reach his beautiful eyes. "I love you too. See you later."

The storm clouds heading our way from the Atlantic were beginning to get thick and dark around us. I crossed my arms against my chest as I watched Joe leave and wondered if the clouds were an omen of what was to come.

CHAPTER 4

Sunshine was gone when I went inside. She'd left me a note to say that she and Detective Malto were doing fine. She was going back to Norfolk, promising to erase any memories of what had happened from Malto's mind. She was always such a clever girl. I wondered what she and her friends had fallen into.

Isabelle said there had been another caller while I was gone, but this one had stayed outside, leaving quickly when no one was home. Before I had a chance to wonder who it was, Dorothy, Elsie and Olivia were frantically knocking at my door.

"Did you get it?" Elsie asked with an excited smile plastered on her face. "Did you look at it?"

"Did I get what?" I asked as I put our leftovers from the restaurant in the fridge. "What's everyone so excited about?"

"I'm not excited at all." Olivia pouted. "No one cares about what happens to you when you're a ghost."

Dorothy held out a beautiful black invitation with gold

embossed words on it. "I can't believe he didn't invite you too, Molly. There must be some mistake. Don't worry. I'll talk to him."

"Talk to . . . what?" There was another person at the door. "Just a minute while I get this."

Elsie and Dorothy giggled, holding each other's hands. "I knew you'd get one too, Molly," Elsie said. "I knew Brian wouldn't just invite us."

I opened the door, and there stood a servant in sumptuous gold and black livery. He was tall and beautiful—probably not really a person. Magic washed from him in waves.

"Molly Addison Renard." His diction was perfect, but his dark eyes never moved and his expression was featureless. "Schadt and Yuriza Fuller invite you to a ball at their residence. Should you accept the invitation, a car will be sent for you. Should you decline the invitation, all is well. Good day."

He vanished as he finished, nothing more than a messenger created for the purpose of giving out invitations in a grand fashion. It was impressive, I admitted as I closed the door with the invitation in my hand.

"It's a ball at the castle," Dorothy's voice squeaked with excitement. "It's Brian's birthday bash, and he wanted us to be there. Is that cool or what?"

"It's amazing!" Elsie was almost dancing with excitement. She'd been quite a dancer when we were younger, but I hadn't seen her dance in many years. "I don't know what to wear. I'm not sure there's anything in my attic that will do. I wonder if I can take Larry with me as a date. It says bring a friend on the invitation."

"I'm pretty sure the Fullers weren't imagining you'd bring a werewolf or a ghost with you to the party." Olivia sighed. Her familiar ghostly features sagged as she fretted. "I've never been invited to a ball at a castle. I guess I wouldn't have to worry about what to wear, as I haven't been able to change clothes since I died. But you all go on without me. I don't want to hold you back."

I glanced at the elaborate invitation. "I'm sure they aren't talking about bringing a non-witch either if it makes you feel any better."

"Forgive me, Molly, if it doesn't make me feel one whit better that Joe can't go either."

"What about using the bottle again?" Elsie asked. "That sort of worked last time."

"It would've worked if Olivia had stayed in the bottle," I suggested. "We were lucky we weren't caught with her. She was lucky too, or she might not be here."

"I think I could come up with something so you could go too, Mom," Dorothy said in the voice of a child who wanted to appease her parent. "I hate for you to miss it. Since Brian is already going to be there, you could be my plus one."

Olivia wrapped her mostly see-through form around her daughter to give her a hug. I hadn't said anything about Olivia's ghostly hugs, but they were more like being suffocated. She couldn't help it, bless her soul. She just wanted to be alive again. She'd been working hard to have a better physical presence and control the many abilities that came with being a ghost. But as yet, she hadn't mastered those abilities enough to fool an entire castle full of witches who intensely disliked ghosts and had the ability to banish her from our world.

"You're the best daughter ever." Olivia smiled at her and patted Dorothy's dark, sleek pageboy hair even though her hand appeared to go through her head. "I'm sure we can come up with something. It's so exciting, isn't it?"

I shook my head, hating to be a killjoy. "I don't think we should go if we're planning to take Larry and Olivia into a castle full of witches—and not just ordinary witches. The entire Grand Council is bound to be there, since it's the Fuller family. I don't want to be thrown out, or worse, try to sneak inside."

"Oh, that's just fine," Olivia said quickly. Too quickly. "I'll just sit this one out. As Molly says, it's too risky. I'll be dandy. Don't worry about me."

Elsie shook her head. "I suppose that means we'll have to think of something or Olivia will guilt us all to death."

"Like I said," Olivia reiterated, "I'm happy to stay home. I think we should be discussing how we're going to hide Dorothy from her father right now instead of thinking about this stupid ball anyway."

"I don't need to be hidden," Dorothy said. "I'm not leaving with him, but there's no reason that I can't get to know my father a little, is there? I mean, you did hide me from him all these years. It seems only fair to establish some kind of relationship with him now."

"Honey, I know you mean well," Olivia began, "but your father is an evil witch who will bend you to his will if he has half a chance. While that might be exciting in a lover, it won't be exciting to you as his child. Besides, I worked too hard to see you become evil. You know I had to live with those awful witches in the Paris catacombs until after you were born. Sometimes I still get the taste of sewer in my mouth."

"Oh great!" Elsie put her hands on her ample hips. "Now we have to hear all about it again for the hundredth time."

"Mom." Dorothy stared at her. "I don't want to hurt you. I just want to be fair. How do we even know if Dad is still evil?"

"He's still evil all right." Olivia tossed her head in the way she always had when she was alive, but the effect on her ectoplasmic form was different. It gave the gesture a streaming quality that came close to making me nauseous.

"We really don't know that," I reminded her, looking

away. I knew how terrified she was for Dorothy, but I also knew she wasn't going to be able to protect her this time. Dorothy would have to make her own decisions and mistakes.

"Molly Renard!" Olivia's shriek was piercing. "What are you saying? How could you betray me this way?"

"I'm not betraying you. You've done all you can to protect her."

"Standing here," Dorothy reminded us.

Olivia folded her arms across her chest. "I'd leave now, if I could. It's stupid to discuss Drago not being evil. He'll ruin your life, Dorothy. Mark my words. If you let him in, he'll take advantage."

"All right," Elsie decided. "That's enough about evil witches. Let's talk about what we're going to wear to the ball. I'm so excited to be invited. Oh! That rhymes. That was fun."

"Maybe now isn't the best time," I suggested.

"If not now, when?" she asked. "It starts at midnight. Didn't you listen to the invitation?"

I glanced at the card again. "This is very little advance notice."

"Witches aren't known for their thoughtfulness." Elsie laughed and spun around. "I'd like a black hat with sequins, please." She loved hats.

To our complete surprise, an imaginative black velvet hat with sequins appeared on her head.

"What the—?" Dorothy wondered.

Mike chose that moment to come home. He was immediately followed by Brian. Brian's shiny new red Corvette filled out the driveway behind Mike's old Camaro.

"Hey, Mom." Mike nodded at Elsie and Dorothy. He couldn't see Olivia, because he hadn't inherited being a witch from me. "Hey, Elsie. Love the hat. Hello, Dorothy."

We all said hello to him. Dorothy asked how school was as Brian came up and put his arm around her—a very territorial move.

"Hi, Mike." Brian shook his hand. "I haven't seen you in a while."

"Hi, Brian. How's it going?" If Mike had any memories of last year's crush on Dorothy, he didn't show it. His eyes, so like mine, were perfect with his father's dark hair.

"Good," Brian replied before turning his attention to us. "I'm guessing you got the invitations by now."

"Yes!" Elsie kissed his cheek. "And we're thrilled."

"Don't look at me," he said. "It wasn't my idea. I'm not going. I hate those things."

"But it's your birthday," Dorothy reminded him. "You have to go."

He kissed the side of her face. "I never go to their parties. I'd rather just go out to dinner with you."

"Oh." She smiled softly, her usually pale cheeks taking on a pink hue. "Thank you. But I couldn't do that and take you away from your family."

"Please. Take me away. I haven't celebrated a birthday with my parents since I was five. And if you'd ever been to one of their birthday balls, you wouldn't want to go again either."

"So it wasn't your idea to invite us?" I asked, wondering whose idea it was. His family had no love for us and had actively tried to keep Brian from being part of our coven. We weren't worthy of the Fuller name.

"No," he denied. "I wouldn't do something like that to you."

Mike grinned at his words.

"I think the rest of us would be very disappointed if we didn't go." Dorothy glanced at Elsie and me. "We've never been to a ball at a castle. It's very exciting."

"Are you ashamed of us, Brian?" Olivia asked and I echoed.

"No—them! They've obviously put some thought into this. It scares me that they invited you when I think we all know how they feel about you." He frowned. "Sorry. I didn't mean that the way it sounded."

"Oh, Brian," Elsie remarked. "I don't care how they feel. I just want the champagne and the castle!"

He shrugged. "Okay. If that's what you want, you go this time, but you won't ever want to go again. Believe me."

"A ball at a castle?" Mike nodded. "Sounds fun. I think you should all go."

"What do you have in mind?" I asked him quickly. "You're a little too eager to get rid of me."

"Just some pizza and friends, since Dad is working a case. Nothing much."

"That's fine," I told him. "Just don't wreck the house. Or clean it up if you do."

He laughed. "Like Isabelle would let me do that. When I have friends over, she gives us these dirty looks, and I can just imagine her reporting back to you! See you later." He hugged me and flopped down in front of the TV as we walked into the kitchen.

"You don't think . . . ?" Olivia suggested.

"No. Mike isn't a witch," I answered. "We'd know by now."

"There was Jerry Doffin's daughter that he swore didn't have magic," Elsie said. "At her twenty-first birthday party, she levitated her cake across the room! He could still be a late-blooming witch."

I thought about it, glancing toward my son. "I've never known anyone that late blooming. Mike doesn't have any magic. As I said, we'd know by now."

"We could test him," Brian suggested.

"That would mean telling him that he could be a witch," I replied. "I don't think so."

He jammed his hands into the pockets of his jeans. "Just saying."

"If we're done with that, on to the shopping!" Elsie said. "I'm not sure about trying to create an entire ensemble with magic. I've been doing pretty well lately. But I don't want to walk into the ball and have my gown fall on the floor."

"Are you going, Molly?" Dorothy asked.

It wasn't exactly something I'd always wanted to do, but my coven was part of my family too. Dorothy and Elsie might decide not to go if I didn't. I wouldn't want them to miss out if it was something they really wanted to do.

"Of course." I smiled as though I'd never considered not going. "I suppose this means a visit to Madam Tunis's Beauty Mark."

"Madam Tunis!" Elsie was in raptures. "I haven't been there since I was sixteen and my grandmother took me there for my senior prom. But I've never forgotten the experience. I've always been nervous about going, since Aleese isn't a witch and neither was Bill. I didn't want it to be too grand and have them wonder how I'd done it. Can we really go there?"

Dorothy was confused. "Madam Tunis?"

"The only witch dressmaker in Wilmington," I told her. "I'd say this is occasion enough for it."

"Really?" Dorothy's eyes got wide. "A witch dressmaker? Cool. Don't worry—I'll be glad to pay, if it's expensive. It's my treat."

"You know the money I left you isn't going to last very long if you go around treating people to expensive gifts every few minutes," Olivia said sourly.

"Like Molly said. It's not every day you get invited to a ball." Dorothy kissed Brian. "I'll see you later. Wait! I have your birthday gift."

"Okay. As long as I don't have to go to the dressmaker too. I've never been inside the place, and I hope I never am." He held her close for a moment. "Don't forget they'll send a car for you. It's the only way you can get to the castle."

"I won't." She snuggled close to him. "Let me get your gift."

She ran to the car and came back with a pet carrier that had a large pink bow on top. "Open it."

He smiled and carefully opened the carrier. "Just what I needed—a cat."

"I thought she was so beautiful." Dorothy smoothed the black cat's fur. "You don't have a familiar. I understand because you didn't have a permanent home until now, but you'll love having her with you. Look how calm and beautiful she is."

"She's really nice." Brian kissed Dorothy. "Thank you. What should I name her?"

"You'll have to ask her," Elsie said. "You can't just pick a name, or you'll end up with a cat named Scooter like Dorothy did. She'll tell you in due time. She is quite a lovely cat."

The nameless cat blinked her pretty, violet-colored eyes—unusual to see a black cat with pale purple eyes. I wanted to ask Dorothy where she'd found her, but the excitement of the ball drew us away. Brian took the cat and the carrier with him back to his apartment.

"We should go if we're going to be ready by midnight." Elsie stormed the door. "Who's driving?"

CHAPTER 5

Madam Tunis ran a one-of-a-kind beauty shop in the heart of the old downtown area of Wilmington. It was in the Cotton Exchange building a few floors above Smuggler's Arcane.

We decided to drive to the shop in Dorothy's car, have our beauty treatment and then meet back at our shop to request a car from there. It would be good for us all to ride to the ball together. Besides, Olivia wanted to wait in the shop for us so she could say good-bye.

"We can't just leave her there while we're out having a good time," Dorothy said as we trudged up the back stairs to the dressmaker. "She looks so sad."

"She'll be fine," Elsie said. "She's probably forgotten all about it by now. Harper is there. He always cheers her up. Let's go. There are probably a lot of other witches getting ready for the ball too."

Harper was Olivia's cat who had been with her for many

years. He was a Russian blue with a gray and white coat and blue eyes. He was very large and told many stories of being a British sailor in his past life. He couldn't live at the house they'd once shared because Dorothy's tuxedo cat, Hemlock aka Scooter, was there now, and the two familiars didn't always get along.

We all had familiars—Elsie had a ginger tabby Manx named Barnabas who had the spirit of a preacher mistakenly hanged for witchcraft in the 1700s. It was only natural that Brian should have a cat too. It was another way his parents had ignored his training as a witch that he didn't have a cat he confided in.

Leaving behind Olivia's fears and woes, we entered the magical realm of Madam Tunis's Beauty Mark. It didn't look like much when you first opened the door—nothing but an empty dusty room. But for those with magic who could enter the shop, a world of glamour and delight awaited.

Madam Tunis was there to welcome us. She was a short, plump witch with strands of hair made from real gold. Her eyes were crusted with diamonds, and she had a single star-shaped ruby near the corner of her red lips. Her silk gown was made with magic fibers that were constantly moving and changing, like the colors of the rainbow.

"Welcome, ladies. Let me guess. You're here to get ready for the birthday ball. As always, my ladies are here to help you become whoever you want to be. Will you want the entire treatment?"

"I'm sure we do," Dorothy decided with a nod at us.

"Except for you, Elsie," Madam Tunis observed. "I adore your hat. It is too perfect. No one here will suggest another."

"You still remember me after all these years?" Elsie was as amazed and beguiled as Dorothy and I were.

"Indeed I do. I never forget a face or a name." Madam Tunis bowed her head. "I am so happy and honored that you returned." She clapped her hands, and three witches appeared. They took each of us into separate rooms, and the doors closed behind us.

I wished I was as excited as Elsie, but I truly felt more nervous and faintly sick at the idea of what would come next. I said as much to my attendant—a woman who looked to be about my age.

"Don't worry. I won't do anything you don't like." She smiled. "Now, what color did you have in mind? I'm thinking a vibrant blue that will show off your wonderful blue eyes. You have lovely hair. It's a good mid-length to work with too. Maybe a touch of red in those brown strands for the night. What do you say?"

As I looked in the mirror, autumn red strands appeared in my hair. Blue highlights appeared on my eyelids. A soft sheen of makeup added glamour to my face. "Wonderful. I wouldn't have thought of adding red highlights to my hair."

She nodded. "Put yourself in my hands, Molly. You're going to be fabulous!"

First came the beauty bath that was filled with so many different types of flowers and essences that I lost track. It smelled heavenly, as did the shampoo and conditioner she used on my hair. The bath and shampoo made my whole body glisten as though I was covered in glitter. It was a wonderful, rejuvenating feeling.

My glittery blue gown was slinky, slit up the right side to give a clear view of my leg from ankle to thigh. It was more daring than anything I'd ever worn. The attendant tried different styles with my hair and finally ended with one that was flattering as well as glamorous. She piled the newly colored locks up to give me more height and left a few strands at my ears and forehead.

"Now jewelry." She mulled it over. "Sapphires seem the obvious choice, especially with your wonderful amulet. Will you be wearing that tonight?"

My hand went to it immediately. Repeated warnings not to remove it had made me a little jumpy when someone mentioned it. "I never take it off."

"No, of course not. I wouldn't either if I were you. Let's try something more unique than sapphires, shall we? What about fire opals?"

I looked at the large earrings that appeared. Blue and silver wound through them. The fire opal necklace hung at the deep V in my dress without being too gaudy. There was also a matching bracelet and a matching anklet for the exposed leg.

"Perfect!" I couldn't believe it was me in the mirror. "I never looked that good twenty years ago."

"You are stunning. You have such a wonderful natural glow about you. It doesn't need a lot of dressing up. I hope you have fun at the ball tonight."

"Thank you." I walked out of the small room, teetering on sandals with six-inch heels. I usually wore flats. I hoped I wouldn't fall down the stairs as I entered the castle.

Dorothy was waiting—a vision in gold and green. "Oh, Molly! You look awesome. I hate that it all wears off by morning. I wish Joe could see you like this."

"It isn't permanent magic," I said wistfully. I wished he could see me too.

"But I bet we could still send him a picture." She took out her cell phone. "Let's do one of each of us and then one together. I'm so excited about going tonight. Is that wrong, since Mom can't go?"

I would have liked to hug her, but I was afraid it would ruin everything that had been done to both of us. I didn't know how durable the magic was. "Your mother has seen and done amazing things in her travels. One ball is nothing. Don't let her fool you. Just have a good time with Brian tonight and don't worry about it."

A third door opened, and Elsie sashayed out. "Well? How do I look?"

Her attendant had matched the black and sequins of her hat with her dress and graced her beautifully with emeralds. She all but dripped them as she turned for us to see her. Surprisingly she wore a short black velvet skirt that showed off her very pretty legs, which were encased in black stockings.

"It's a shame Larry can't be there tonight." She hiked her skirt to show us emerald-studded garters. "I would've liked to see the look on his face."

"Probably just as well," I said. "He might've had a heart attack when he saw you."

"Okay. Pictures of all of us," Dorothy said. She glanced at her cell phone. "Good thing too. It's almost midnight."

She snapped a dozen photos, and we were ready to go.

Madam Tunis came out to wish us a wonderful time at the ball. "And don't forget—the magic ends at dawn. Your previous clothing will be under what you're wearing now, so no need to panic about being caught out in the altogether. You look wonderful, ladies. Come back for our specials at Summer Solstice."

We waved good-bye and went slowly and carefully down the stairs again to Smuggler's Arcane. None of us had the kind of money it took to boost our magic to the point where we could appear and disappear at will. We had always been lower-level witches and had been happy with it. Magic was something we were born with, passed down through our family lines, but not our goal in life. Not like the Fuller family and Drago.

Larry surprised Elsie by waiting at the door to the shop. His eyes never left his glamourized girlfriend. "Woo-hoo! Seeing you like that is enough to make me howl. You look delicious, Elsie."

She blushed and flirted, but I thought his description of how she looked was a poor choice for a werewolf. Even though he'd sworn off eating people for many years, sometimes being around him still made me a little uncomfortable. Werewolves and witches weren't friends by nature. They'd come to accept one another, but anything else was purely by accident.

"Why are you here, you old rogue?" Elsie asked.

"I got your phone call about being all dressed up and how I should come by to see you." He waggled his shaggy brows and grinned. "I wouldn't have missed it."

"You know I didn't call you," she said. "How did you guess what we were doing?"

He sobered a little before he started slobbering. "No. Really. I got your phone call." He took out his cell phone to show her. "That's funny. It's not there now, but I talked to you."

"That's strange," Elsie told him. "I wish you could come with us, but you know those witches on the council have sharp noses. They'd smell a werewolf a mile away."

"I don't want to go to something where I'm not welcome anyway, sweetie." He carefully kissed her. "I'll see you when you get back. Have a good time. But keep the dress, huh?"

Elsie laughed and said good-bye, not bothering to explain that it was temporary. I called for the car, and Dorothy checked her makeup again in the mirror behind the counter.

"Where's Mom?" she asked, her eyes toward the ceiling, as Olivia frequently floated up there.

"She's here somewhere." I nodded toward the staff that was in the corner. "She couldn't leave without it."

"She's been practicing, you know," Dorothy explained. "She says other ghosts don't need a physical prop, so why should a witch? It's not going to be long before she can go wherever she wants. She can levitate stuff easily now too."

"Sounds like our witch is really becoming a ghost," Elsie remarked.

I looked for Harper but didn't see him either. "They might be downstairs." I peeked down the opening into the cave below where we conjured and held training for Dorothy and Brian, calling for Olivia. The cave connected directly to the Cape Fear River, an old rum run for pirate smugglers. "But I'm not attempting those stairs in these heels."

"Yeah. Me either. They don't hurt my feet, but I feel like I'm going to fall over." Dorothy glanced down at the intricate gold sandals on her feet. "I guess she'll be okay. I wish I didn't have to leave her. I don't understand why witches don't like ghosts."

"It's just one of those things."

"Look. I must've left my bracelet here." She picked up her mother's bracelet. "Maybe I'll wear it to remind me of her."

"Ladies!" Elsie's voice was edged with excitement. "The car has arrived."

CHAPTER 6

Both times we'd been invited to the Fullers' castle, a car and driver had been dispatched for us. Tonight, it was the same black limo in front of Smuggler's Arcane that had picked us up the last time, and the same driver.

This visit was much more auspicious. The last time—I couldn't even bear to think about it. The circumstances weren't something that I'd ever want to do again. Just thinking about it made me want to cry.

It seemed no one drove or otherwise arrived at the castle. We'd speculated that this was because it wasn't in our world. Elsie thought it might just be in another country, but I wasn't convinced that was true. Whatever the location, the Fullers were very conscious of their security. Sending a car for each visitor took a lot of magic, but they could keep out the riff-raff that way and keep the location of their home a secret.

The driver was stiffly polite as he helped us into the car. Unlike the messenger with the invitation to the birthday ball, the driver was a real person. He still wore the Fuller livery well with his height and broad shoulders. When the door was closed behind us, he assumed his position behind the wheel and we were off.

I tried to see out of the windows, but they were too heavily tinted to view anything moving in the darkness. I finally sat back with nervous butterflies in my stomach, not at all sure we should be attending Brian's birthday bash. The last time we'd been at the castle, I'd felt like a stranger in a strange land. We all had. We were housewives, mothers, teachers and librarians. Hobnobbing with celebrity witches wasn't fun or relaxing.

I was sure Olivia would have fit right in. As I'd said to Dorothy, her mother had spent her life traveling the world and meeting wealthy, famous witches like Drago and the council. She wouldn't have felt intimidated at all. But this had come too late for her. It had to be enough for her that Dorothy was there in her place.

Being part of Brian's family now as his coven meant that we had to support him in times like these. We had to set aside our feelings about this glittering world he'd grown up in. It also helped to know he didn't want to be there either.

Dorothy didn't stop talking. She had a tendency to be that way when she was nervous. Elsie was grinning and staring at the rings on her fingers. I fingered my amulet, feeling its coolness against my skin, and hoped for the best.

The entire trip didn't take more than a few minutes—at least we didn't have to spend much time worrying about what was to come. When we emerged from the car, we were in a different weather pattern with unusual landmarks.

"I really don't think this is our world," Elsie said, glancing around as we got out of the car.

"Maybe it's a magical realm created by the Fullers," Dorothy suggested.

"If that's the case, I don't want to see the monthly bill

for additional magic." I took the driver's hand when he offered to assist me from the car.

We were outside the same castle as last time. It was a huge, imposing structure with mullioned windows and immense double doors. But this time the stone was glowing a soft pink color.

"I think the castle is happier this time," Dorothy said as we started up the wide staircase to the front door.

"I should hope so, since the last time we came for a funeral," Elsie said. "If they have so much magic, why don't they have moving stairs?"

Dozens of people in elaborate, expensive clothes were moving slowly toward the arched, open doors where Abdon, Brian's parents and Brian were greeting their guests. Dorothy waved to Brian and then stumbled in her very high-heeled sandals. I caught her arm to keep her from falling, but Brian was there a moment later.

"Are you okay?" he asked with an arm around her.

"I guess I should've worn flats like usual," she said. "I'm kind of clumsy in heels."

Unexpectedly, Brian lifted her in his arms and kissed her. "Maybe, but you're also beautiful, and I'm so glad you're here with me tonight."

People around us stared but didn't remark on the gesture as Brian carried Dorothy the rest of the way up the stairs.

"I don't suppose he'd be willing to come back for me," Elsie wondered as she huffed and puffed up the stairs.

"Probably not." I took her arm and drew her close. "But you can lean on me."

"Can I take off my shoes when we get inside? I'd forgotten how much I hate being dressed up."

"That's why we don't go to many of these things, I suppose. We're just too settled and we're happy to be comfortable."

Elsie chuckled. "I suppose we are, Molly. But we can do this for Brian, right?"

"That's right."

There was no sign of Brian or Dorothy by the time we reached the entrance. A few guests milled around at the top of the stairs after being greeted by Brian's family, but most descended into the ballroom right away.

We were greeted by the Fuller family. There was as much warmth in that greeting as one might expect from frozen fish. Not so much as a smile graced the three party-givers' faces. We barely touched hands and then moved on through the doorway. They didn't want us there and we knew it. Always a fun way to start a party.

We stood at the top of another set of stairs, this one leading down to the bottom of the large ballroom. With dozens of crystal chandeliers above us, we watched the glittering crowd of wealthy witches as they stood in groups to chat, drank champagne from sparkling flutes or whirled around the dance floor past the colored fountain and ornate furniture.

"It might have been worth it just to see this," Elsie murmured. "I've never seen so many diamonds in one place. It's almost blinding."

"Don't forget that they probably came by their jewels like we did, and they'll all disappear at dawn."

"Not hers, I'll bet." She nodded toward Yuriza Fuller, Brian's mother. "I'll bet those are real."

"They most definitely are." Council member Makaleigh Veazy joined us. She had an open, interesting face that was both stern and merciful in its countenance. There was a ring of gold in her dark eyes, and her black hair was coiffed to become a ring around her features. She had been born on the Nile River centuries before and had been instrumental in starting the first Council of Witches. She was dressed in a bright orange floor-length robe but had come without any jewels. "Just ask her. She'll be glad to tell you."

We smiled at her remark but were careful with what we said. Makaleigh was my favorite of all the council members, but our first meeting had shown that she had a streak of maliciousness too when it came to the laws of the council regarding witches and non-witches marrying and having children. I couldn't agree with her ideas, probably since I was married to a non-witch and had a son who had no magic.

The council's strict policy about erasing the memories of magic and witches from non–magic users' minds was a thorn in many witches' sides. The punishment was swift and could be badly done—using magic to erase memories was tricky business. I'd known too many lives that had been ruined by it. I understood the fear of the Inquisition and other witch hunts down through the centuries and certainly didn't want them to happen again, but this was a different time.

No one could convince the council of that.

"You know, Molly, I've thought a great deal about what you said when we first met," Makaleigh said. "I think you may be right."

"Really?" I could hardly believe she would have softened her stand on this major rule of the council. "That's amazing."

She nodded regally. "I believe you are correct about the council playing too much of a role in protecting magic from the families of witches. We have been harsh in our judg-ments. At the next council meeting, I intend to bring up changes in that code of conduct."

For Elsie and me, and thousands of other witches who had children without magic, that was good news. The idea of protecting your child from being marked by the council was a frightening thing. You never knew when someone might hear a careless whisper, and then your life would be changed forever.

"Thank you for considering it," I said. "It means a lot to many witches."

She patted her orange turban–wrapped head. "Thank you for being bold enough to say it. I think the council should go out amongst the people more often and gain back their trust. We must hear what they have to say and try to make their lives better. That was my intent when the council was formed. We lost it along the way."

I was too stunned to speak. No one on the council ever talked like that. I glanced at Elsie. She shrugged and wiped a tear from her eye.

"I hope I can count on you to support me in this, Molly." Makaleigh smiled. "Elsie. We can make things better, you know. There is always room for improvement. I shall speak with you later. Have a wonderful time."

Elsie and I hugged each other after she left us to head down into the ballroom.

"Did she really say what I thought she said?" Elsie asked.

"She did." I cleared my throat. "I don't know what to say."

"It would be so wonderful to tell Aleese about magic, even if she won't ever be able to use it herself. I know she's thought I was crazy all these years. But I was so afraid of what could happen to her if she knew about witches."

"I know what you mean." Would I tell Mike? It was hard to say, but at least I could tell him if I wanted to, or needed to, as I had Joe. I could protect them from the council, but how wonderful it would be not feeling as though they had to be protected.

The world would tilt for many witches who were afraid to share that part of their lives with their families. I would certainly support Makaleigh in that quest. I knew many others would too.

Of course there would be many who weren't ready for a broad change like that. I knew there would be stiff opposition. But Makaleigh led the council, and that could make all the difference. The evening took on a shimmering highlight that had nothing to do with diamonds or champagne.

Elsie and I still hadn't moved from the large stone landing. We stared at the array of blue diamonds on Yuriza's chest, making a few impolite remarks to ourselves, before we finally turned away.

I hadn't bothered looking for Dorothy, since I knew she was with Brian and was probably busy being introduced to his other family and friends. But there she was suddenly marching back toward us.

"Isn't this amazing? I've never seen anything like it, have you?"

"That's just what we were talking about," I said, not telling her what Makaleigh had mentioned. It had no direct bearing on her as yet. Maybe never would, since she might marry a witch and have witchlings. "Where's Brian?"

"He brought my birthday present and went to get it so he could show her off. I wish he wouldn't have. Did you notice the gift table over there?" She pointed to the far end of the room. "A cat isn't going to seem like much compared to all those other things."

We gawked at the tremendous pile of gifts—some wrapped, others open to scrutiny. There was a new red Harley-Davidson that only had a bow on it. Probably supposed to match his Corvette. I had to assume the motorcycle came from the same source.

There were wrapped boxes that size as well as smaller gifts. One of them was a moving waterfall that we speculated might contain a vacation gift. Another was wrapped in rainbows, and still another was encased in a pyramid that had fiery torches on it.

"These people go all out, don't they?" Elsie shook her head.

"There are real golden fish too," Dorothy said. "Made out of gold. Brian and I saw them. My cat is really pathetic."

"But I'm sure it will be well loved," I assured her. "What do you do with real gold fish anyway?"

"You can't eat them," Elsie said. "I'm starving. Has anyone seen the food table? I hope it's better than it was at the funeral."

The three of us went to search out the food as trays moved magically past us containing glasses of champagne and other colorful beverages, including some that were on fire.

"What do you think that is?" Dorothy asked.

"Let's try one and see." I grabbed two of the fiery beverages and handed one to her.

"I want one too," Elsie said, and grabbed one for herself off another passing tray.

The drink that was on fire was surprisingly frosty and tasted like pineapple. Dorothy took a second one from another tray going in the opposite direction.

"I wouldn't want to live this way, would you?" she asked over the top of her drink. "I hope this isn't what Brian expects after we're married. This isn't normal."

"Brian has made it very clear that this isn't the lifestyle for him," I assured her. "He said he wouldn't even come tonight if it wasn't for you."

"I know." She watched Brian as he tried to get across the crowded room carrying the pink cat carrier with the pink bow. "But things change, don't they, Molly? You and Joe aren't the same now as you were thirty years ago. What if Brian becomes like his parents?"

"I don't think Brian will ever be like them," Elsie said. "He was born a rebel, Dorothy. He's going to do what he wants to do, not what they want him to do."

Dorothy smiled. "I think I need another drink to get through this."

"Oh, look!" Elsie pointed. "There's the food. At least we don't have to grab it as it waltzes by. Come on. We'll all feel better after we've eaten."

The food was as elaborate as the rest of the party. I'd

never seen so many large, dead animals displayed in a buffet before. There were also huge amounts of vegetables and fruit, some of them on fire as well, many artfully carved. Several ice sculptures of Brian at different ages graced the long table too.

As we were filling our plates with the help of white-gloved servants, Dorothy began shaking her wrist.

"What's wrong?" I asked her. "Is the bracelet too tight?"

"No." She frowned at her wrist. "It's something else. I don't know—"

Suddenly, there was Olivia. Her ghost form had slipped out of the bracelet where she'd hidden to get into the ball.

"Oh bother."

CHAPTER 7

"What are you doing here, Olivia?" Elsie demanded. "Are you trying to get us thrown out before we even have a chance to eat?"

"I'm so sorry," Olivia said. "I just wanted to come to the birthday ball so badly. I've been practicing this spell to hide for a while. Well, not really a spell, since my magic is gone. It's more like harnessing my energy to do what I want. I know you all understand. No one wants to be left behind."

"*Shh!*" I cautioned as they started getting louder.

"We don't care what it is," Elsie continued her rant but at a lower pitch. "You have to go."

"I can't just go," Olivia wailed. "I managed to move some of my runes from the staff to the bracelet, which I thought would be much more attractive than Dorothy carrying around that big staff. You all look so lovely. I'm so jealous, even though I went to Madam Tunis's myself many times. Dorothy, you are just beautiful."

"Thanks, Mom." Dorothy walked into a shadowed corner

of the room with Olivia following her, tethered by the magic in the bracelet. "Why didn't you tell me? I would've helped you. I felt terrible leaving you home."

"You are so sweet. I just didn't want to get you in trouble."

"And yet here you are floating around," Elsie said.

"We need to get her back in the bracelet," I interrupted. "Let's not have to sneak out like last time and embarrass Brian. Elsie, find him. We may need his help making this bracelet work again."

Elsie took her plate with her to find Brian. Dorothy and I stood in the corner, hoping no one would notice that we had a ghost with us.

"I'm so sorry, Molly," Olivia said. "I thought I had the spell down perfectly. Well, not really a spell—"

"I know. *Shh.* If we can hear you speaking, so can every other witch in this room." I glared at my old friend even though I understood how she felt. "This is why you should have included us. We could've helped you and made sure what you were doing was solid."

"I know. I know. Do you think you can get me back in the bracelet?"

"We'll see. Now please, stop talking and keep very still."

Brian and Elsie were finally coming toward us. They had to part the ocean of sparkling witches who stood between us, each one wanting to wish Brian a happy birthday.

"What happened?" Brian asked when he got close.

"The inevitable," Elsie said. "Olivia screwed up again."

"You don't have to be so harsh," Olivia responded.

"We have to get her back in the bracelet," I told Brian. "You know what will happen if they catch us here."

Brian grinned at Olivia. "Nice disguise. I didn't even see you there when I was holding Dorothy."

Olivia preened at his compliment. "You really think so? I also managed to make a call to Larry's cell phone to distract everyone. That's the first time I've been able to do that."

"So you were the one who called Larry to meet us. That's why it wasn't on his phone!" Elsie exclaimed.

"I think it's great." Brian laughed. "I love that you're here. There's no reason why ghosts and witches, and werewolves too, can't mingle. It would be good for this crowd to get the sticks out of their butts."

"But not right now, please." Dorothy looked frantic. "Not tonight. We need to get her back in the bracelet before anyone sees her."

He shrugged. "Okay. Whatever you want. But I still think it's funny."

"Is there a small room where we could go to work this magic before anyone notices what we're doing?" I asked him. I agreed with Brian in principle, but I didn't want our group to be embarrassed again in front of his family.

"Sure. There are hundreds of small rooms. Follow me."

Dorothy, Elsie and I huddled around the smallest Olivia could make herself as we followed him. People kept stopping and talking to him, but they ignored us. We probably looked ridiculous—as though we couldn't walk without one another. But better that than for them to guess that we were hiding a ghost.

Brian finally opened a door. The room it revealed was as elaborately decorated as the entire castle seemed to be. The walls were covered in pink gauze with silver shot through it. The fireplace was made of pink marble, as was the floor. The furniture was delicate pink and deeply cushioned. Mirrors of different shapes and sizes hung everywhere.

"What a beautiful room," Elsie exclaimed. "Does your mother spend a lot of time here?"

"My mother doesn't spend a lot of time anywhere. My parents are always going somewhere or other. This should do to give us some privacy until we can get Olivia back in the bracelet."

Olivia was flitting around the room, admiring the

gorgeous decorations. Dorothy called her back to us so we could get on with it before Brian was missed.

"What's this?" Olivia zoomed down to the floor behind the silver and pink velvet sofa.

"Mom! Please, let's do this." Dorothy tried to get her attention.

"Oh, girls!" Olivia's head appeared through the back of the sofa. "Something terrible has happened! Makaleigh Veazy is back here. She's been hurt. I—I hope she's all right."

Brian shoved the sofa out of the way, and we all gathered behind it. Makaleigh was lying on the pink marble, which was rapidly turning red with her blood. A large, elaborately made knife was sticking out of her back. It glistened with heavy jewels in the gold hilt.

"She's still alive." Dorothy checked her pulse. "We have to get her to the hospital."

Makaleigh's eyes fluttered open in her gray face. "No. There's nothing you can do. The knife was poisoned."

We joined hands and each placed one hand on Makaleigh before we called on several strong healing spells. I could feel our strength together as we fought for her life. It felt as though she was slipping away. With all her magic, and all ours too, there was no way to bring her back. She was lost to us.

"Who did this to you?" I took her hand, squeezed hard and stared into her fading eyes. "If we can't save you, we can at least avenge you." With her died our hope of ever making the Grand Council of Witches consider changing the stranglehold of fear they held on us. No doubt there were plenty of suspects. I wished Joe was here to take charge.

"Come closer." She pulled my head down to her. "They must stop, Molly. The council must stop persecuting the witches. Promise me."

"I promise to do what I can," I said tearfully.

"Remember this." Makaleigh muttered a few words that

I couldn't clearly understand. They sounded like gibberish. Maybe the passing of a soul from one world to the next. There was no time to ask her to repeat them. I cried as her hand released mine.

"So much for not having a funeral while we're here," Elsie sobbed.

CHAPTER 8

It all seemed to have happened so quickly. One minute Makaleigh was with us, and the next she was gone. I felt confused and angry. Why had this happened? Why now of all times when the most important revolution in the last few hundred years of witch history was about to take place?

And maybe the answer to that question was what had doomed Makaleigh and her new ideas.

We didn't touch anything and left Makaleigh as she lay. Being the wife of a homicide detective, I knew the rules. Even if the police wouldn't handle this murder, things needed to be done right so that the killer could be found.

Brian went to tell his grandfather what had happened. Dorothy, Elsie and I huddled in a far corner of the room away from the dead council member. Even though this tragedy had occurred, we still had to put our magic together to get Olivia back into the bracelet. I hated to think what the other members of the council would think if they found us here—with a ghost and a dead body. We wouldn't be able to cover her presence in the castle with dozens of witches looking at us for answers as to what had happened to Makaleigh.

"Concentrate, ladies," Olivia encouraged. "I know I shouldn't have done this, but it's too late to go back now. They can't find me this way, for all our sakes."

"Brian should've stayed and helped us with this before he went off to tell everyone," Elsie grumbled.

"People had to be notified. Knowing the time of death is very important to a police investigation," I reminded her.

"I don't think that's gonna happen," Dorothy said. "The council won't let anyone else help with it."

"That's for sure," Elsie grunted. "They'd have to wipe the memories of the whole police department!"

"Let's try this again," I encouraged. "Olivia, you got yourself into this bracelet. We can help, but you need to make it happen again."

"And quickly," Dorothy urged. "It won't be long before the whole council is here."

"Not to mention all those other people who are going to want to know what's going on," Elsie said.

We joined our magic one more time, and Olivia closed her eyes. She slowly began to merge with the bracelet again. Everything but her eyes became part of the enchanted metal. It was creepy watching her eyes move back and forth across the bracelet as she tried to see what was going on, but someone would have to look closely to notice. Elsie and I finished off with a hiding spell with no more than an instant to spare.

"Where is she?" Abdon demanded as he marched like an angry general into the sitting room. "You three. I should have known you were involved."

We had to hope that Olivia had been well enough hidden in the bracelet by the time he barged in that he didn't notice.

Dorothy put her hand over her wrist, holding it against her side.

I winced to think of her putting her hand on top of Olivia's eyes.

"Move your hand, honey," Olivia whispered. "I can't see a thing."

We all shushed her at the same time, gathering closer to Dorothy. Not that it would help hide Olivia completely, but it felt as though there was solidarity when we were close.

"Are you daring to tell me to be quiet?" Abdon roared.

Brian appeared a moment later. "Don't give them a hard time. I was with them when we found Makaleigh. She was already near death. I came to get you right away. But we didn't kill her or have anything to do with it."

"Nearly dead? Did she say anything?" he demanded.

I immediately thought that his words seemed suspicious, since she had muttered those few words, which may have implicated her killer—if I could have understood her. I went back to that moment and went over what she'd said to me. It didn't make any sense, and I wasn't planning to randomly share until I knew the person who heard me wasn't her killer.

After all, Abdon may have been one of those people who didn't like the change Makaleigh was urging me to fight for. I knew that no matter what the rest of us did, with Makaleigh gone, it was unlikely that her ideas would have any impact on the council.

Not to mention that not just anyone could have killed her— though a witch of Abdon's strength would be at the top of the list. So I kept my own council on Makaleigh's last words.

Everyone was staring at me, waiting for me to say something. *Thanks, Brian!* "I'm sorry. She just thanked us for our help." It was a lie, but it might be an important one. If not, I could always tell the truth. Probably not to Abdon, but to someone.

"Of all the half-witted, incompetent witches to find someone important dead, you three are the worst!" He went down on one knee to be near her, taking her hand in his and murmuring, "Oh my dear. This should never have ended this way for you."

He was right, of course. Most witches had an idea of when they were going to die. Our magic helped us avoid accidental death, even murder. Makaleigh shouldn't have died this way. She should have been able to avoid it, just as Olivia should have. I couldn't imagine how hard this was for her, even if she couldn't see what was happening as well as we could.

Though witches were born with the information regarding their deaths, it was forbidden to share it with anyone else. No one would know when Makaleigh's death was supposed to happen. It took powerful magic for it to circumvent what should have been the natural order of her life.

As it had taken powerful, evil magic to kill Olivia.

As Abdon mourned her, more witches joined us in the small room. Brian's parents saw what had happened and came to stand with their son. Members of the council filed in, most averting their eyes from their friend's death. Because it was unnatural, many witches would try to keep themselves apart from it. It was a means of protecting themselves from further happenings away from the natural order.

The room was filled to capacity with whispering, suspicion and fear. If this could happen to Makaleigh, it could happen to anyone. No one was safe. What could be done to protect other witches from the threat?

Abdon finally got to his feet in jerky movements and wiped a hand across his tears. "We must find the witch who did this. No matter what it takes. Makaleigh's killer must be found and made to pay for his or her crime."

Everyone agreed and shouted encouragement for the idea.

I felt sure most of them wouldn't want to be actively involved in that procedure, but like other mob activities, they wanted someone else to take care of it.

"Summon the witchfinder!" Sarif Patel, one of the other council members, called to Abdon. "Bring him forward until the killer is identified."

"Witchfinder?" Elsie whispered to me. "Is that what I think it is? Is that really a thing? I mean, I've heard old stories from my grandmother, but I didn't believe it was true."

Abdon held out his hands for quiet as the shouting demands for calling the witchfinder increased.

Dorothy looked curiously at me. Like Elsie and probably every other older witch in the room, I'd heard the old tales and put them down to mythology. Many of the younger witches would have no idea what they were talking about. From the stories I'd heard as a child, it had been hundreds of years since the witchfinder was called.

The witchfinder was one of the oldest legends—at least I'd always thought of it as such—a witch's bogeyman. *If you're not good, the witchfinder will come for you.* He was supposed to be one of the original members of the Spanish Inquisition who went above and beyond his calling to bring witches to trial and finally to flame in the early 1500s. They said he was responsible for the deaths of a thousand witches. He had a knack, almost magical, for finding his prey, and he took great pleasure in getting them to confess and killing them in ghoulish ways.

When it was over, it was said that a powerful spell was cast upon him to make him the slave of the witches he'd wronged for all time. The witches could call upon him to serve them in anything they might need. His body was said to be hidden somewhere and reanimated—when they called.

It occurred to me that Makaleigh, and maybe Abdon, had helped make the decision to punish the witchfinder by this means. What spell had they used that was powerful enough to trap the man forever?

"What exactly is that?" Dorothy had never heard the old stories that Elsie, Olivia and I had grown up with.

Brian took her hand and explained in muted tones, bringing all our nightmares into real life. "I've never seen the witchfinder. He hasn't been called in hundreds of years," he whispered. "But a council member hasn't been murdered in that long either. Anything is possible now."

Even the molecules in the air around us seemed different. The passing of an ancient, powerful witch like Makaleigh was no trifling matter. I couldn't imagine how it was possible for someone to have killed her. I thought she'd be above that kind of thing. I thought all the members of the council would be better protected.

I fingered my amulet, feeling the power of the sea trapped inside it. While there was still a great deal of magic in it, it wasn't as strong here as it was in Wilmington. It had to be that we weren't near a large body of water. With the river and the sea in proximity, water witches like myself were strongest. Makaleigh was a water witch too.

"Where are we, Brian?" I asked him softly as the other witches in the room were still expressing their outrage over Makaleigh's death.

"We're still in our world, but slightly set apart in reality," he explained. "It's a powerful spell set by the Fuller family a thousand years ago. I've never had anything to do with it, but that's why no one can just get here and they had to send the cars. Leave it to the Fullers to go overboard in paranoia."

"That explains the loss of water energy that I feel around us."

"I feel the same about the earth energy," Dorothy said. "I noticed it right away. How can we not be on the earth?"

"Did I also mention the dampening spell that protects the castle from magic assaults against it?" Brian grimaced.

"That's right, ladies. My ancestors tried to think of every-thing. All the witches here are operating on half power."

"Which made Makaleigh's death possible." Elsie sneezed and looked around at us. "What? It's what happened. I hate she's gone too, but someone carefully set this up."

CHAPTER 9

My brain began going over Makaleigh's death as probably few witches here would. How many cases had I sat through, half asleep in many instances, listening as Joe droned on about what he'd done and why they couldn't find the killer they were looking for? I almost had the mind of a homicide detective after so many years.

I looked at Abdon. He was certainly powerful enough to kill Makaleigh, but then so were the other members of the council. Yet with all of them at half magic, which was placed on everyone in the castle including the Fullers, even Elsie and I could probably have killed her. That made it possible that anyone here could be guilty.

"Except the killer would be at half strength too," Dorothy echoed my thoughts as I used her as my sounding board.

"That's true," I had to agree. It wasn't going to be as easy to solve Makaleigh's murder as I thought.

"Since we are pretty sure we know why she was killed," Elsie added, "all we have to do is figure out which of the witches had the most to lose by her instituting the new plan to take away the penalties for non-witches finding out about magic."

Dorothy laughed. "You wouldn't want to say that five times fast!"

Brian commended her. "You are on the ball, Red. Are you taking new vitamins or something?"

"It's love." Elsie sniffed and put her handkerchief to her nose. "Something in here is making me allergic." She sneezed a few times.

"Girls, we should get out of here." Olivia's voice was like a tiny chirping sound when she spoke. What she said made sense, but it was harsh on my ears. "I'm kind of nervous being surrounded by a bunch of angry witches, not to mention all this talk about the witchfinder and all."

Dorothy pointed out that we would be even more noticeable if we tried to leave. "We're squished in here like sardines. We can't even move without hitting someone. This is mob mentality. We have to be careful."

Elsie, Brian and I quietly agreed.

"Just be patient," I whispered, staring into the two dots that were her pretty gray eyes in the bracelet. "We'll get out of here soon."

The two dots blinked—a little weird—and she started to say something else. Dorothy quickly put her hand across the metal, silencing her mother.

Abdon was holding out his hands for silence again. "My good friends, this is a terrible tragedy, but calling the witchfinder is no easy task, nor is it something we do lightly. We should explore all possibilities before that dread solution. Thanks to an immediate response by council member Erinna Coptus, no one has left or entered the castle since Makaleigh's death."

That made everyone start talking again. The room buzzed with it, and the sound carried from the outer areas.

Not all the hundreds of witches present could fit in the pink sitting room.

"Are you saying that we're prisoners here, Abdon?" a stout witch with a pointed white beard asked in a tone of pompous disbelief.

"Calm yourself, Sir Hardsley," Erinna said. "The spell only lasts for twenty-four hours. I'm sure that will be enough time to find Makaleigh's killer."

"I suggest we all adjourn to the main hall again," Abdon said. "We will quickly start conducting interviews of each and every witch present. The killer is still here in the castle. It won't take long to choose the guilty witch."

His emphasis on the word "choose" made me nervous. Killers weren't chosen in my experience. They were carefully discovered by unraveling their actions and the facts of the case.

"Who's going to be responsible for that?" Owen Graybeard, another member of the council, asked. "You, Abdon?"

"I'm not sure," Abdon admitted. "Perhaps the members of the Grand Council should sit together in judgment on this. That might be a better response than calling the witchfinder."

With Makaleigh dead, there were only eleven members of the council. Most of the witches present were unhappy with that idea.

"What if one of the council killed Makaleigh?" an older witch demanded. Her very fine white hair was piled a foot high on her head.

"Do you have a better suggestion, Madam Ernst?" Larissa Lonescue haughtily demanded. She was another member of the council.

"Yes." Madam Ernst was just as haughty. "It should be a combination of council members and non–council members. Just using council members isn't fair."

"I agree," Sarif Patel said. "Bring forward the witchfinder. He is impartial and won't stop until he finds the killer."

"Oh my gosh!" Dorothy put a hand to her mouth. "I forgot all about your present, Brian. She can't just stay wrapped up that way."

"Yeah. Sorry. I didn't think about her being alive." Brian quickly followed her as Dorothy pushed her way out of the room. Loud grunting and a few curses followed them, but it was Brian, so no one dared say much about his departure.

Abdon stared at me and Elsie. He appeared to be trying to put something together, and I was pretty sure I wasn't going to like it. With the bracelet containing Olivia gone, I wasn't so worried about standing out in the crowd, even with him. I stared right back until I grabbed Elsie's arm and the two of us followed Brian and Dorothy through the crowd.

"What in the world was wrong with him?" Elsie asked. "I feel as though I've had the third degree, and he didn't even speak."

"I don't know," I muttered. "But we just needed to get out of that room. I'd rather not find out what he's thinking. I'm sure it has something to do with him 'choosing' a murder suspect."

We emerged through the throng of angry, depressed witches back into the nearly deserted ballroom. Dorothy was pulling Brian behind her as they approached the ceiling-high pile of gifts.

"She's right here. You don't have to worry. I mean, it's not like she's in a closed coffin or something. She'll be fine."

Dorothy carefully picked through the gifts until she found what she was looking for. "Oh no! She got out." She held up the empty pink cat carrier. "No telling where she is now."

Brian started searching in earnest too. "Don't worry. She's just a cat. She was probably terrified and has hunched down in a corner around here somewhere."

"You can tell he's never had a cat," Elsie said. "That cat has probably been all over the castle a few times by now!"

"Oh, Brian." Dorothy rested her head against his shoulder. "That poor little kitty. We have to find her."

"I'm sure she's fine, honey," Brian said. "She's locked in too. She's here."

"Wait," Elsie said. "Let's do a locator spell for her."

"With the magic already diminished here, I don't think we can find her that way," I said to Elsie. "We might just have to look for her the old-fashioned way."

"So this is what it's like to have a cat." Brian smiled at Dorothy. "Fun."

"It's not always like this," she told him. "Once you get to know each other, this won't happen. You'll have a rapport with her, and she won't run away."

"Sounds like a wife."

Dorothy frowned at him.

"Uh-oh," Olivia whispered. "That look means trouble."

"Just kidding." Brian hugged Dorothy and took her hand. "Come on. Let's find the cat."

She laughed and they sprinted toward the stairs.

"You know, I wonder why I was sneezing in the other room." Elsie put away her handkerchief. "There are very few things that I'm allergic to."

"It's a castle," I said. "Lots of mold and mildew, even if it is maintained by magic."

"That's true, I suppose. Although I've never been allergic to mold or mildew. I'm glad it's not that way out here. I could sneeze myself to death. A fine thing to do. Lock all of us up in here with a killer. Someone's brain wasn't working when that spell was cast."

"What would you have done?" Erinna Coptus was standing behind us. Her long black hair was shining with blue highlights from the chandeliers.

"I would've called the police." Elsie didn't back down.

"It's ridiculous keeping all of us here with no way of knowing who did it."

Erinna smiled slightly, the barest upturn to the edges of her lips. "I have not lived in the human world for many years. What would these police do to find the killer?"

"You should talk to Molly." Elsie nodded at me. "Her husband is a police homicide detective. He could take care of it for you."

I was shaking my head and miming "no" as hard as I could once I understood the direction she was heading, but Elsie's words had come out anyway.

"And where is your husband, Molly?" Erinna asked.

"He doesn't have magic," I told her quickly. "Naturally he couldn't be here because he doesn't know anything about magic or witches."

"Naturally." Erinna regally inclined her head. "But we could, of course, bring him here and then clear his mind of everything that happened while he was finding Makaleigh's killer. As you can see, our resources in this matter are not the best. I'm certain we could benefit from his experience."

Elsie's expression froze as she realized what she'd done.

There were several problems with the suggestion, but I had to tread carefully. Erinna could simply decide to bring him here. She didn't need my permission. I'd worked too hard to protect him from having his memories—possible the memories of his whole life—stripped from him. I had to be careful how I declined her offer. Bringing Joe here could make the council realize that he was protected from them and they couldn't see or hear him and that he knew all about magic. I couldn't let that happen.

I nodded respectfully to Erinna. "That would have been such an honor. Alas! My husband has been ill recently, as non-witches sometimes are, and has lost many of his powers of deduction." I laid it on thick and smooth as peanut butter with a smile to sweeten the pot. "I'm afraid he is not the man he once was."

Erinna actually lightly patted my shoulder. "Poor dear. Probably for the best anyway. Whoever killed Makaleigh might have killed your husband as well if he was here investigating, Molly. I suppose that means we shall have to find another way."

"What about the witchfinder?" Elsie immediately jumped in to help me get Joe out of the conversation. "If he's so good at finding guilty witches, why not let him do it?"

Several witches had been standing around us in the ballroom, listening to our conversation. They echoed Elsie's words. Erinna shuddered and hurried away.

"I'm so sorry, Molly," Elsie muttered when the council member was gone. "I don't know what I was thinking suggesting Joe's help. I guess I thought I was with normal witches who didn't want to rule the world."

"It's all right. We got her mind off him. That's what matters. I don't think she likes the idea of the witchfinder."

"I don't think anyone who knows who and what he is would, do you? It's still hard for me to believe he's real."

She gasped as she finished speaking and put a trembling hand on mine. Her eyes were huge and terrified as she stared behind me. Witches were backing slowly away from us with the same expression on their faces.

"What the—?" I glanced behind.

"Molly Addison Renard." A deep voice called my name. "You are to be judged."

CHAPTER 10

A long, bony finger pointed toward me as I slowly faced him.

The man was tall and thin, dressed in black velvet with silver trim on the seams. It would have been considered a costume from the 1500s today, something Shakespeare or his contemporaries would have worn, with its puffed sleeves and short pants that went down to black stockings and knee-high leather boots. A real-looking sword hung at his waist.

His face appeared to be made of wax or plastic. Only the dark eyes were alive beneath it, staring out at me. Gray-laced long black hair hung to his bony shoulders in rattails.

A chill went down my spine when I looked into those dead eyes. I knew I was facing the witchfinder, Antonio de Santiago.

Elsie grabbed my arm. She was shaking and cold yet prepared to defend me. Words wouldn't come from her lips as she tried to think of what to say. I was no better, though I clenched my jaws so that my teeth didn't chatter. Just being this close to him was horrible. The evil that he had been was intensified knowing the evil that had been visited on him.

Someone had freed the demon on us. It was easy to imagine Abdon releasing him with no thought of the consequences. Who else would immediately put him after me? I wished I could laugh at Abdon with his ridiculous notions that he could use me to intimidate Brian.

The legends that accompanied the release of the witchfinder were enough to make anyone nervous. I wasn't as terrified of him as I might have been after facing down the Bone Man on Oak Island. That experience, and my amulet, had left me armored for this encounter. I was terrified but was able to stand near him without crying and begging for mercy from those relentless eyes.

"I am Molly Renard." I was proud that my voice wasn't shaking.

He wore one leather glove, slapping the other against his leathered hand as he spoke. "You discovered the victim, did you not? You shall be the first one questioned in the death of Makaleigh Veazy."

Elsie squirmed a little more under his regard before she finally laughed. It seemed to erupt from her as though she'd tried to hold it in.

"What's wrong with you?" I hissed, keeping one eye on the grim man in front of me.

"I'm so sorry," she said but laughed again. "I mean, he's a little like Michael Jackson, you know? With the one glove and all. Is he the witchfinder? I had expected him to be scarier. I guess after the sea witch, it's going to take more to scare me."

"I think you must be light-headed. Maybe you should sit down for a while," I suggested. "I'll be fine."

"No. I'm not letting them question you alone." She held her head high. "We all know that the witchfinder can use any means necessary to find out what he needs to know."

He shook his finger at her. "That's right. Do not tempt me to make you my first victim."

The dreaded witchfinder struck a pose with one knee bent and his head turned away from us as he took a pinch of snuff from a gold and enameled box.

"Oh for goodness' sake." Elsie shook her head as she snatched away his snuffbox. "That's not good for you at all, you know. I realize you've been locked in a closet, or whatever it is that they do to you between jobs, but we've discovered now that tobacco will kill you or at least shorten your life. Maybe you should try sugar-free gum or mints."

The eleven members of the council were still in the ballroom, though not close by. They carefully kept their distance from the monster they'd created. But I could hear their indrawn breaths at her audacity.

The witchfinder leaned closer to her, one dark eye closed as he peered into her face. "Give that back to me. I hardly worry about how long I shall live considering I am already more than five hundred years old."

He held out his hand, and Elsie returned the snuffbox.

"Don't say I didn't warn you," she said. "It's bad for your teeth too."

Antonio de Santiago studied her pink face for another moment before his hand closed on the snuffbox and he resumed his painfully erect posture. "You shall come with me, Molly Addison Renard, or be dragged to the cellar in chains for your interrogation."

"Wait!" Elsie interrupted us again. "This isn't ancient Spain, my friend. Everyone nowadays gets a lawyer. Molly has to have someone represent her."

"It's fine, Elsie." I was terrified that he would drag both of us to the cellar in chains. I didn't imagine that anyone would be willing to help us. "I'll be fine. Don't worry."

"No. You can't go alone." Her brilliant green eyes landed on Richard Brannigan, the witch lawyer who had helped

Olivia settle her estate. "You!" Elsie pointed to him. "You're a lawyer. Go with them."

Richard glanced around as though he was hoping she'd meant someone else. When it was clear that there was no one else, he straightened his deep blue tuxedo on his short frame and approached us. "I am not a criminal attorney," he said.

"That's all right. Molly's not a criminal," Elsie told him. "But she needs your help."

The dwarf turned his spectacled face to the council. "Must I go with her? Is there some sort of precedent that precludes this?"

Abdon shrugged. "She's asked for an attorney. You may be the only one here. I think it's fair."

His stare burned through me for a moment, and I wondered what his game was. Surely he must have been the one who decided the witchfinder should question me first. I knew the rule Joe always went by when he questioned the suspect that had found the body, but there were several of us in the room at the time.

"By that fact, I would have to sit in on hundreds of interrogations, Mr. Fuller. Who is going to pay for my services?"

Cassandra Black, the herald of the Grand Council of Witches, stepped forward. "I'm sure we would all appreciate your services, Mr. Brannigan. Think of it as a goodwill gesture that will be paid forward. These are trying times, sir."

Still not appeased by her response, the lawyer grudgingly agreed to go with me. "But does it have to be in the cellar? Have you been down there, Mr. Santiago? Not exactly the most pleasant of places."

"I do not care where the interrogations take place." The witchfinder casually withdrew a foot-long needle from his boot. "Let us quickly get to the truth of the matter."

There were gasps at the sight of the needle. We all knew

how that had been applied during the Inquisition. No one wanted to see it again. And yet I was expected to walk out of the ballroom calmly with him to my fate.

"Good." Mr. Brannigan nodded. "May I suggest we adjourn to the brandy room, then? I don't know about you, but I feel the need for a drink or two."

"This is all highly irregular." The witchfinder paced back and forth across the expensive blue Persian carpet.

Mr. Brannigan had me sit in a turquoise velvet chair beside an alabaster statue of Aphrodite, the goddess of love and beauty. It was a fully naked pose of the goddess as she rose from the sea in her oyster shell. Across the room was the large, well-stocked mahogany bar of which the lawyer had quickly availed himself.

"What's irregular about it?" the lawyer asked as he poured another brandy.

"The subject of the interrogation should be seated in a plain wood chair with her arms and legs bound to it with leather. It is the way it has always been done. This is wrong, sir. Such comfort and softness will yield us no answers."

Elsie laughed again. She'd refused to stay behind and was sitting on a matching velvet sofa across the room from me. "I told you, Antonio, it's been a while. Things have changed. Women aren't the easy targets they once were. You and your kind were able to take advantage of mostly midwives and hedge witches who were charged with witchcraft. You won't find today's witches as easy to intimidate."

Mr. Brannigan applauded. "Brava! Well said. Now, shall we get on with it? I don't want to sit in here any longer than I have to."

The witchfinder remained unhappy with his surroundings but finally came to terms with them. He still had the long needle in his hands, no doubt to intimidate me. It had once been used to decide whether or not a woman was truly a witch—and still had the bloodstains on it to prove its usage.

"It was you who found Makaleigh Veazy dead on the floor, was it not, Molly Addison Renard?"

"Please, just call me Molly and save us all some time." I flicked a glance in his direction. It was said that a witch couldn't lie to the witchfinder. I knew I would have to, since Olivia was actually the one who found her. "Yes. I found Makaleigh behind the sofa with the ceremonial dagger in her back."

The witchfinder grinned and shook his finger at me. "You are lying to me. Why is that?"

"I'm not lying," I said. "I went behind the sofa and she was lying there. I turned her over and asked her who attacked her."

"And what did she say?"

"I couldn't understand her. She was nearly gone and her voice was too weak. We whispered healing spells for her, but none of them helped. She died. And our world is the worse for it."

"Why is that?"

"Because she was about to instigate changes that would have made life so much easier for witches who live with family members who don't have magic."

"I can still sense that you are lying to me," the witchfinder said. "Did you kill Makaleigh Veazy?" He peered closely into my face.

"No. I'm sure if there were forensics we'd be able to tell whose fingerprints were on the knife," I said. "Also, there would be blood splatter on the person who actually stabbed her."

"Yes. That's right," Elsie added. "They could use that chemical and ultraviolet light to detect blood on the surrounding surfaces. I watch *CSI*."

"That's right," Mr. Brannigan said. "Clearly a police homicide detective could get to the heart of this matter faster. Why are there no witches who are police detectives?"

"Maybe there are," Elsie said. "But they aren't elite enough to be here at this party."

"Silence!" the witchfinder yelled. "You two should not be here." He waved his hand, and Elsie and Mr. Brannigan disappeared.

I guess it was me that was transported from them. I found myself alone with him in a damp, dark place—tied to a crude wood chair with leather thongs. "Where are we?"

"Where we should be, madam, to get the answers we need. Now you will only speak to me, and we shall get to the bottom of this. I will do what is necessary to have the truth from you."

CHAPTER 11

I can't say being alone with him in that terrible place didn't make me nervous. I had no idea where we were or if my friends knew where he'd taken me. It was obvious that the witches' council had given de Santiago a heavy dose of magic to use at his discretion. The irony of a witchfinder with magic put a grim smile on my face.

As though it didn't bother me to be there, I slowly looked around the prison. The room surrounding us was made of rough concrete with rusted iron bars on one side. There were other chains on the walls, and reddened torture devices hung from the ceiling. I couldn't see or hear anyone else around us. The stench was horrible, even though it was cold. I didn't want to know why it smelled so bad. I didn't want to know how many terrible things had happened here.

Were we beneath the Fullers' castle? It seemed likely to me. I doubted that the council would let their prisoner go very far. There had to be some limit on the witchfinder's magic to keep him in check.

My amulet was softly glowing in the dim light. It wasn't surprising, since it was tethered magically, and by my family line, to me. I was in danger. It was letting me know that magic was available for me to use to free myself.

The witchfinder saw it too. He bent close and stared at it. He smelled of cloves and other spices that made me want to sneeze. "This will not do. You cannot have access to your tools of magic, witch. I shall have it."

But when he tried to touch it, he received a strong shock from the living current of the sea that filled the ever-moving amulet.

"What have you in there, madam?" He moved back a step and nursed his finger. "That is magic I have never seen."

"It's old magic," I explained. "Much older than you, Senor de Santiago. The amulet can't be removed by anyone else, even someone with magic given by the council."

"We shall see," he promised. "There is more to you than appears, Molly Addison Renard. Your magic might be powerful, but I have been gifted by the council with the means to take it from you. It is my 'gift' from the council by which to break you and have your confession."

Streams of water had begun to flow from cracks in the walls and floor around us. The scent of sea life grew stronger as the water began to flow faster and pool in depressions in the old concrete. Having the water nearby made me stronger and caused the amulet to glow even more fiercely. I didn't know where the water was coming from, and I couldn't tell if the witchfinder had noticed it. He seemed so intent on what he was about to do that I thought it might have eluded him.

I had a feeling that I knew what was happening, and I didn't give it away. If it was what I suspected, Antonio was in for a big surprise.

The witchfinder took out a crudely made pair of pliers and came toward me to cut the amulet's chain from my neck.

His booted foot splashed in the pools of water as he moved. He glanced around, watching the water fill the chamber. His quickly worded incantation did nothing to stop the water from spilling into the cell—if anything, it came faster.

He swore softly in Spanish but kept coming at me with the pliers. "Water will not avail you, madam. I have taken the lives of water witches in the past."

I closed my eyes and recited every spell I knew to break bonds and get free. I felt the leather loosening around my wrists, but it wasn't fast enough. I knew he couldn't cut the amulet chain, but I was worried about what he might do with those nasty-looking pliers once he found out.

I could have been home eating pizza with Joe and Mike, I reminded myself, breaking my concentration, when I realized I couldn't get away fast enough. My heart was pounding in my ears as fear took hold of me and I grasped why even the witches with magic during the Inquisition couldn't get away. It was difficult to retain control of the necessary concentration to make magic work when you were terrified.

"My dear Molly," a familiar voice said. "What are you doing down here?"

I opened my eyes to the awful—but right now wonderful—face of the Bone Man. He was too tall for the chamber and had to bend his head to stand. His black eyes were normally frightening, but compared to the witchfinder, I was happy to see him.

"What is this?" the witchfinder demanded. "I said I would be alone with this lady." He snapped his fingers again and again, thinking he could dismiss the Bone Man from his sight as he had Mr. Brannigan and Elsie.

The Bone Man laughed, his bloody red mouth stretched to its fullest. "You can't wish me away. The power of the Grand Council of Witches means nothing to me."

"You do not belong here, sir." The witchfinder was

beginning to understand what he was dealing with. "Your magic has no place here."

"I belong where that amulet is used." The Bone Man nodded toward me. "This witch is under my protection." His neck creaked as though it might fall from his shoulders. A necklace of dried bones clicked together when he moved. It hung above a black suit that had been fashionable in the 1700s.

"I am Antonio de Santiago." The witchfinder curtly nodded to him. "Molly Addison Renard is my prisoner."

The Bone Man's laugh still made my skin crawl, even though I knew he was on my side and was there to help me. His black eyes fastened on the witchfinder with deepening fury. "Then you and I have a problem, dead man."

"I have everything in good control," I assured my erstwhile protector as I held up my hands so he could see that I had finally worked them free between the magic and the water. "I was about to get away. I appreciate you coming for me, but I can take care of myself."

Water had begun spraying from every direction and was ankle deep on the floor, probably ruining my shoes from Madam Tunis's. It seemed pressurized, as it started spewing in very quickly, making eddies and ripples across the concrete. I couldn't see where, if anyplace, it was going back out. Bits of sand and plant matter from the ocean were mixed with it, swirling in the warm salt water.

The Bone Man shrugged, his eyes appearing much larger than they should have been in his gaunt face. "Very good. But I shall still see you out of this place, Molly. I am prepared to offer you a very good bargain to rid yourself of this council trash. Part of it will be my pleasure."

"Council trash?" The witchfinder was obviously offended by the term. "I am the chosen of the Council of Witches, sir. Begone before they realize you are here and come for you."

"We both know the council has no power over me, dead

man." The Bone Man smiled slowly. "I'd love to see them come."

"No." I tried to stop the discussion. "He's here to do a job." I stared at the witchfinder. "I'd rather you not get rid of him. He may yet be valuable."

"Then it seems my work is done." The Bone Man cracked his prominent joints in his large, bony hands and feet. "Another time."

Though he was gone, the water continued filling the chamber. It was up to my knees by then. I was free of the chair restraints but had no idea how to get out of that terrible place.

"I do not recognize that man." The witchfinder still pondered the mystery of the Bone Man. "I am not even certain he was a man. Where did he come from? Where has he gone? Why was my magic nothing against him?"

"Right now, we should think about getting out of here." I wasn't a witch who could snap my fingers and be elsewhere. While I loved the water and felt stronger in its embrace, I could also drown. It might be harder for me to die that way, but I didn't want to find out. "Perhaps we should go back to the brandy room."

"Perhaps you are correct." His curious gaze was steady on mine. "You have powerful friends. But I still know that you are lying to me."

With water approaching my thighs, I said, "Let's leave this place, and I'll tell you what you want to know."

"Simple enough." He nodded and we were back in the brandy room. Elsie and Mr. Brannigan were gone. It was only me and the witchfinder. I staggered, unsure of my feet and not used to using so much power to get places.

"Now, the truth." His eyes were sharp behind the mask.

"Someone else found Makaleigh," I confided. "But it was not a witch."

I explained about Olivia as I grabbed a hand towel from

behind the bar to dry my shoes and legs. I was surprised to find the shoes in good condition, barely wet at all. It had to be part of their magical properties. It would be awesome to have a pair of my own.

Unfortunately the magic would be over at dawn, but the spell to keep us in the castle would still be in place. Dorothy, Elsie and I wouldn't be naked, as Madam Tunis had promised, but I was hoping we wouldn't be the only ones to be de-glammed.

"This I believe," the witchfinder said as I finished my story. "No wonder that creature from the sea came to protect you. Not everyone would have walked into a company of witches who hate ghosts knowing she has a ghost pressed into a bracelet. You do not appear to be unintelligent, so I must believe you are brave," he acknowledged, "but fool-hardy."

"Thank you." I didn't explain that I had no idea Olivia had hidden herself in Dorothy's bracelet. It felt like a good time to leave without telling the complete story.

"And so you are exonerated. I move on to interrogate that foolish friend of yours who dared defy me." His bearing became stiff and rigid again as he took a pinch of snuff and sneezed.

"I'm afraid that's a waste of your time too, Antonio. I was in the room with Elsie, Dorothy and Abdon Fuller's grandson, Brian, when we found Makaleigh. None of us were with her alone. You need to look elsewhere for the killer."

He sat slowly on one of the velvet chairs, fingering his pencil-thin mustache. "I am quite confused by this turn of events. But how shall I redeem myself if I do not question your friends?"

"Well, you could say you questioned them," I suggested. "Call them all in here, but then let's strategize. One of the witches in the castle is still guilty of murder. It would be my honor to help you discover who that is."

"And you would do this for me?"

"Makaleigh was a very special person. I would do it for her."

He jumped to his feet and held out his hand. "Then let us begin, madam. The truth awaits."

CHAPTER 12

The witchfinder did as I suggested, grimly summoning my friends into the brandy room one at a time until all of us were together. Brian immediately poured himself a drink when he heard why we were all there.

"That's amazing." Dorothy was surprised when she heard the tale of the Bone Man and the witchfinder. "We have good news too. We found Brian's cat. She somehow managed to get out of the box and was wandering through the castle. Brian and I did a locator spell and found her."

"Great." I looked around the room. "What did you do with her?"

"Brian and Dorothy put her back in the carrier and took her upstairs to their room. I guess we all get rooms, since we have to stay here," Elsie said. "Brian, pour me one of those too, please. I feel a headache coming on, and it needs something stronger than an aspirin."

Brian handed her a drink.

"But as soon as he saw her he knew her name," Dorothy continued her story. "It was amazing. At least she was okay."

"Really? What are you going to call her?" I asked.

"Kalyna." Brian laughed. "It sounds crazy, but that's what I got from her, and Dorothy said that's how you name them."

"I can't believe you never had a cat," Elsie added. "Your parents really neglected your childhood. What witch doesn't have a cat?"

The witchfinder had been restlessly moving about the room as we spoke. He finally gave up all attempts at keeping still. "While you prattle about your cat, a killer is free in the castle. He or she may kill again. This is no way to run an investigation."

We all sobered at the reminder of why we were there. Once he had our attention, Antonio asked us on which witch he should begin his interrogation.

"I think that's where you're missing the point," Elsie told him. "In this day, people aren't interrogated so much as those looking for the truth find it with scientific means."

"There is no torture?" he demanded indignantly. "No scalding of the feet nor pain?"

"Definitely not." Dorothy shuddered. "We just don't do things that way anymore—well, at least not here. There are some places where torture is still used. It's usually waterboarding or sleep deprivation. Sometimes they use drugs."

"Thank you." I smiled at her and gave her the finger-slicing-across-my-neck sign of that being too much information. "But what Elsie said is true, Antonio. We use scientific ways of approaching evidence that will lead us to the killer. This is what my husband does every day as a homicide detective."

"What are these scientific methods you speak of?" he asked. "How do you utilize them?"

"Well, as we mentioned before—someone out there

should have blood splatter on them from using the ceremonial knife," I explained. "We'd need some luminol and a black light to see blood where it seems invisible now."

"And there would be prints on the knife," Elsie said. "They would match the killer's prints."

"Prints?" Antonio swore in fluent Spanish. "What are these prints you speak of?"

"Let me show you." Dorothy took out a tiny notepad and her makeup brush. "You put some powder on someone's fingertips and then push them down on the paper." She showed him her fingerprints on the notepad. "Everyone has different prints. Let's do yours and we can compare our prints."

She carefully dusted the witchfinder's fingertips and then pushed his fingers on the notepad beside her print. "There. You see? Our prints are completely different. If we did one for everyone in the room, they'd all be different."

"And that's the way we find out who killed Makaleigh," Elsie added.

Antonio looked carefully at his fingers and at the marks on the notepad. "Where do we start this scientific examination? Every witch here could be guilty."

"We should start with the knife," I told him. "Where is it?"

"I do not know, since I could not interrogate the blade." He looked exasperated with the turn of events he wasn't expecting. "I shall inquire as to its resting place." He bowed slightly to us and left the brandy room.

Olivia's ghost popped out of Dorothy's bracelet. Even for Olivia, she looked stressed.

"What are you doing, Molly? I can't believe you all are trying to reform the witchfinder. Have you lost your minds? This man is a monster. We all know that. He can't be bargained with or taught new ways of finding killers. We have to get out of here. He said you were innocent—let him and the council take it from here."

"But we may never know who killed Makaleigh that way," I argued. "It hasn't been easy getting to this point with him, Olivia. I don't think he's a monster—just a man obsessed with his job and finding the truth. We can help him not to have to use enhanced interrogation techniques."

"It's crazy. Dorothy, you should at least get out of here. Brian, get my daughter somewhere safe."

"We can't leave the castle," he reminded her. "This room is as safe as any other with the killer still wandering around out there. At least he or she is only at half magic. Once the spell wears off, everyone will leave, and Makaleigh's killer could go free. This is the best shot we have, Olivia. I agree with Molly on this one."

"Anyway, I'm not leaving, Mom," Dorothy said. "We're going to find the killer, just like we figured out who killed you. We can do this. I wish Joe was helping us, but we'll have to do it without him."

"Don't wish that too hard," I disagreed. "I wouldn't want him here. This is an ugly side of being a witch I hope he never has to know about."

The witchfinder returned. He wasn't alone, accompanied by Abdon. The elder witch and council member was angry. He shook the Spaniard, nearly lifting him off his feet before he tossed him to the Persian carpet as though he was a rag doll. If there had been witches like Abdon during the Inquisition, things would have gone much differently.

"What game are you playing at, Brian?" Abdon's voice shook with his fury. "For hundreds of years, the witchfinder has used extreme measures to get to the truth. Now you have him wanting to find fingerprints on the knife that killed Makaleigh. What next—he'll be asking pretty please for information?"

"Grandfather, this is a better way. Every study ever done has showed that torture doesn't work. People say whatever you want them to say just to stop the torture. If you allow us to proceed, with the help of the witchfinder, I think we'll catch the real killer."

Staring at Abdon's livid face, I wasn't sure what his response would be. He was used to doing things his own way. The Council of Witches never took rationality into consideration when making their judgments.

But then his features softened when he gazed on the handsome face of his only grandson. "All right, Brian. On one condition." He put a hand on Brian's shoulder. "I want you to take Makaleigh's place on the council when this is over. I won't be here forever, you know. But there has always been a member of our family on the council. You should be next in line."

I could see that Brian was struggling for words. If he had any political aspirations to follow in Abdon's footsteps, I'd never heard him mention them. I thought he was as polar opposite from the old man as possible. I wondered why Abdon planned to skip a generation—shouldn't he be talking to Schadt about replacing Makaleigh?

Even though the council was political, with members of the same families coming and going as sitting participants, there were no elections. The council decided who took empty spaces, though to my knowledge, there had never been a place open on the council in my lifetime.

"Well?" Abdon asked impatiently. "You want to change things, do things your way, don't you? The only way to do that is to join the council. Make the changes you want to see. How do you think things got to be the way they are now?"

"That's not saying much," Elsie muttered.

"It's easy to say that now," Abdon continued. "During the time of the witchfinder and those like him, witches would have given anything to have an authority like the council. We protect witches, provide ways for them to prosper. I'm sure your girlfriend would approve, right, Debbie?"

Brian's jaw tightened. "Dorothy. Not Debbie. And I don't

want to be on the council. If you don't care whether or not you have the right witch who killed Makaleigh, why should I? What way is that to convince me that I should join a useless organization that I don't agree with? Excuse me. The air is kind of thick in here for me."

He brushed passed Abdon in a disrespectful way, his blue eyes hard on his grandfather. Dorothy followed closely behind him with a subtle glance at me and Elsie.

Abdon stared at us too. "I suppose you're pleased with that. You've been trying to turn him against me since you forced him into your coven."

"I'm not happy about it," Elsie said plainly. "I think Brian would be great on the council, and I wouldn't mind being friends with people in high places. But he's probably right— the stuffiness might kill him. As for forcing him into our coven—that boy never even had a cat! For being such powerful witches, you and his parents have done nothing for him as far as I'm concerned."

His mouth opened and closed like a disbelieving fish out of water. He obviously didn't realize that Elsie always spoke her mind.

"We really aren't your enemy, Mr. Fuller." I tried to smooth things over. "It doesn't seem to me that Brian has ever been on the same wavelength with his family. I agree with Elsie that we could use his fresh ideas on the council, but coercing him to do it won't work."

"When I need advice from two witches who are so far beneath me as to almost be invisible, I'll let you know."

He stared at the witchfinder, who was still on the floor where Abdon had thrown him. "Get up and get on with your job. You know the consequences if you don't find the witch responsible for Makaleigh's death."

The door slammed behind him, and Elsie poured herself another drink.

"I thought this party was going to be fun," she said. "I'd rather watch Larry catch fish than be here."

Without considering my actions, I went to Antonio and offered my hand to help him up. He ignored me to begin with and then suddenly caught hold of me and rose to his feet.

"Are you all right?" I asked him.

He tried to smile, I felt sure of that, but the mask that covered his face barely moved. Still, I saw something in his dark eyes that wasn't there before. I didn't know what to call it—hope? Understanding? I wasn't sure.

"I'm sorry you had to go through that. I guess you'll have to do what the council tells you to do," I said.

Antonio took my hand and pressed it to his face where his lips would have been. "Dear lady, you have given me something wonderful. I will not dishonor it by taking the old roads. We shall investigate this murder according to your scientific methods, not using torture. What more can the council do to me?"

"They could kill you." Elsie snorted.

"There is so much worse than death," he said. "I have seen all of it. I no longer fear what may come of me. Let us away and find the blade that was used by the killer."

CHAPTER 13

He held out his arm, and I took it with no trepidation. There was only the feeling of bone and sinew beneath the velvet of his clothing. The council had further tortured him by leaving him as a living man all those years.

"Where are we going to look for the knife?" Elsie hurriedly polished off her drink. "It could be anywhere by now."

We left the brandy room and found Brian and Dorothy beside the large pile of birthday gifts. Brian was stroking the small black cat Dorothy found as a familiar for him, Kalyna. She reminded me more of the black dragon in *How to Train Your Dragon* than any cat I'd ever seen. Her eyes were a violet color as she stared at me. She didn't look happy to see us, but I couldn't read her thoughts as I could Isabelle's. Maybe this was simply her response from being trapped in a birthday box for so long. Some familiars were also naturally standoffish to anyone but their witches.

"We're looking for the knife that killed Makaleigh," I

told Brian as I stroked the cat. "Any idea where it came from or where it might be?"

Brian glanced at Antonio. "He's gonna help us?"

"Yes. He's ready to move on from his past." What I said was followed by a yelp as Kalyna scratched me. "Someone needs to learn some manners."

"Sorry, Molly," Brian apologized, taking her from me. "I think she's just freaked-out by all of this. I'll sheathe her claws until she calms down."

As good as his word, tiny sheaths appeared on each of Kalyna's claws. She meowed loudly and hissed at Brian but didn't try to get away from him.

"Maybe we could ask Oscar. He manages the castle for my family. He was more like a father to me than my father or Abdon when I was growing up. And he knows everything that goes on around here. If anyone knows where the knife went, it's him." Brian took the lead across the ballroom.

Black-and-gold-clothed servants were offering rooms to the witches who were trapped in the castle until the spell wore off. It hadn't been long enough for any of Madam Tunis's magic outfits to change as yet, but many of the guests were looking bedraggled and unhappy as they waited for word of what happened to Makaleigh and when they could get on with their own lives.

"Where is Oscar?" Dorothy asked.

"He's bound to be around here somewhere," Brian told her. "I'm sure giving rooms to everyone was his idea. I can't imagine my parents caring if anyone needed a place to get away from the crowd."

Kalyna took a swipe at Dorothy, catching her on the wrist. The claws were covered but still managed to lightly scratch her arm.

"I don't know what's wrong with her," she said of the exotic-looking black cat. "She wasn't aggressive like this when I bought her."

"Sometimes it's hard for a familiar when they first meet their witch." Olivia's voice sounded tinny coming through the bracelet. "I understand how she feels. Being in this bracelet isn't easy either."

"It's true," Elsie agreed. "Kalyna will be fine after a while. She's very beautiful."

The cat meowed at her and didn't try to scratch her.

"Maybe that's the answer," Dorothy said. "She just needs a lot of compliments."

Kalyna was too far away to scratch her, but she hissed loudly at her and flattened back her ears.

"Or maybe not," Dorothy reconsidered.

Brian seemed too worried about finding Oscar to be concerned with the cat. "There he is. Oscar! I need to talk with you."

Oscar was a tall, bald man with one gold earring. It might have been terrible to think it, but he reminded me of Mr. Clean, the personified cleaning product. He was muscular and dressed completely in black.

"I was wondering when I'd see you." Oscar hugged Brian with a big smile on his face. "You're looking good! The outside life agrees with you. I'm surprised you came for your party."

"I know." Brian curled his lip. "I probably wouldn't have, but Dorothy wanted to come."

"The girlfriend." Oscar turned to her and hugged her. "I'm glad Brian finally found someone important."

"Thanks. He's told me so much about you." Dorothy smiled. "And this is the rest of our coven—Molly, Elsie and, inside this bracelet, my mother."

"Inside?" Oscar frowned as he examined the bracelet. "A ghost!"

"Pleased to meet you," Olivia whispered.

"For goodness' sake!" Oscar slapped Brian's back. "What else have you brought with you to upset your grandfather?"

The two men started walking away, catching up.

"That's more than Brian gets from his whole family," Dorothy said softly. "They are the coldest bunch of people I've ever met."

"What about the council seat?" Elsie murmured as Brian spoke with Oscar. "Is he going to do it?"

"I don't think so," Dorothy replied. "He's completely against the idea. I keep wondering why Abdon didn't ask Schadt. He and Brian's mother seem very political. I'm sure they'd love for one of them to be on the council."

"That's gotta be a hard pill for Abdon to swallow," Elsie said. "Even witches like for their sons to follow them in the family business."

Brian brought Oscar back to where we trailed him in the crowd. "Oscar saw the blade after they moved Makaleigh's body," he said. "He knows where they put it."

"Follow me," Oscar said. "The blade is an ancient one belonging to one of your ancestors, Brian. It's always been kept in a sealed glass box until now."

"Was the box spelled?" Elsie asked.

"No. Not as far as I know," Oscar replied. "There are daggers, knives and swords all over the castle. No one has ever killed a visitor with one—at least not for hundreds of years."

He led us back to the pink sitting room, where we'd found Makaleigh. It had been thoroughly cleaned. Until it appeared as though nothing had happened there earlier.

Brian picked up the glass case that held the dagger. "It's in here again. I don't think they saved the fingerprints. Probably didn't even think of it. It was probably wiped down like the rest of the room."

Of the group, the witchfinder looked most distressed by the news. "How can we use scientific method if there are no fingerprints?"

"Just because the knife was wiped clean doesn't mean anything," I told him. "Trust me—it might appear clean, but there are always microscopic cracks in the metal, and blood gets trapped there. And no matter how well they wipe it, usually there are at least partial prints left, especially on something this ornate. It would be hard to wipe them all off."

"Look at that big red ruby on the hilt." Elsie pointed without touching. "There's something smeared right there. On *CSI*, they use prints that get trapped in blood all the time."

"We need some gloves." I took the glass case from Brian. "We're going to need a few other things too. Do you have any superglue?"

"In the kitchen." Oscar grinned. "Not everything that breaks needs magic to repair it."

"What are you doing, Molly?" Elsie asked.

"Joe showed me this. He used superglue in a case to find the fingerprints. It reacts with the chemicals found in fingerprints and leaves a white film that you can take a picture of."

"What next?" Dorothy wondered.

"The kitchen will be perfect to heat the box," I told them. "We need something like a coffee or tea warmer, low watt."

We walked across the ballroom and down a long stone hallway to a kitchen that made the gigantic ballroom look like a pantry. There were dozens of workers preparing food at the long stainless steel tables and the large stoves. Refrigerators and freezers lined the walls. Modern lighting had been installed here, so things were easier to see. It appeared the Fullers liked their food made to specification.

"What about using one of these candle warmers?" Dorothy picked one up as we walked by it on a shelf.

"That should do it," I agreed. "We need a small bowl of water too."

"I'll get the superglue," Oscar volunteered. "Brian, you can handle the water, right?"

Brian grinned. "Yeah. I think I can do that."

We got all the ingredients together and put the knife, warming tray and water into a cardboard box. I tried to remember exactly what Joe had told me, but I wasn't sure I could have put the whole thing together without Elsie's help—she recalled someone doing something similar on television. She loved all the detective and mystery shows.

When everything was set up, we had to wait ten minutes for the development of the fingerprints on the knife. Brian questioned Oscar about Makaleigh, asking if he'd ever noticed her arguing with someone or being threatened by one of the other witches.

Oscar ran his hand over his smooth face. "You know the council is always bickering with one another. Those are the only ones I've ever heard Makaleigh argue with. She and Abdon seemed like they couldn't agree on anything. This new idea she had of not punishing non-witches for knowing about magic was a hot button for almost everyone on the council."

"Enough that one of them might have wanted to kill her to keep her from doing it?" I asked. I'd heard Joe talking about even less important reasons, so I wouldn't be surprised.

"They're afraid," Elsie summed up. "Like with Antonio here, everything is always supposed to stay the same. People fear change, you know."

"They do," the witchfinder agreed slowly. "I know this better than most."

"But Makaleigh and Abdon were always the ones most likely to cross swords," Oscar said. "You know how he gets, Brian."

"I do. Thanks." Brian's face was grim when he looked at us. "We can't rule out that my grandfather could have killed her, or it could have been another member of the council."

"Difficult no matter," the witchfinder said. "And deadly."

CHAPTER 14

The chiming of the timer we'd set for ten minutes couldn't have come at a worse moment. Everyone, except the witch-finder, jumped.

"I guess that's it," Dorothy said. "Will you do the honors, Molly?"

"You know we still have nothing to compare this to even if there is a print on the knife," Elsie reminded me. "And no national fingerprint database to look it up. I don't know if this will work without police assistance."

"Perhaps it would be wise to find the fingerprints of the witches who seem most guilty," Antonio suggested. "That is normally where I would start my interrogations."

"Good idea," Brian agreed. "And that's why you started with Molly."

"Yes." Antonio took my hand and kissed it. "Forgive me, dear lady."

"Not a problem." I started dismantling the fingerprint

box. "My mother always told me that I had a guilty expression even when I didn't do anything wrong."

After taking the knife carefully out of the box, I could clearly see fingerprints on it.

"It looks like a thumb and forefinger to me." Elsie examined it closely.

"Quick!" Brian took out his phone. "We need pictures."

At that point we all pulled out our phones and took pictures.

"We don't have to worry about not having enough evidence." Dorothy smiled as she looked at the burst of pictures she'd just taken with her camera. "Now what?"

"Now we do what Antonio said. We get fingerprints from our top suspects." I looked at the single picture on my phone camera. "It could be anyone."

Oscar, who'd waited in the kitchen with us while he checked on food preparations, came back when he saw the pictures being taken. "I assume you got something."

"Yes. Now we have to be creative and get prints from everyone on the council, since they seem to be our main suspects." I showed him the fingerprints on the knife. They were already fading as the fumes from the superglue escaped. Lucky we had the pictures, and that the evidence didn't have to hold up in court. "Anyone have any suggestions?"

Antonio cleared his throat. "I am the witchfinder. I am expected to conduct the interrogations of the guilty. Perhaps this is slightly different, but nevertheless, it should be my job to secure what is needed to find the guilty. And I shall take possession of this blade as the weapon of death."

"That's not gonna happen," Oscar said. "The knife belongs to the Fuller family. You'll have to get permission from Abdon if you want to take it."

The witchfinder formally nodded. "I am certain that can be done."

"Until then." Oscar took charge of the knife, replacing it in the glass case.

"Okay then." Elsie cleared her throat. "Sounds like a good idea to me."

"Great," Brian agreed. "I'll get Kalyna into my room so I don't have to carry her around with me everywhere."

"While the witchfinder does his job, why don't I see each of you to a room where you can refresh yourselves?" Oscar offered politely. "It's nearly morning. Breakfast will be served promptly at seven A.M."

"Yes." Dorothy smiled at Brian. "I could use a shower before my clothes turn back to rags and I'm not wearing glass slippers."

"Then allow me to lead the way." Oscar started toward the kitchen door.

"Are you sure you'll be all right doing this?" I asked Antonio as everyone else started to leave. "I could go with you. I don't want to see you get in trouble because you aren't torturing people."

His eyes behind the mask were alive with mischief. "Who says no one must be tortured to procure their fingerprints?"

"I guess that's true."

"I do not plan to torture anyone, Molly," he assured me. "Not again for the witches or for anyone else. Though it may cost my life, I swear it is so."

I understood that he was joking with me, probably in the only way he knew how. "Just don't make it worse for yourself. I know what you were, but you don't have to be that person anymore."

"You are too kind." He kissed my hand again. "Trust me. It shall be done."

He and I walked out of the kitchen together before he went on ahead. Elsie had waited for me while Dorothy and Brian had gone ahead with Oscar.

"Does anything seem off to you about that cat?" Elsie asked.

"Besides her scratching everyone but Brian, no. Does she seem off to you?"

"I don't know." She shook her head. "It's probably too much brandy and not enough food. Do you really think the witches' council will agree to being fingerprinted by the witchfinder?"

"I'm almost too tired to care," I admitted. "I need some way to call Joe and let him know what's going on. Mike is home, and they'll be worried about me."

"I left Aleese a note and told her I was going on a cruise with Larry." She laughed. "She's getting used to that now, and it makes it so much easier for me. I should have made up a boyfriend years ago."

"Elsie!"

"I know. My mother always said I was such a good person. I think she just never really knew me." She grinned. "Let's get up to the bedrooms and get some rest. We'll see if we can patch you through to Joe somehow. Even if our magic is at half power—we're used to that. The kids can help us. We'll find a way. We always do."

Oscar put Dorothy in a room with Brian. I thought about it being a little obvious, but then I realized that this was the twenty-first century. People didn't think that way anymore. Besides, I wasn't her mother—Olivia was, and she going to be with her the whole time. She could handle the details.

After he'd finished with Brian and Dorothy, I asked if Elsie and I could bunk together. I knew neither of us wanted to be in a room alone. Oscar was very gracious about showing us to a large room right next to Dorothy and Brian that we could share. He nodded when we thanked him, and he left us with a reminder about breakfast.

"If you need anything, please ask. We have clothes, shoes, toiletries, anything you might need."

"Thank you, Oscar," I said.

He nodded and was gone with no doubt thousands of things to attend to.

The room was gorgeous, as everything in the castle seemed to be.

"The dungeon or wherever it was Antonio took me wasn't so nice," I told Elsie as we examined the burgundy silk comforter on the oversized bed with a matching canopy. "I never expected to see the Bone Man there. I thought he was done with me."

She was delighting over the large bay window nook that overlooked a wonderful garden far below us. "I don't think he's ever going to be finished with you as long as you wear that amulet."

"You might be right. I could have gotten away without him." I stood next to a marble fireplace that was taller than me. "I didn't need him."

"Really, Molly," Elsie chided as she studied the crystal chandelier above us from the comfort of a red velvet chair. "I don't think the witchfinder would have let you go except that the Bone Man was there and he was afraid of him. You may as well give credit where credit is due."

"I know you think I should give up the amulet."

"I do," she agreed. "It hasn't brought you a moment's peace since you put it on, and I don't think it ever will."

"It makes my magic stronger."

She tsked. "I'm sure Dorian Gray used a similar argument about his portrait being evil."

"I'm not Dorian Gray!"

Olivia's ghost came through the magnificent wallpaper that portrayed a complete scene from the Middle Ages as it progressed around the room. "Yoo-hoo. Girls? Are you decent?"

"Since when did that matter?" Elsie demanded. "I don't

know how many times you've seen me in the altogether since we were young. Sometimes, I thought you did it on purpose."

"Don't be absurd," Olivia denied. "I was just curious, and you are older than me. I had questions about the female body."

"That was a long time ago," I said. "I thought you'd be chaperoning Dorothy and Brian."

"They don't need me." Olivia flitted around the room, looking at everything much the same way Elsie and I had. "In fact, I think they were glad to be rid of me. And I was longing for a bit of intelligent conversation that didn't have anything to do with giggling or the cat. Did you two notice anything strange about that cat? I wasn't with Dorothy when she bought it."

"That's what I was saying to Molly." Elsie glanced at herself in the full-length mirror and adjusted her dress. "I don't know what it is, but something's not right."

"I think we should focus on helping Antonio find Maka-leigh's killer," I said. "I need to call Joe first, and the cell phone doesn't work here. Elsie, let's give it a try before I ask Brian and Dorothy for help."

"I'm so sorry I let you down by being murdered," Olivia said. "I still can't believe it happened to me. I know I'll be a lot happier once I can use my ghostly abilities."

"One of those ghostly abilities wouldn't include talking to other ghosts, would it?" I wondered. "If so, maybe you could contact Makaleigh and this would be all over. We'd know who killed her, and we could go home."

"Good idea." Elsie backed me up. "What about it, Olivia?"

"I can certainly give it a try," she said. "I'll start down there in the pink sitting room where she was killed. We're both witches who were murdered. We should have some-thing to say to each other. I'll be right back."

"While she's gone, why don't we try to get in touch with Joe?" Elsie said. "I don't like to hurt her feelings by doing magic around her if I can help it. I can't imagine what it's like for her to feel so powerless."

"That's what I was saying about the amulet." I tackled the ongoing argument again. "It makes me stronger. Larry makes you stronger, you know. I can tell a difference in you."

"Oh for goodness' sake! He does no such thing!"

"And you say I won't admit things! Your relationship with him has made a huge difference. When was the last time you messed up a spell?"

"I don't know," she hedged. "Not recently, I suppose."

"You were unhappy and lonely," I said. "Larry came into your life and changed that."

"Along with other activities we've undertaken recently," she replied. "But that's different than you relying on that amulet anyway. Larry isn't the Bone Man. I don't see how anything good can come of a relationship with him. And you can see by him showing up that you do have a relationship, Molly."

"I know what you're saying, Elsie. But this still belonged to my mother and going back several generations in my family. I don't see it as being bad."

"Then we'll have to agree to disagree."

"All right." I nodded, not liking being at odds with her. "Let's see if we can make that call to Joe, huh?"

"Let's do it."

We held hands and used a simple communication spell. There was no need to use the enchanted bubble, since Joe wasn't here with us. The bubble protected communication from the council—or other witches. I wasn't worried about anyone else overhearing us.

"Joe?" I could faintly see him.

"Molly?" He was in his office at the police department, looking around for me. "Is that you?"

"Yes." I tried to concentrate harder. "I'm not going to be home for a while but I'm okay. I just wanted you to know so you wouldn't worry."

"Okay. Is this a witch telephone? You sound like you're on a bad cell," he joked. "Can you get a clearer signal?"

The link between us went completely dead. I couldn't see Joe at all.

"Nuts." Elsie opened her eyes. "We're going to need the children. I was hoping we could do it ourselves. I hate when they get all over us because their magic is better."

"Me too, but this call might have been worse than Joe not knowing anything. I have to get through to him again."

"All right. But next time, make up something short and sweet before you talk to him."

We knocked on the adjoining door between our rooms. There was no response.

"Sounds like they could be dead in there," Elsie said, pressing her ear to the door.

"That heavy breathing sounds like they're alive," I whispered.

"Which one?" Elsie asked. "I don't want to know what's going on in there."

I grinned and nudged her with my elbow. "It hasn't been that long! I think you know what's probably going on."

We both heard Dorothy giggling.

"I guess I haven't forgotten after all." Elsie smiled. "Too bad Olivia isn't here. She'd really like this."

We knocked again, but there was no answer.

"We know you're in there," Elsie called out. "It's only me and Molly. You're adults. It doesn't matter what you do anymore."

I tried the door, pushing it open when it stuck.

There was still no sign of Dorothy and Brian, but a young, dark-haired beauty was holding Brian's shirt to her face as though she were smelling it.

"Who are you?" Elsie asked.

"Look at her eyes," I said. "It's Kalyna."

CHAPTER 15

"The cat?" Elsie's cinnamon-colored brows shot up above her amazed green eyes.

"I think that's why we all felt something odd about her. She's a shifter."

"Don't tell Brian," the girl asked of us. "He doesn't need to know."

Dorothy and Brian came up behind us. We all stared at one another like owls caught out during the day.

"Hello." Dorothy smiled. "Did you need something?"

"We actually came because I need your help contacting Joe. I don't want him to worry about me."

"And then we found something more interesting," Elsie said with a nod toward the bed.

But the clever young woman who was also a pretty black cat had changed form and was sitting on Brian's shirt on the bed. She looked at us from behind those violet eyes with total calm.

"The cat?" Brian asked. "You're right. That black hair

will be all over my shirt. Scoot." He moved her to the other side of the bed.

"No. She's not just a cat," I told him. "Kalyna is a shape-shifter. She's also a very pretty young woman."

Dorothy and Brian exchanged questioning looks.

"She's not a shifter," Dorothy said. "I would've noticed when I got her, wouldn't I? Isn't shifting magic? She's just a cat with a bad attitude. I think she's jealous of me. She scratched me twice a few minutes ago. That's why we went to get bandages from Oscar."

"We both saw it," Elsie insisted as though that made it gospel. "She was a girl when we walked in, and just now she became a cat again."

"Okay." Brian smiled. "Kalyna, change shape. Become a woman. No one is going to hurt you. If you're a shifter, we're good with that. Go ahead and change."

The cat didn't move, purring softly from the bed.

"I don't think she's a shifter," he decided. "But I'll be glad to help you contact Joe."

"We know what we saw," I disagreed. "She asked us not to tell you."

"Can we do a spell or something to turn her into a woman?" Dorothy glanced at the cat uncomfortably.

"We could," Brian agreed. "But how would we know if she was a woman *before* we used magic on her? That could be a disaster."

"Any other ideas?" Elsie requested.

"Why don't we contact Joe first?" Brian suggested. "Then we can worry about the cat."

I wanted to get in touch with Joe, so I agreed. Elsie and I could always make our point about Kalyna once that was done. There were spells to reveal shifters and other magical creatures. It didn't have to be the way Brian had explained it. I didn't know why the cat shifter had decided to trick Dorothy, but we were going to find out.

We went back into our room and held hands, closing our eyes. I envisioned my husband—black hair with silver strands, kind face and dark eyes. "Joe. Hear me."

He was standing next to his locker at the police station when we could see him again. "Molly? Is that you, honey?"

The next moment, he was slammed hard against his locker and pinned there. "Molly!"

"Oh. I'm so sorry, Joe." I smiled at him. "It's really difficult getting past these blocks to our magic, so we had to team up. I didn't mean to hurt you. It took a lot more power to get through."

He was suddenly released from the tight hold against him. "I thought you were going to Brian's birthday party. Why are there blocks on your magic?"

"They do it to keep witches from using all their magic. Kind of a safety thing, I guess," I told him. "And there was a murder. I'm trapped here for twenty-four hours while they hunt for the killer. I'll be home as soon as I can."

"A murder? Are you okay? Can I do anything?"

"I wish you could, but we'll have to take care of this ourselves. I love you."

"I love you too! Be careful!"

Brian, Elsie, Dorothy and I finished with a spell for cleansing and released our hands.

"That went refreshingly well," Elsie said. "Now we can address the issue of the shape-shifting cat."

But when we went back next door and looked around the room, Kalyna was gone.

"Don't worry. I'll find her," Brian told us. "But I really think you're wrong about her."

"We aren't," I said. "She's hiding something. Be careful."

"I've never liked shape-shifters," Elsie said. "They're all sneaky."

"What about Larry?" Dorothy asked as she searched under the side of the bed.

"He's a werewolf," Elsie replied. "Two different breeds."

"What now?" Dorothy sat in an upholstered chair. "What do we do next? I don't want to be trapped here with someone strong enough to kill Makaleigh Veazy."

"We have to help the witchfinder," I said. "That's our best way out of here. We have the fingerprints from the knife. All we have to do is match them to the killer. Case solved."

"That might be easier said than done," Elsie said. "Witches are a stubborn lot."

Olivia returned to check on them and went back into Dorothy's bracelet, though she groaned and complained the whole time. "I don't see why I should be stuffed in here," she said. "I didn't do anything wrong."

"You did, Olivia," Brian told her. "You knew you couldn't be out in the open here at the castle. We're just continuing what you started."

"Et tu, Brian?" Her eyes blinked at us from the bracelet.

We went downstairs together past dozens of disgruntled witches who were very unhappy about being trapped at the castle. Despite every luxury, there was always something to be said about leaving when the party was over. For all of us, the party had been over when Makaleigh was found dead.

Oscar was unhappy too. He was finding that most of the witches didn't want to share their fingerprints. "Unless we can get Abdon to proclaim a general command that everyone must submit, I'm not sure what to do."

"We can collect all the glasses and check the prints against the prints on the knife," Elsie suggested. "I saw it on TV. That seems possible."

"There are more than two hundred people here," Brian added. "It might be hard to get fingerprints from their glasses and then keep them all straight."

"Well, we know Abdon isn't going to work with us on this," Dorothy said. "We have to find another way."

"But there aren't two hundred members of the council,"

I said. "And they're our best suspects. I can't think of any witches outside the council who wanted their husbands or children without magic subjugated by the rules we have now. Everyone would have been behind her. I'm sure that's what Abdon and the other council members were afraid of."

"And why Makaleigh was killed," Dorothy said.

"Besides, most witches would have been afraid to try to kill a council member," Elsie said. "It has to be someone with more magic than your ordinary witch, and a lot more brass!"

"There were plenty of council members who didn't want anything to change," Oscar agreed. "I don't know how we can collect the council's fingerprints, but if you're going to investigate, they're probably your best bet. The emphasis is on the word 'careful' on this. If the council got wind of any of it, we'd all find ourselves in trouble."

Elsie laughed. "And by trouble, he means abandoned without magic on a remote island, locked away in a deep dungeon, or flying in a plane over an endless ocean."

Brian blinked. "Really? Are those real things? I've never heard of them."

"I don't know," she admitted. "Those were right off the top of my head."

"Are those the worst things you can think of?" Oscar asked. "Because I'm sure I've heard of punishments that were much worse."

"Like being imprisoned still alive in a wall for hundreds of years," Dorothy added with a shiver. "That is awful."

Brian put his arm around her. "That's not going to happen to us for trying to help find Makaleigh's killer," he promised.

"I hope you're right." She looked up at him with worried eyes.

"There are eleven members of the council left," I said, trying to get us back on track. "Let's split them up between us. Brian, you take Zuleyma Castanada and your grandfather, since he's less likely to do anything to you if he finds out you're trying to get his fingerprints. Elsie, you take Owen Graybeard, Arleigh Burke and Sarif Patel. Dorothy, you take Joshua Bartleson, Larissa Lonescue and Bairne Caelius. I'll take Rhianna Black, Hedyle and Erinna Coptus."

"How are we supposed to do it? I don't watch those TV shows that Elsie loves so much. Can we use our magic?" Dorothy asked. "Do we hand each of them a glass and then whisk it away to check for fingerprints when they aren't looking?"

"You should get as close as you can without getting caught," I agreed. "Just remember that getting caught is a bad thing. Be sneaky. Don't let them know what we're doing."

Elsie took a deep breath and cracked her neck. "Okay. I'm ready. I know what to do. You can come with me, Dorothy, if you want to see it done."

"Okay." Dorothy smiled at Brian. "Maybe you should come too."

"I'm not worried about it," he said. "Not to mention that one of my assignments is my grandfather. You go on with Elsie if you're scared. I think I can figure it out."

We set off around the castle to get the prints from the council members who were still alive. It was a big castle, and the witches, including the council, were spread everywhere inside it. I kept an eye open for the witchfinder in case he had found some answers, but I was afraid that he might be out of his depths without a torture device in his hand. I thought he meant well in trying scientific methods, but he'd been out of circulation for a long time.

It seemed for an hour or so that the only council members I saw were the ones I wasn't looking for. But there were Brian, Elsie and Dorothy, lurking around behind their designated council members, trying to think of creative ways to steal their fingerprints without getting caught.

It was interesting watching the guests talking and drinking champagne. A fountain had been set in the middle of the great hall where the party had originally taken place. I supposed it was easier to conjure than to have servants going from glass to glass refilling drinks.

I finally located Erinna Coptus and followed her from her room to one of the sitting rooms downstairs. She stopped to converse with Arleigh Burke on the way down the wide stone stairs. Elsie and I nodded at each other with grave, secretive smiles on our faces. I had a difficult time stopping myself from laughing. We were the most unlikely spies.

Though I listened carefully, Erinna and Arleigh had nothing of great importance to say in their exchange. They both were ready to leave the castle and concerned that Makaleigh's death might mean something bad was about to happen to each of them. They didn't speculate on who had killed their fellow council member. Maybe they were too afraid to question it.

They parted company a few minutes later, going off in different directions.

Elsie and I watched them descend the stairs before daring to speak to each other.

"Bring any fingerprint powder with you?" Elsie asked. "I think Arleigh touched the banister right here. Maybe I could get something from that."

"I didn't. I'm sorry. It seems like it won't be that simple. I'll see you later."

Erinna went into the brandy room. I casually followed her there, glad to see there were other witches imbibing alcohol to while away the day. I carefully kept my eye on a glass of Sazerac as she drank it. She casually put it on a side table as she flirted with a handsome older witch who got her attention.

They spoke for several minutes with a lot of hand touching and serious eye contact before finally leaving together with Erinna's hand in the crook of his arm. She left the half glass of amber liquid on the table.

I swooped down on it with all the major excitement of a department store find and snatched it up.

"Excuse me," a polite voice said. "I'll take that glass for you, ma'am."

It was a servant dressed in black. His smile was firmly in place as he held out his hand.

"No. That's all right. I really wanted a drink but not a whole one, you know?" I forced myself to take a sip, careful that I didn't smudge where her hand had been.

"I'll be happy to make you any size drink you'd like," he replied, still reaching for the glass.

I took another sip and tried not to make a face—not a big fan of Sazerac. "Oh no. This is fine. I'll bring it to you when I'm finished."

"Of course." He finally nodded and walked away.

I let out a sigh of relief and left the room quickly before he came back for the glass again. My next thought was panic. What should I do with it? I couldn't carry it around with me. I might mess up the fingerprints. I'd have to continue to sip at it to keep it in my hand as I walked quickly toward the kitchen. It felt like every servant was watching me, waiting for me to falter so they could ask for it.

In my imagination, no doubt. I was just nervous. Lucky I could get those awful sips in my mouth!

I had to find Oscar so we could come up with a safe place we could all put our glasses, or whatever, with fingerprints. The kitchen would make the best staging area. It was out of the way, and most guests wouldn't go there. I kept my head down, hoping no one would notice me, and ran right into Cassandra as I tried to hurry down the hall.

"Molly." She was radiant as usual in a long black and silver gown. Everything seemed to hang perfectly on her. It wasn't just magic either. She was tall—no hips or chest— like a fashion model. She wore huge silver earrings that moved in and out of her waist-length black hair as she spoke. The distinct smell of roses always accompanied her.

She claimed to be a thousand years old. I didn't know if

it was true, but if it was, she'd spent that time making herself look as fabulous as possible.

"Cassandra." I raised the Sazerac to my lips again, barely tasting any of the liquid.

"This is a horrible situation, Molly." She shook her head slowly. "It was a tragedy losing Makaleigh. No one will ever be able to take her place. As one of the founders of the council, her vision will be missed."

"Yes," I agreed. "I liked her. She seemed very wise."

I couldn't claim more than a brief acquaintance with her since Olivia, Elsie and I had never even met one of the council before last year. We'd only seen Cassandra a few times. We had lived very modest lives for witches.

"She was," Cassandra, the herald, confirmed. "She will be sorely missed."

"I wonder who'll take her place on the council." I felt sure my idle speculation would be on every witch's mind. It wouldn't seem out of place, or suspicious.

Her laugh was dainty, a tinkling sound like tiny silver bells. "Why, Brian, of course, Molly. Abdon has asked him to sit on the council. I've never heard of a witch who refused that singular honor."

"I suppose so." I sipped more Sazerac. It was starting to taste much better. "But then no one on the council has died in a very long time. No one has given up their seat. We don't really know what will happen, do we?"

I couldn't believe those provocative words had come out of my mouth. What was I thinking?

Finding Makaleigh's killer was more important than standing there talking to Cassandra. I could already see that she was surprised that I had spoken to her that way about the council. Usually it was Elsie or Dorothy who gave her a hard time. "Excuse me. I'm looking for someone," I said.

"Surely." She nodded graciously. "I do wish you'd give

sweet little Dorothy a message for me, Molly, if you don't mind?"

"Of course, Cassandra." I hiccupped and excused myself. "What is it?"

"Tell her that I know she's hiding that disgusting ghost of her mother in her bracelet. When we're out of quarantine and our magic is at full strength again, I plan to rid her of that vile revenant once and for all." She smiled.

CHAPTER 16

I knew it was best to ignore her threat, at least for the time being. It wouldn't do any good to get into an argument about Olivia's right to survive. The council was as clear about not wanting ghosts around as they were about family members without magic not knowing about witchcraft. It was an indisputable law to them, not to be questioned or disobeyed. Frankly, I was surprised they hadn't taken Olivia before now.

We needed to move Olivia out of the bracelet for the rest of the time we were stuck here. And then we needed a way to protect her from the council, maybe like the way Joe was protected, except not with the help of the Bone Man. There had to be a way.

Brian joined us with a half glass of orange juice in his hand. "Cassandra. Molly. What's up? You both look kind of serious and scary. Are you talking about Makaleigh?"

Cassandra looked pointedly at each of us with partial glasses of liquid—or was that my imagination thinking she could possibly have any idea what we were doing? My hand shook a little, and I steadied the glass on my lips.

"We were talking about Makaleigh and her terrible fate." Cassandra bowed her head. When her head came up again, her eyes were sharp on my face. "But we were also discussing Olivia's fate. I know Molly and Dorothy have a soft spot for her, but I hope you'll be more objective and a good influence on your coven by making sure they get rid of the ghost. There's no room in the world for her. Olivia should move on. It's part of nature to die. As witches we accept that."

"I don't really understand the whole witches hating ghosts thing." Brian wasn't afraid to disagree with her and certainly didn't mind issuing his opinion. I wondered if Abdon and the rest of the Grand Council were ready for that kind of new voice. "Why can't we all be friends?"

"It's unnatural for a witch to become a ghost," Cassandra reiterated as though Brian may not have understood her position. "We don't do it."

He grinned. "Maybe I should take that spot on the council my grandfather just offered me. I'd like to change that law and a few others that have been around since the Dark Ages. This is a new world for witches, Cassandra. It's about time that you and the council realize it." He glanced at me. "I'm headed to the kitchen to find Oscar. Care to join me?"

"Yes!" I moved a little closer to him in case there was any doubt. "I'd love to join you. I'll be sure to deliver that message to Dorothy, Cassandra."

She didn't say anything in return, but her beautiful face expressed her distaste of the subject. She turned her nose up and stalked by us. Would she go to Abdon and tell him to rescind his invitation to Brian to join the council? I doubted it. She probably wouldn't dare question his choice.

The kitchen was filled with cooks and servants working on breakfast prep and taking various items back and forth to the rooms. The smell of eggs, toast and coffee made me realize that I was starving. No wonder the Sazerac had such a strong effect on me so quickly.

"What was that all about?" Brian whispered as we searched for a quiet spot in a corner of the kitchen.

"She knows about Olivia being here, of course. How Olivia ever thought she could disguise herself from a couple hundred witches in tight quarters is beyond me."

"She might have gotten away with it, Molly, if it had only been the party. I feel bad for her. She just wanted to be here with us. I don't understand why it's such a big deal. What's the history behind the council's feelings that ghosts shouldn't exist?"

I shrugged, uncertain. The question hadn't come up in my life until Olivia had come back. "Maybe Oscar knows. I'm sure your grandfather could tell you. It's been that way for as long as I've been a witch. Whose orange juice is that?"

He carefully held up the glass. "I believe I have a thumb and index finger on this glass from my grandfather. He'd probably kick me off the council before I ever got on it if he knew we thought he could be Makaleigh's murderer."

"I doubt that." I studied his handsome young face. "Are you going to take the open seat, Brian?"

Elsie and Dorothy came upon us quickly in our hidden corner. There was no time for Brian to answer. I wasn't sure he would have if there had been. He might not even know the answer himself yet.

"You two were lucky," Dorothy said. "All I got were some candy bar wrappers that Joshua dropped on the floor. Can fingerprints be on paper?"

"I don't know, but what a slob," Elsie said. "I found Owen's fancy cigarette lighter." She took it out. "Pretty cool, huh?"

The lighter was shaped like a dragon. It blew fire from its mouth when the button was pushed—a clever piece of technology and magic, since it had no place to add fuel to it.

"We better get going," Brian suggested. "I think he's bound to miss that. He smokes like a fiend."

We were able to get fingerprints from everything but the candy bar wrapper. Oscar joined us while we were working and found a magnifying glass to compare them to the prints on the knife.

"None of these match." I sat back from my turn looking at the items. We'd each agreed to compare them and decide.

"So we can cross Abdon, Owen and Erinna off the list of suspects," Elsie said. "That still leaves eight more to go."

"Still need Joshua's prints." Brian kissed Dorothy's forehead. "Nothing paper, I guess."

"And we have another problem." I stared at Olivia's tiny visible gaze in the bracelet. "Cassandra is onto this bracelet. We have to find something else to do with Olivia."

"I thought she was looking too close at the bracelet," Dorothy said. "What now? We're still stuck here. Where else can we hide Mom?"

"We could hide her in our room and put a no trespassing spell on it," Brian said. "No other witches would be able to get inside, but she wouldn't be able to get out and look around either. I'm sorry, Olivia. I hate that it has to be this way right now."

"Oh. It's not your fault, Brian," Olivia replied. "I guess I should've known better."

"What are you talking about?" Oscar asked. "Perhaps I can help."

We explained about Olivia, and he peered closely to see her.

"That's the darnedest thing I've ever seen." He grinned. "You're either the bravest witches I know or the craziest."

Elsie cleared her throat. "Speaking only for myself, I'd say the bravest. Crazy doesn't run in my family."

"Tell you what—there's a very nice poison ring in the Fuller family. I'd be glad to get it out for you, Brian, if you'd like to put the ghost in there. It's spelled to avoid detection, so that could keep any other interested eyes away."

"That would be great." Brian accepted his offer. "Maybe that can get us through until we're released from the castle. Olivia normally isn't out in public so much."

"I'll take care of it myself." Oscar nodded and left us.

"In the meantime, we have other prints to get." I smiled at Dorothy. "I think it has to be something solid. We don't have the resources the police do. Joe says they can even take fingerprints from skin now—but we need something solid."

Dorothy understood. "I'll get it this time. Sorry. I thought the candy wrappers would work."

"Let's get it done." Elsie fist-bumped each of us.

As we left the kitchen, she and I held back a pace or two from Dorothy and Brian.

"Didn't you think it was Abdon?" Elsie asked. "I could've sworn he did it."

"Joe always says not to form preconceived ideas about who the killer is," I told her. "I guess that's why."

"You don't think he could've known Brian was looking for his fingerprints and magically changed them, do you?"

"Anything is possible, but it seems like a remote chance to me. Look at all these other witches—they rely heavily on magic. I don't think he'd consider us using science instead."

She smiled. "I'm sure you're right. I guess I was kind of *hoping* it was him, you know? He's so obnoxious. That way we'd have him and Makaleigh off the council. It would sort of balance out. There would be two seats available. Not that I didn't like Makaleigh, but she's been part of the problem all these years, after all."

"That's true, I suppose. I guess I was hoping she was going to change things, but there was no way to know for sure."

"And now we'll never know." She adjusted her dress. "I'll

be glad when this thing is gone. It's not as comfortable as it was to begin with. See you in a while, Molly. Be careful."

"You too."

I was on the prowl for my next fingerprint victim when the witchfinder came up beside me and took my arm.

"How is the investigation going?" he asked.

"Slow, but we're making progress." I glanced at him as we walked together. "What have you been doing?"

"Interrogating suspects." His mask was firmly in place. I couldn't tell if he was serious or not.

As we started through the crowded halls of the castle, the other witches averted their eyes and walked on the other side of the hall. They either didn't want to be noticed by Antonio or were frightened by him—maybe some of both.

"Has anyone cracked yet?"

He stared at me, muttering in Spanish. "Cracked? What does this mean?"

"Told you their secrets," I explained. "Spilled their guts."

"No. My interrogations have been less intense. There have been no revelations, and the time is fleeting. Abdon will destroy me if I don't know who killed Makaleigh Veazy by the time the spell wears off and all are free to go."

I stopped walking and pulled him into one of the many shadowed alcoves that lined the castle walls. "Let me help you. We know that several of the council aren't guilty. Maybe if you tell him that, he'll leave you alone."

"My dear lady, I find it remarkable that you care one way or another." He pointed at two witches who walked by, shuddering and changing course when they saw him. "That is what I expect from everyone. I am hated and reviled by all witches, a symbol of their unpleasant past."

"If that were the case, the council shouldn't have enslaved you to do their bidding. They should've killed you and been done with it. In my opinion, you have worked off your crimes, Antonio. That's the way I feel. Everyone makes mistakes."

He brought my hand to his covered lips. "You have a good heart, Molly. But we are wasting valuable time. Tell me who those witches are that you believe to be free of guilt, and I will concentrate my efforts elsewhere."

I gave him the names of the three council members whose fingerprints didn't match the ones on the knife.

"Are you certain of this?" His voice was intense but kept low so as not to be heard.

"Yes. Well, at least according to the fingerprint tests we've done. Did you think it was one of them?"

"No." He shook his head. "Not precisely."

He paused, and I asked, "What is it? Do you have some evidence to the contrary?"

"I do not." He sighed. "I suppose I was hoping it was Abdon Fuller, as he possibly is the only one left alive who knows the secret to imprisoning me in the wall again."

"What about Hedyle? Isn't she the oldest of the council? Wouldn't she know the secret?"

"I do not know. Makaleigh carried the secret. I thought Abdon did as well." He shrugged. "Alas! I was hoping to seek my freedom, but perhaps it is not to be. Be wary, Molly. There is danger all around you."

He left the alcove, disappearing quickly in the hall. I left immediately behind him, considering his plight, understanding how hated he was and the terrible things he'd done but certain that he'd earned a spot of redemption.

Reaching the main hall again, Rhianna Black was in my sights with a sterling silver fork moving cheesecake from a silver plate to her mouth. She was laughing at one of the other witches, who seemed to be doing stand-up comedy for the guests. It was a perfect opportunity. All I had to do was wait until she finished.

But a delicate hand took mine, and a pair of sky blue eyes peered into my face. "You are Molly Renard, are you not?" Hedyle, the eldest of the witches on the council, inserted herself between me and Rhianna's cheesecake. "I should love to have a private conversation with you."

CHAPTER 17

I hated to leave without getting Rhianna's fork, but I could hardly tell Hedyle that I didn't want to talk to her. She was an ancient Greek poetess whose work had been recorded on scrolls before being translated into books during the 1800s. She had a wealth of flowing white hair and a wonderful, calm manner that put me immediately at ease.

We went into another small room. This one was empty. A single window looked out on a romantic view of the ocean. I wondered if it was the Atlantic and we were closer to home than we thought. The color scheme here was suited to the ocean view, all shades of blue and green. There was another massive fireplace with carved statues of mermaids on it.

"Would you like some tea?" she asked, taking one of the two upholstered blue chairs in the room.

It was a perfect setup to get her fingerprints on a spoon, cup or saucer. But it was difficult to think about those things when I was faced with her clear eyes. I couldn't help but recall how old she was, and how much she knew and had seen in her time.

"No. Thanks." I smiled as I said it, thinking how remarkable she was. I'd read her poems when I was a teenager. She had great clarity of thought—it reflected in her gaze, which was very open and honest.

I reminded myself that she was still a member of the Council of Witches and I needed to take care what I said to her. She was very powerful and probably shared the other council members' viewpoints on behavior and rules of witches.

"If you don't mind, I'd like a cup." She rang a tiny silver bell, and a servant appeared, holding a beautiful flowered tray with a tea service for two on it.

"Please do." I stared at her hands as she poured the tea and dismissed the servant from the room. They weren't gnarled or blue veined as one might think with her age. They were as smooth and free of old-age spots as a young woman's hands. Strong magic accomplished this.

"What about baklava?" she invited. "It has always been one of my favorites."

"I'm not partial to sweets." It wasn't a lie, exactly, but I enjoyed good baklava in the right company where I didn't feel threatened.

"Oh, come on, Molly! It won't hurt you to break some baklava with me," she coaxed. "It's not poisoned."

"All right." I took a piece of the honey and nut sweet from her on a tiny saucer. "Thank you."

We were finally settled with tea and baklava. She sat back in her chair, her keen eyes searching my face. "All of this running around, summoning the witchfinder and so on. I've known the whole time that the answer is in *you*, Molly. Something passed between you and Makaleigh. What did she say to you before she passed?"

I choked on a bit of baklava and excused myself, putting

a tiny cloth napkin to my lips as I gathered my thoughts. I had only myself to blame for allowing her to put me at ease with sweets and tea. "I'm sorry. Makaleigh said something to me before she died, but it was impossible to say what it was. Her words were so low, and possibly in another language. I couldn't understand. I'm sorry to disappoint you."

"Don't be sorry." Her lips became a straight line in her unblemished face. "We'll figure out what it was. What she said holds the answer to everything, Molly. Do you understand? It's imperative that we know what she said. You may not realize consciously what it was, but it's there in your brain. All we have to do is dig it out."

That didn't sound inviting. Neither did the tone she used. It reminded me more of a threat if I couldn't tell her what she wanted to know. Was she afraid of what Makaleigh had said to me? What real difference did it make?

"I've thought of almost nothing else since it happened," I assured her, putting down my saucer and cup. "I wish I could be more help. It's possible she didn't see her killer, since she was attacked from behind. Her last words might give us no clue as to who it was that killed her."

"*Ah.*" Hedyle's gaze held mine. "Did I say we were looking for the killer's name or face? No. That is not all that is at stake. Makaleigh had secrets she left with—secrets we need to know. No doubt she told you but you couldn't understand on a level of your mind that will help us."

"I don't understand what you're saying." I was really afraid. Her calm demeanor meant nothing to me now.

"There is very old magic that can give us the answer to this question. Do you submit? I shall not use it on you unless you agree, that I promise you. Relax. You need not fear me."

My heart was pounding and my hands were shaking. I was having trouble thinking as I felt the fierceness of her gaze. Her eyes seemed to bore into mine, trying to force the secrets from me whether I gave permission or not. I wanted to know what Makaleigh had said, but old magic—the sort she was referring to—was never a good idea. No doubt Hedyle knew countless spells I would never guess at and couldn't keep from falling under. She was more powerful than I would ever be. Even the amulet might not be able to protect me from whatever she had in mind. I was terrified to agree with what she wanted, yet I could feel her trying to bend my will to hers.

"I see you have some doubt in you as to whether or not I should use the spell." Hedyle sipped her tea, but her eyes remained on me. "Perhaps there is something you are hiding? Something you fear the council will learn if you submit to a discovery spell?"

A discovery spell! I'd heard of these spells. They were like truth serum for witches, forcing you to reveal anything and everything you know, even things the questioner might not ask.

She was right in thinking I would never submit—I couldn't think of a witch that would. That was why the council didn't just use them on everyone here at the party to figure out who'd killed Makaleigh. Admitting that her words were true would be like telling her I was keeping something from the council—which I was. Joe was invisible to them. They didn't realize that he knew about magic. I couldn't jeopardize that secret, not even to find Makaleigh's killer.

I fumbled, picking up my cup from the tray and sipping from it to mask my nervousness and uncertainty, partly because I needed a moment to consider what I should say, and partly because there were baklava crumbs stuck in my throat. I sipped the fragrant brew slowly and tried to gather my wits.

"I'd like to help you," I finally said. "But I was there. I know what I heard. It was gibberish from a dying woman. I don't think it would help find her killer, or whatever you're looking for."

Hedyle nodded slowly. "And if I insist?"

Her will came down on my head like the crash of ocean waves, pulling at my senses until they were spinning. It was all I could do to tell up from down as I was dragged deeper into her eyes. I didn't raise my hand to my amulet, but it began glowing softly in response to the threat.

That water magic brought me back to myself with a start. It made me want to run from the room to get away from Hedyle. She'd almost trapped me into agreeing to the discovery spell, letting her search my mind and my soul for what she wanted. Realizing the threat she was posing, I held the amulet flat against my skin. If necessary, I decided, I would call for help from the Bone Man. There wasn't much I wouldn't do to protect Joe and Mike from the council.

"I see." Her gaze broke from mine and focused on the amulet and the ocean waves breaking inside it. "An interesting piece of jewelry. A gift from the sea. Very potent." She reached a hand to touch it and was stung by a mild shock issued from it. "You are correct. It might deflect my magic from working on you."

From what I could tell, it had worked to keep her magic from reaching its tendrils into my brain and sapping my will. I had almost fallen into an apathy as she'd been speaking, ready to give her what she wanted and allow her to use the discovery spell on me. Thank goodness I hadn't left it at home as Elsie was always trying to convince me to do.

Hedyle held her hand against her, obviously unpleasantly surprised by the power of the amulet. "Suppose I made you a blood oath that I shall not divulge to another living being the secret you hide? Would that influence your decision?"

"No." Nothing she could say would make me feel safe telling her that Joe knew about magic. I had seen too many people lose their loved ones to the strict council edict that made erasing all memory of magic ruin their lives. "You may be able to force me. That I can't say. But I won't willingly allow you to use that magic on me. Too much is at stake."

"The power in that amulet is wild magic, you know. Unsanctioned by the council. You could be banned from using it."

"I know what it is and where it came from," I told her plainly. "I won't give it up. It has been in my family for many generations. The council shouldn't think it can get rid of everything it fears."

She sighed and played with the shell bracelet on her wrist. "You have something from Makaleigh in you, Molly. But I won't force it from you. I hope you will reconsider and allow me to bring it out. It may be the only way we will ever solve this mystery."

"I understand, and I may be able to find another way to bring it out." I had no idea how, but it made it sound like I was trying anyway.

"Indeed." Her gaze seemed even more disturbed after I'd said it.

What was she hiding? What information did Makaleigh have that she didn't want other witches to know?

There were no pleasantries ending the conversation between us. The servant came back for the tray. Hedyle walked slowly from the small room. I stayed behind to consider her words.

It occurred to me a moment later that I'd missed my opportunity to get her fingerprints, but that seemed unimportant compared to her certainty that knowledge I possessed from Makaleigh was something earth-shattering, worth dragging from my head. I was scared even though the amulet had protected me.

How could I withhold that information? Would she allow me to withhold it? I wouldn't allow Hedyle to take Joe's secret from me with it. That I was certain of. I hoped I could keep her at bay and not be fooled into giving her what she wanted.

Maybe there was another way—one with fewer potential side effects. Elsie, Brian and Dorothy might be strong enough to create a discovery spell and use it on me. They knew about Joe, and I trusted them with that secret. Whatever Makaleigh had said to me, I trusted them with that too.

I stalked back into the kitchen, where Brian and Dorothy were excited to have taken fingerprints from Zuleyma and Larissa.

"We're looking at them now," Brian said. "I think I missed my calling. I kind of like being a cop."

"A witch cop." Dorothy smiled at him. "That might be interesting."

"What's wrong, Molly?" he asked me.

"Nothing, really. I need to speak with all of you at one time. Maybe later."

"Did you get any prints?" Dorothy asked.

"No. I missed a few opportunities. Something else has come up."

Elsie raced in holding a silver butter knife. "I got Sarif's print! Two down, one to go."

But none of the prints we'd taken matched the one on the knife that had killed Makaleigh. It was frustrating. I had a taste of what Joe went through every day.

"That only leaves five people on the council that we haven't printed," Brian said. "And speaking of the council, my grandfather and my parents talked to me again about taking Makaleigh's place. They're really giving me a hard sell. My grandfather said he wouldn't take no for an answer."

"I don't understand why they aren't asking your mother or father to do it." Dorothy pouted. "They probably want to be on the council. You don't. What else is there to say? How much clearer can you make it?"

"It is odd that Abdon wants a family member on the council and he doesn't want your father," Elsie considered.

"And I know my father would be more than happy to take the seat." Brian frowned. "I don't get it either. Maybe I should ask my parents about it away from my grandfather. My father might be afraid to speak up around him."

"I spoke with the witchfinder," I told them. "Nothing is turning up for him either—whatever he's doing. Someone is very good at hiding their tracks. We have to get these other fingerprints."

"And then what?" Dorothy asked. "What if none of the council members' prints matches the one on the knife?"

"Then we have to start with the other hundred and ninety or so people here," Elsie responded. "Not to mention the staff. I'm exhausted just thinking about it."

"There's something else too." I looked each of them in the eye and knew I could trust them with my life and Joe's. "I didn't get Hedyle's fingerprints, but we did have a chat about her forcing a discovery spell on me."

"My grandfather mentioned you hearing Makaleigh's last words again too," Brian replied. "He didn't say anything about Hedyle wanting to do a spell on you, but he was very concerned about you keeping what she had to say a secret from the council. It made me wonder what they're worried about."

"Me too." I shared my fears with them as well as the moment in the blue room with the spectacular ocean view when I thought I might succumb to Hedyle's will.

"I'm surprised she didn't just do it." Olivia pushed herself out of the Dorothy's bracelet enough to speak. "Why didn't she just force the spell on you, Molly?"

"She wasn't sure if she could," I told her. "When she began to weave the spell around me, my amulet started glowing and she backed off. She asked me for permission—I wouldn't give it."

Dorothy looked puzzled. "Why not? Maybe you really did hear something and you don't realize it. It could make a difference and we could all go home."

Elsie came behind me, lightly touching my shoulders. "Because you don't know what someone will find with a discovery spell. Hedyle could find out about Joe and the Bone Man's agreement to protect him from the council. There is no stopping a spell like that, especially with a powerful witch like Hedyle. It could ruin Molly's life."

We stood in the noisy kitchen, out of the way of the cooks and servers, surrounded by the scents of cinnamon rolls and biscuits.

"But the three of us could do a discovery spell without taking anything from you, Molly." Dorothy took Brian's hand in hers. "Let's at least give it a try."

I nodded, glad that I didn't have to ask them to bear whatever secret might come from it with me. "Thank you. That's exactly what I was thinking."

CHAPTER 18

We ate breakfast on the way upstairs to our rooms. It was delicious, and the orange juice was filled with champagne. Elsie ate strawberries until I thought she might pop. Brian was quiet and didn't eat much. I thought he might be worried about being forced to take the council seat he didn't want. Dorothy stayed close to him, watching him as though he might slip away when she wasn't looking. She ate only a few bites of French toast.

I thought about discovery spells. They weren't difficult usually. They could be more complex depending on the depth you were trying to reach. I was willing to fight not to have it done, so Hedyle would have had to use strong magic to coerce me.

Olivia, Elsie and I knew discovery spells. They weren't the good ones that we would have had if our spell book hadn't been stolen. We were still waiting for our new spell book from Elder Magics, but that would be a while. Even then, the old spells that had been handed down from our ancestors were lost. We'd decided to start fresh with the spells we remembered—few enough—and add new spells as we went along. It was better than nothing.

But not helpful with a discovery spell of this nature.

We were upstairs with the door locked and the room carefully cleansed for a big spell. Candles were lighted, and Brian had smudged the room with sage and rosemary for memory.

"Just take off that old amulet, Molly," Olivia said. "Probably anything will work on you if you aren't wearing it."

"And if Hedyle thought it was too powerful for her," Elsie said, "it would make mincemeat out of one of our spells."

"Except that I trust you not to give Joe and Mike away," I replied with a smile. "I trust you to hear whatever Maka-leigh said to me that might mean something important about her killer. I don't trust Hedyle or anyone else on the council with that information. You know it's different. That was why she asked me to cooperate before she tried to force me to do it."

Brian had been silent on the matter, standing away from us with a frown on his young face. "You know, I think Molly is right. I don't think this is going to be a problem. It's not like we don't know a few discovery spells, and together, we're pretty powerful. I think we should give it a try."

"But here?" Elsie glanced suspiciously around us. "Can we trust this room not to have ears even though we spelled it?"

"We could create an enchanted bubble," Dorothy said. "As I understand it, you could use it downstairs in the heart of the council, and they still couldn't listen in. Right?"

"That should be correct," I agreed. "We could create the bubble and protect ourselves from whatever information comes out of me, just as an added precaution."

"Right." Brian nodded. "Let's do this."

Between us we made a closed bubble that witches used for privacy. Not even the council could peer inside it or hear what was said, although too many energy spikes of that nature could bring the council down on whoever was doing it. They were very aware of the way magic was used and protected it zealously.

Olivia came out of the bracelet while we were in the bubble. "Oh, girls—and Brian—this is such a mess. I don't know if a discovery spell is a good idea or not."

"It could be exactly what Hedyle was trying to goad you into doing, Molly," Elsie warned. "Maybe she knew she couldn't do it herself but you'd try it."

"I don't see where we have any choice," I told her. "It sounded like muttering to me when Makaleigh died, but I guess I owe it to her to find out."

"Why?" Olivia demanded. "She only talked about changing things. We really don't even know if she meant any of it."

"I was still the last person she spoke to," I reminded her. "I don't want to do this either, but I think we should."

"Let's get on with it," Brian said. "If what she had to say doesn't amount to the name of the killer, we're going to need those other fingerprints. We don't have time to waste. Ready, Molly?"

I nodded and closed my eyes, standing between them while they joined hands around me. As far as I knew, there were no other deep, dark secrets in me. My friends knew everything. I had to trust that it would be okay. I let myself relax and lean on the affection and faith we shared. They wouldn't hurt me and would guard my secrets with their lives, as I would theirs. This was the nature of a coven and why it was important for the right people to belong to one another.

Brian began the spell, stronger and more confident in his magic than Dorothy or Elsie. They joined in, holding hands, eyes closed. I could feel their magic building. There was a protective nature to it that wouldn't have been there if Hedyle had done the discovery spell. I was glad that I had resisted.

I was in the pink parlor again. Everything looked as it had when we'd found Makaleigh. Olivia called us over behind the pink sofa, and I reached Makaleigh before Dorothy, Brian or Elsie. I heard a voice murmuring close to my ear— *Makaleigh*. She was beside me on the floor, her life energy draining away as she fought to say one last thing.

She kept repeating the same words, trying to tell me something important, but it made no sense to me. Was she speaking in another language? If so, I couldn't interpret it. She was saying the same words over and over. Three words that I couldn't understand. She was desperate to tell me. Her eyes focused on me, and her hand grasped mine tightly.

Aba. Mho. Ord.

I was repeating the words again and again as I opened my eyes, coming out of the discovery spell. Nothing seemed real, as though I had just stepped out of a dream world and was having trouble finding my way back into the real one.

Brian, Dorothy and Elsie were all staring expectantly at me. They weren't moving. I wasn't sure they were breathing. I reached to touch Elsie's arm but found I couldn't move either. My amulet was glowing brightly. I wasn't sure if this was a backlash from its magic or something else.

"A discovery spell?" the Bone Man harshly laughed. He was inside the bubble with us. *How was that even possible?* "You should know better than to let someone invade your inner secrets. Do they teach witches nothing these days?"

"You can't be here," I told him. "No one can break through the sanctity of the protective bubble."

"No witch," he agreed with a smirk to his red lips. "I, however, am not a witch, as you well know. There is more at stake here than protecting your husband and son. You are privy to a few of *my* secrets as well, Molly. Did you think of that before you allowed your friends to rummage in your head?" He tapped my forehead sharply with his bony finger. "I think not."

"I told them everything the last time I left Oak Island," I confessed. "They're my friends, and my coven. I would trust them with anything, including *your* secrets."

"I see." He grinned horribly, showing rotted teeth. "I do not. I have given you the words you seek. Do not try this again. I know you have other plans for your life, but I could put them on hold so you could spend the rest of your time on Oak Island with me."

"You can't just pop in and out of my life whenever you feel like it, because I know who you really are!"

He tipped his ragged hat to me. "Never make a deal with the Bone Man if you don't intend to keep your part of the bargain!"

He was gone before I could ask about the meaning of the words. I assumed he knew but wouldn't just share unless I made another deal with him. That wasn't going to happen. He already had access to more of my life than I was happy with.

An instant later, we could all move. Brian, Elsie and Dorothy were still chanting the discovery spell.

"I know what she said," I told them, startling all of us.

"What?" Dorothy demanded. "Was it the killer's name?"

"I don't know." I repeated the three words that were racing through my brain aloud again.

"Maybe it's the killer's name in code," Elsie suggested. "Who brought their secret decoder book?"

The protective bubble slowly dissipated around us.

"I don't understand," Brian said. "What do those words mean? What's the big secret?"

"That's what I thought too," I agreed. "I remember hearing Makaleigh say those words now, but I don't know what they mean."

"They must be something important," Dorothy said. "Why else would Hedyle be so anxious to get them from Molly?"

We all agreed on that, except Olivia. "Gibberish," she declared. "A wild-goose chase."

"Maybe you should write the words down anyway so you don't forget," Elsie suggested. "Maybe it's one of those things where the time isn't right yet but when it is, you'll need the words."

"It could be anything," Olivia said. "And it doesn't sound like it's gonna get us out of here any faster. We still don't know who killed Makaleigh."

"Until we can figure out how to decipher the words, I suggest we get those other fingerprints." Brian watched as Dorothy wrote down the words. "Maybe we should keep them with us in case someone gets in here while we're gone. We may not know what the words mean, but I'll bet Hedyle does."

I agreed with him, shaking my head to clear a faint buzzing sound in my ears.

"Are you okay after the spell, Molly?" Elsie asked. "You look kind of pale."

"Like you've seen a ghost." Olivia laughed.

She didn't realize how close she'd come to the truth. I might have needed the Bone Man's help when the witchfinder was ready to torture me, but even that was debatable. I didn't need him in the enchanted bubble. It seemed he was entwined in my life now and there was no way to get him out. His magic was stronger and not part of our witchcraft. I had no idea how to get rid of him.

Not a pleasant thought.

Abdon was waiting in the hall, about to knock on the door, as we were getting ready to walk out. Dorothy almost walked into him and apologized before she got quickly out of the way.

"Good. I was hoping to find you all together." His keen eyes fell on us with much the same impact as the witch-finder's needle. "I'd like a word with you. It seems, for better or worse, that you are Brian's coven now. I don't pretend to like it, but he needs you to stand behind him."

"Grandfather—" Brian's voice was dry and embarrassed.

"No. I won't be silenced about this. It is an opportunity that may not come again," Abdon said to him. "Brian needs you to encourage him to take Makaleigh's place on the council, ladies. Think of the advantage and prestige to your coven and your magic. Consider what a remarkable addition he would make to the council as my heir. I urge you to discuss this with him and help him make the right choice."

"What about Schadt?" Elsie asked daringly.

"What about him?" Abdon responded impatiently.

"Why isn't he taking Makaleigh's place?" Dorothy added. "He's older and a member of your family. He'd like to be on the council. Brian isn't interested. Have you asked Schadt?"

"It's curious why you wouldn't want your only son to take your place on the Grand Council." I put in my two cents' worth. "Why would you pass him over to take Brian? How does he feel about it?"

Abdon's blunt features twisted his mouth into a snarl. "There is no question of what is going to happen. I only asked for your help because I thought you were Brian's friends. I suppose I was mistaken. But make no mistake—with or without your support, my grandson will be on the Council of Witches at my side by the time the doors open to the castle."

With a last sneer, he left us. We were glad to see him go—Brian was relieved.

"He really wants to see you on the council, doesn't he?" Dorothy said. "I don't know if he's going to take no for an answer. Are you sure you want to go against him?"

For a moment there was a sneer on Brian's face that resembled his grandfather's. "He's going to have to live with my answer. I'm not interested in being part of the council. I have never been interested. Come on. Let's see if we can find Makaleigh's killer before the doors open. Because I'm ready to go home. Aren't you?"

CHAPTER 19

I was hot on the trail of Rhianna's fingerprints. She flitted around the castle like a moth, going from group to group, drinking and eating. Each time I thought I had her, I was wrong.

Hedyle was in several of those groups. I avoided her, though I felt her gaze on me. Should I tell her that I knew the last three words Makaleigh had spoken?

But what if Hedyle was the killer?

None of the other council members had approached me about trying to decipher what Makaleigh had said. I carefully watched Hedyle. She looked so innocent. It was difficult to imagine her plunging a large knife into a woman she'd known for hundreds of years.

Yet I couldn't imagine who else could have been strong enough to kill Makaleigh. There was also the part about her half threatening to force me to tell her the words she wanted to know. That didn't make me feel gracious toward her at all.

I kept the words to myself. They swam through my head as I tried to decipher them and learn their meaning. I agreed with Hedyle that Makaleigh wouldn't have wasted her last breath telling me those three words unless they had some meaning. It was maddening knowing that our release could be immediate if we could just figure out what Makaleigh was talking about.

The Bone Man might have known what they meant. It was just as likely that he didn't. As he was so fond of reminding me, his magic was different than ours. He saw things we couldn't see, but I was convinced he felt the same way about us, despite his words to the contrary.

Rhianna was leaving the scene of another quick snack stop—this time caviar and smoked salmon. No knife or fork, but I was sure her fingertips had touched the silver plate she ate from. All I had to do was get there before the fleet-footed servants came to take it away.

"I think you've got her now." Elsie was standing beside me.

"Sorry. I was lost in thought." I was startled when she spoke to me. "Maybe you could distract the servant while I grab the plate."

"I believe I could do that." She nodded. "Molly, I know I've been hard on you about the amulet. With it connected to the Bone Man, it makes me nervous. I know we're all looking for something that will keep us going. I guess this is it for you. I don't want you to think that I love you any less for it. It just scares me sometimes."

"I feel the same way about you and Larry." I kept my eyes on Rhianna. "Since you got together with him, you've been like a different person."

A thin red brow arched. "I hope you mean that in a good way."

"I do. He's given you back your old spark. I like it."

"Thanks. You know I never loved Bill. Back then, it was a good thing to marry someone without magic, remember? The council thought it was good then. Not like now when they want all the witches to only marry witches. I always wondered what changed." She shrugged. "Anyway, my mother pushed hard for me to marry him. I was just a dumb kid. What did I know?"

"I don't remember a lot about your mother, but I remember she was really strong-willed. When she said you were going to eat cheese toast, you were going to eat cheese toast."

Elsie laughed. "You're still talking about that time you spent the night when Abby was born, aren't you? You didn't have to eat the cheese toast."

"I was afraid not to eat it."

"I understand what you're saying. I guess that's what I mean. She was strong-willed." She sighed. "It still hurt when Bill cheated on me, but not as much as if I had loved him. With Larry, it's different. I love him to pieces. If he cheated on me, someone would be sorry. I'm not a fire witch for nothing!"

"I know." I hugged her yet continued watching Rhianna wolf down salmon. "And I think it's that happiness that has given you that extra sparkle—and magic."

She blushed. "I think so too. And I want you to be the first to know that I accepted his marriage proposal. I don't want this one to get away."

"You're going to marry Larry?" Tears spilled from my eyes. "That's so wonderful. When?"

"I don't know yet. We're supposed to talk about it when he gets back this month. I don't have a ring yet." She showed me her bare finger. "But I'm already the happiest woman in the world."

"And I'm so happy for you."

"Don't tell anyone else. I'm afraid it will jinx it." She pointed toward the group. "I think she's finally done eating. How docs she stay so thin eating like that? You get the plate. I've got the servant."

Elsie "accidentally" tipped over several glasses of champagne that had already been poured. Rhianna set down her plate to see what was going on, and I snatched it. I hoped she didn't want to use it again.

At the moment I laid my hand on the plate, the spell from Madam Tunis was over. Those of us who'd purchased magic one-night clothes for the party from her saw them disappear and become the clothes we'd worn to her shop. I was surprised how many witches had taken advantage of that opportunity. Probably half the witches in the room were now dressed in plain jeans and sweat suits instead of glitter and lace.

"Oh well." One pretty young witch laughed. "I guess you can see what I wore shopping."

She was beautiful and completely naked. Evidently she hadn't worn any clothes before the spell.

If I'd been worried about the transition for me, I didn't need to be. She drew all the attention to herself from everyone around the room. I carefully hid the silver plate behind my back as I hurried away. Elsie came quickly behind me.

"Stop!" The servant who should've been engaged by the naked witch shouted and pointed. "Stop! Thief! That woman is stealing a silver plate. Security!"

It suddenly occurred to me that he was yelling about me. I faltered, thinking I should explain myself, but Elsie pushed me forward, urging me toward the kitchen, before she stopped to confront the servant.

"Oh, all right," she confessed loudly. "I wasn't stealing them, just taking a look at the style." She took a handful of silverware from her bag and put it on the buffet table. I'm sure we can discuss this like rational adults."

I kept going. Elsie was right—there was no point in both of us being called thieves. I realized she'd put one fork in my pocket. It had to be the important one, Arleigh Burke's fork.

Two security guards had her arms. Someone was walking rapidly toward them. I didn't stop to see who it was.

Brian and Dorothy were absent from the kitchen, but a large group of staff was there preparing more food and drink. I went into our tiny corner area where the box and superglue still waited. With Arleigh's and Rhianna's prints, that left only three council members uninvestigated. I hoped one of them was the killer—I really didn't want to face Hedyle again.

But I was disappointed to find that those prints didn't match the ones on the knife either. Dorothy brought Bairne's, and Brian got Joshua's. None of them matched.

"That only leaves Hedyle," Brian said. "We've still got about twelve hours until the spell is gone. We have to get her prints."

"Or we could just assume she's guilty, since the rest of the council is clear," Dorothy suggested. "I mean, let's face it—only other council members had a reason to kill her, right?"

"That's assuming someone couldn't figure out how to stop her from trying to change the rules," I added. "It could be about something else."

"Like someone who thought he or she would be nominated for the council after Makaleigh's death," Brian said. "I'm the front-runner, mostly because my grandfather wants a Fuller on the council."

"But not your father?" Dorothy shook her head. "Why not? Pardon me, but he seems the type, if you know what I mean? No offense. Your family has a political bent to it."

I knew what she meant. "Who else would like to be on the council?"

Brian grinned. "It would be easier to ask who *didn't* want to be on the council. I could be the only one on that list."

"Not the only one," I disagreed. "None of us want to be on the council either."

"Yep. Good thing they won't ask us," Dorothy said.

"I should go check on Elsie." I tried to see through the

crowd that had formed around Elsie and the servant. "I'm sure she can talk herself out of this whole theft thing, but just in case."

"Let me take care of it," Brian offered. "Elsie and I will meet you upstairs. The five of us need to think this through."

Dorothy giggled. "That's one reason I love you. You always include my mother, even if she is a ghost."

Brian kissed her. "Of course I do. But we have to take this seriously. There's still a killer in the castle for at least another twelve hours. It seems like we might need a miracle to find him."

CHAPTER 20

Dorothy and I went upstairs, leaving Brian to sort through the mess we'd created. Dorothy was right—he was a very congenial person. I hoped it wouldn't be long before we heard wedding bell news from them too.

Olivia was glad to see us. She was never good at being alone. "Thank goodness you're back! I was beginning to wonder what was going on!"

We explained everything that had happened, and then Dorothy made a decision.

"I'm going to sneak up on that cat," she whispered. "It's crazy for us to be afraid of her. I'm sure she's just frightened and needs someone to talk to." She slowly began opening the door between our rooms.

"Be careful," I warned. "She already doesn't like you, and she has claws."

"So do I when I need to," she assured me as she smoothed back her dark cap of hair. "I'm not afraid of some shape-shifting cat. And I don't want her in there sleeping on Brian's bed like she owns it. She's got some explaining to do, sneaking in here without letting us know that she was more than just a cat."

"Be careful, Dorothy," Olivia warned. "Some of those shape-shifters can be vicious and nasty."

"We don't know that about her," I reminded them both. "She might be in hiding or didn't know that we didn't understand what she was."

"Oh, she knew!" Olivia disagreed.

"Do you want my help?" I asked.

"No," Dorothy whispered. "I've got this."

Two minutes and a few howls and hisses later, Dorothy ran back through the doorway and slammed the door behind her, locking it for good measure. "That cat thing is insane. I think she was trying to kill me. Look what she did to my arm."

I didn't repeat myself that the shifter could be scared and react accordingly. I examined the deep, long gouges where the cat had scratched her. "Let's see if we can heal those. They look angry."

As I uttered a spell for healing and held my amulet, I had Dorothy sit down and relax. "I'm not going in there again. Brian is going to have to handle her. But he can't keep that cat."

"*Shh.* If you want to heal, you have to think healing thoughts. Let go of what happened. Let yourself heal quietly."

She closed her eyes and complied, relaxing on the bed. I could feel her energies aligning with mine to make the magic stronger.

As the scratches began to heal, I agreed with her assessment of the cat situation. "Funny how she was so docile and quiet when you first gave her to Brian. Maybe it's something here at the castle that's bothering her."

"That wouldn't be surprising," Olivia added. "None of us should have come to this terrible place."

"Where did you get her anyway?" I asked.

"There was a man by the library with a box of kittens he needed to give away. He said he couldn't keep them because he had to move. That's how I got Hemlock too. I thought getting a rescue cat would be great. I didn't know she was an evil shape-shifter."

Listening to her tell the story made me suspicious. "Let me look at you," I suggested. "I'm just wondering if that was a witch who gave you Kalyna. You could have been spelled not to notice the cat was a shape-shifter. Normally witches recognize werewolves, shape-shifters and the like."

Dorothy held very still, and I gazed deeply into her confused brown eyes. Because she was new at using her magic, it was still possible to take advantage of her. But if she'd been spelled, there was no sign of it in her.

"Am I okay?" she asked as I moved back from her.

"You're fine. It was just a thought." I smiled at her and stroked her hair. "You're still in training. Anything could happen that you wouldn't recognize yet. We should have thought about that in the first place."

"It won't be long though, sweetie," Olivia said, "and no one will be able to take advantage of you—not with your daddy's magic."

I sighed, wishing Olivia wouldn't glorify Drago's dark magic in one breath and disparage it in the next. I supposed it reflected her own feelings of uncertainty about him in her life. Not that anyone was ever truly all good or all evil. We were all a mixture of both.

Brian and Elsie knocked and then quickly entered the room as though demons were chasing them. When the door was shut tight and spelled, we all joined hands, glad that we were together.

"What happened?" Dorothy asked. "Is everything okay? They didn't arrest you did they, Elsie?"

"She was fine," Brian said with a grin. "I felt sorrier for

the servant and the security guard who tried to detain her until Oscar could get there."

"It was stupid for them to think I was stealing something," Elsie huffed. "I would've told Oscar or Abdon the same if it came down to it."

"Well, it's over now." I hugged her. "I'm glad you're okay."

"And I'm afraid it was for nothing. The fingerprints we got didn't match." Brian broke the circle and put his arms around Dorothy.

"So only Hedyle is left." Elsie sat in a corner chair. "I know you don't want to talk to her again, Molly. I'll get her prints. She doesn't want anything in my head."

"We have another problem too, Brian." Dorothy held out her arm for him to see. "You have to get her into the carrier. Once we can leave the castle, I'll take her right back to the man I got her from. She's a little devil."

"I'm sorry." He winced when he saw the scratches, which were now mostly healed. "Let me see what I can do. Stay here, honey. I don't want her to hurt you again."

They kissed again, and Brian disappeared into his room, closing the door behind him.

"I think we need to take some time here and figure out the meaning of those three words that Molly heard Makaleigh say as she was dying," Olivia said in a stern voice. "We've been running around, trying to figure this out the way the police would. That's not working. We need some magic—I'm willing to bet that those words are magic."

"Maybe you're right." I sat at the desk and took out a sheet of plain white paper before I wrote the three words at the top. "All right. There they are. I have to assume the spelling, since I only heard them. If we can find something close to that, maybe we can figure it out."

"Let me take a look," Dorothy said. "I learned the entire Dewey Decimal System in three days. People were amazed. If I can do that, I can figure out anything."

We were about to get started when there was a knock at the door. Elsie answered it. One of the many servants in the castle said that our presence was required in the ballroom. "All witches are required." The servant nodded and left us.

"I probably should just wait up here anyway, and you can tell me what they said," Dorothy suggested. "This is likely much more important than whatever they're going to say. And I don't want to leave Brian alone with that she-devil."

"What about Brian?" Olivia asked. "That man is still knocking on his door, but he's not answering."

"Let's go through the communicating door and find out," I said.

The servant had given up, moving to the next door down the hall. I walked into Brian's room and abruptly stopped when I saw him.

"What's wrong?" Elsie almost bumped into me. "Oh, Brian."

"Let me see." Olivia swooped around us and went toward the bed where Brian was sitting.

"Why are we—?" Dorothy quickly followed us.

Brian was sitting on the bed, staring blankly as he stroked the black cat that was perched on his lap. His eyes were fixed and glazed. His movements, slow and sluggish.

"What has she done to him?" Dorothy ran toward him.

The small black cat became a much larger, person-sized black cat with six-inch-long claws that extended as Dorothy got closer. The cat had to be a few hundred pounds of lean muscle covered by shiny black fur. Her yellow green eyes focused on Dorothy with angry intent.

"He is mine now, witch. Stay away."

"The kitty talks now." Elsie frowned. "I don't think that's a good thing."

"I'm not afraid of you." Dorothy continued to advance.

One of the cat's long claws grazed Brian's throat. "Before you move, I shall rip the flesh from his vein and he will bleed to death. There is nothing you can do. Leave him to me."

She stopped and glared at the cat. "I don't believe you. You didn't go to all this trouble to enchant him only to rip his throat out. What do you really want?"

"And don't say you want Brian," Olivia challenged. "That's not happening."

"Go away. I will kill him if I must. It would not be my choice, but your actions could force my hand."

"Or paw, as the case may be." Elsie was ready to fight for Brian. "You want him? You'll have to get through us."

All of the claws on the paw came out on Brian's neck. The cat hissed at us and seemed ready to fulfill her promise.

"Let's take a step back on this," I suggested.

Dorothy, Olivia, Elsie and I went back into the other room.

"What do we do?" Dorothy whispered. "We can't leave Brian with her."

Elsie shook her head. "The ladies certainly have a thing for him, don't they? I thought the sea witch was bad, but now it's the evil cat. How does he do it?"

"Actually he didn't do this." Olivia defended him. "Dorothy got the cat for him."

"Mother!" Dorothy was on the verge of tears. "I didn't know the cat was an evil shape-shifter. She seemed like a pretty black cat. Nothing else. I would never have taken her if I'd known."

"Of course you wouldn't," I agreed. "No one here thinks you're responsible. Brian doesn't blame you either."

"That's nice, but it doesn't matter," she said. "Is there a spell or something we can use to get rid of her? Maybe we can shrink her down again? We can't just leave him in there with her."

"I'm sure there's something we can do." Olivia looked at

me hopefully. "Well, maybe not me personally, but the three of you."

"A spell to make her reveal her true form?" Elsie considered. "Then when she turns back into a woman, we can hit her with something."

"But what if her true form is the cat?" Dorothy asked. "That could make it worse."

"I don't see how it could be much worse." Olivia fretted. "Oh, I wish we were home. I wish we wouldn't have come to this ball at all."

"What about a sleeping spell?" Dorothy suggested. "It wouldn't matter what form she was in if we put her to sleep, right?"

"That's a good idea," I agreed. "Between the three of us, we can probably manage a pretty potent sleeping spell. She doesn't have to be out for long."

Elsie clapped her hands. "I can even remember one. How's that for serendipity?"

"Let's do it," Dorothy said. "Let's get her out of there. I want Brian back in one piece."

We agreed on a sleeping spell—the one Elsie could remember—and practiced it a few times before we moved back into the bedroom where Brian was on the bed with the cat.

We could have stayed in the other room for the spell. It would have been safer, but the magic would be stronger if we could see Brian and the cat, especially with using only half magic. Normally that wouldn't have been a problem, but we didn't know how powerful the shifter was. Some shifters had other magic that could fight against ours. Some could only shift form. Either way, we'd be covered.

Elsie began the spell for once. She knew the incantation perfectly as she closed her eyes and called on her fire magic. Dorothy and I joined in, adding water and earth magic. Even

Olivia voiced the spell, though she had no air magic anymore. Together we chanted the spell for sleep as we felt the power surge through us and join together.

"Look!" Dorothy called out a few minutes later. "It worked! She's asleep."

"I knew we could do it," Elsie exclaimed. "Now all we have to do is get her off Brian."

Olivia went close to the big cat. "That's a lot of cat. Let me make sure she's out." She made a few of the dangling curtain edges dance across the cat's nose. "I think she would have responded to that if she could, don't you? Maybe you could make her shift back again. She'd be easier to move. I doubt the woman weighed as much as the cat."

"We don't want to do that," I said. "If we try to do another spell on her, it could negate the first one and she could be awake when she changes right back into the big cat."

We carefully walked up to Brian and the sleeping cat. Dorothy smoothed his brown hair back and told him she loved him. He was still staring straight ahead, a vacant expression on his face, despite the spell on the cat. His hand still moved in the familiar stroking pattern the cat had set up.

Elsie had poked the monstrous cat a few times, and it didn't move. She shrugged, and we managed to slide it from the bed to the floor. Dorothy had to hold on to Brian to keep him from sliding off with it.

"That thing is dead weight," Elsie whispered. "Now it's down, what do we do with it?"

"Couldn't we spell the closet to hold it?" Dorothy wondered. "If so, we could use the moving spell on it and put it in there."

Olivia managed to rattle the closet door. "I don't think this is strong enough even with a spell on it, ladies. Maybe you should put it in the bathroom."

We put our heads together and created the spell for moving heavy objects. We'd used it before to bring books from the New Hanover Public Library, where Dorothy worked, to Smuggler's Arcane. It seemed to work well for the cat too, until there was a loud banging at the bedroom door and we lost focus.

The cat that had been slowly, beautifully levitating across the room suddenly dropped hard and fast to the floor again with a bang. It was enough to wake the beast. She snarled and growled at us.

Abdon, who'd been pounding on the door, opened it abruptly. "Why are you witches still up here? Didn't you get the message that all witches were to come to the ballroom at once?"

As soon as the cat saw the door open, she pounced on Abdon, knocking him to the wood floor. She growled low in her throat, her face in his, and then leapt from his chest through the open doorway and into the hall. Before anyone could react, Kalyna had disappeared.

"What the—?" Abdon was furious and holding his hand over his chest. "That thing broke one of my ribs. Why is it here?"

Elsie gently helped him to his feet. "Just stand still now. We can have that fixed in no time."

"No, thanks. I'll see my doctor. Why was that cat up here? How did you get it past security? I believe we said no familiars."

"Hey." Brian looked around as though he'd been asleep and had suddenly awakened to a room full of people. "What's going on?"

"That's what I want to know," Abdon demanded. "Did you bring your familiar with you, Brian? I didn't even know you had one. You know, I've always seen having a familiar as a sign of personal weakness."

So that's why he never had a cat. It made sense. Brian had always been expected to live up to his grandfather's strict standards of conduct.

"It's a long story," I replied. "Did you want to hear it now or after we go downstairs with everyone else?"

Abdon frowned and then grimaced as he was reminded that his rib was damaged. "Never mind. Come downstairs. We'll discuss the cat later."

That was fine with us. Maybe he'd forget about the incident later. We could only hope.

Olivia had immediately hidden in the elaborate sunburst light on the ceiling when she saw Abdon. "I'll just stay up here until you all get back," she whispered. "This is one time I'm glad I'm not going."

I agreed, the last one out of the room following Abdon to the meeting downstairs. "I'm sure we won't be long," I told her. "I don't think Kalyna will be back right away."

"Not that I'm worried about her." She dismissed the idea. "But I'll let you know before you come in. How are we going to catch her now that she's somewhere in the castle?"

"One thing at a time. Let's see what Abdon wants us to do now."

CHAPTER 21

It looked as though all the guests who'd started the evening so joyfully before were now in attendance again in the ballroom.

They weren't as happy now.

The party mood had evaporated long before, even though the food and drink was constantly refreshed. Champagne still flowed, and servants answered food requests. It didn't matter. The fun had gone out of the event. Everyone wanted to leave and wondered how much longer they would be trapped there.

It was a grumpy, half-dressed crowd that waited for Abdon to appear. Almost everyone needed a shower, even though they'd been given accommodations. The women wore little makeup, and the men needed a shave. They could have done this with magic. It seemed to be a silent protest to what was happening at the castle.

Abdon moved to the top of the stairs. I thought it was probably to be above the rest of us. Elsie, Brian, Dorothy and I blended in with the others in the impatient group of witches. People around us murmured angry words they didn't dare say loudly for fear of council retribution. I shuddered to think of being trapped here for much longer if we didn't find the killer.

Abdon held up his hand for quiet, and everyone stopped talking. The other ten members of the council joined him on the wide landing.

"None of us could have foreseen Makaleigh's death yesterday." Abdon began his speech in a stern, demanding tone. "Yet it is our obligation to find her killer before the spell wears off in about eleven hours. Once the door opens to the castle, the killer will be free. I don't know about you, but I don't want that on my conscience."

"Like he has a conscience," Elsie murmured close to me.

I half expected Abdon to point her out and say, "I heard that," but he continued without acknowledging her remark or glancing her way.

She put her hand to her mouth and glanced at me with laughter in her green eyes. Elsie took very few things seriously.

"We have the witchfinder searching through all the clues that have been left by Makaleigh's killer. I urge all of you to consider what you've seen since you arrived. Anything out of the ordinary should be reported. If a witch seems suspicious, he or she could be guilty of murder."

A chill went through me. It seemed apt that the witchfinder from the Inquisition should be here at a time that sounded like witches turning against witches. What had we become?

A riot of questions and comments erupted from the group when he'd finished speaking.

"I don't know anything about Makaleigh's death," one woman shouted. "But you can't just hold us here for another eleven hours. I want to leave now."

"We all want to leave, madam," Abdon said. "But the spell is cast. We will be here until it is done. We have to find the killer before that moment."

"I'm afraid to say who I think the killer is." The thin witch with long gray sideburns glanced from side to side at the witches around him. "You've taken so much of my magic, I'm not sure I could defend myself."

"That is why we have security," Abdon said. "Just tell one of my security men if you suspect someone. They don't need to know that it was you that turned them in. I guarantee your safety."

"I think we've heard enough," Dorothy whispered. "We have a big cat to catch."

"Do you suppose she could be responsible for killing Makaleigh?" Elsie questioned.

"Why bother using a knife?" I queried. "She could have done it with one swipe of her claws."

"Wait a minute." Brian laughed. "We must be talking about a different cat. Kalyna has sharp claws, but I don't think she's dangerous. Come on. She barely weighs a pound or two."

"Yeah, well, you didn't see her rapid weight-gain issue," Dorothy warned. "I'll fill you in while we look for her."

Brian and Dorothy went to find Oscar and tell him about the situation with Kalyna. They were more afraid of Kalyna attacking other witches than I was. I felt as though she'd set her sights on Brian and would come back for him. We needed to watch him.

Had the mysterious man who'd given Dorothy the cat purposely done so for this reason? Or was it a simple mistake? At this point it was hard to say, since so much had happened since we'd arrived.

"It's hard for me to imagine that Dorothy with all her young magic didn't even notice the cat was a shifter," Elsie said.

"None of us did when we first saw her," I added as we walked slowly up the stairs, leaving the main group still asking questions as we looked for the cat.

"But that was different, Molly. We barely saw the cat for a few minutes. She had been living with Dorothy before Dorothy gave her to Brian. I think there's more to it." She shook her faded red curls. "What if Makaleigh's death has something to do with the cat? In her human form, she could've put that knife in her. We'd all think about her killing as would a cat and dismiss it. What if that's the whole point?"

I nodded, thinking about what she was saying. "And we sneaked her into Brian's birthday bash where we all knew the council would be."

"Exactly."

A servant went by with glasses of pink champagne and matching pink cupcakes.

Elsie took one of each. "At least they feed us well."

I sipped some champagne. "That's true. I'm surprised they don't conjure the food instead of making it the old-fashioned way."

"You know it never tastes as good. This cupcake is delicious. Want a bite?"

Her upper lip had pink frosting on it. "No, thanks. Here's a napkin."

"Have you ever noticed that the best-tasting foods are also the messiest?" She wiped the frosting from her lip.

We'd been wandering through the hallway for twenty minutes or more. We were never going to find a creature who could slip between being a cat and a woman whenever she felt like it—at least not this way.

"We really need an incantation to locate Kalyna," I insisted. "Let's try to find Brian and Dorothy and summon the shifter with magic. It's bad enough trying to decide who killed Makaleigh without looking for a shifter at the same time."

Elsie agreed, and we returned to the main hall. We zig-zagged around the ballroom, where too many witches were drowning their sorrows and still complaining about being trapped in the castle. Neither of us wanted to get caught up in that.

"They should put that energy to better use," Elsie remarked. "Too bad we can't harness the witches into a group that could get things accomplished."

"As usual, we think a lot alike." I smiled. "It must be because we're both retired schoolteachers."

"Maybe so."

We took a set of back stairs that were away from the ballroom—there seemed to be hundreds of stairs and hall-ways throughout the castle. We hadn't gotten lost yet, but most witches did have an inner sense of direction even in the dark.

This set of stairs led us to a short hall with a balcony that overlooked the ballroom. We could see another set of stairs only a few yards from where we stood. It seemed like someone had mistakenly added an extra flight of stairs that weren't needed and didn't quite fit in.

Elsie sniffed and sneezed. "I smell something. It's the same scent from the pink room where Makaleigh was killed. What about you?"

My amulet had begun to glow as though it was agreeing with her. "I don't smell anything except that cupcake, but I feel something. The hall and the stairs are wrong. They shouldn't be here. They aren't part of the castle."

"It doesn't happen often, but I'm kind of scared, Molly. We've wandered into someplace we shouldn't be. How are we gonna get out? I'm sure there's a reason behind this magic. I don't think I want to know what it is."

We both heard footsteps—heeled shoes—coming from the other end of the hall.

"Quick. Let's hide behind this drape." I pulled aside the

heavy red velvet and stepped behind it. Elsie joined me. We were both breathing hard.

Another set of footsteps, this one without heels, made a soft swishing noise on the stone floor. Elsie and I stared into each other's eyes. She touched the silver sword that she wore around her neck as a symbol of her power as a fire witch. I wished that she had a real one.

I put my hand on my amulet. It was as much a symbol of my power as a water witch as the tiny cauldron that I wore around my neck. Maybe together if we had to, we could fight off a more powerful witch if that was who was coming toward us.

"This is very dangerous."

I knew that voice. It was Hedyle. Was this her magic?

"Everything we do is dangerous now."

The man's voice made both my brows and Elsie's raise in surprise. It was Drago Rasmun, Dorothy's father. Why was he there with Hedyle? How could he even be at the castle, since he was reviled by the council? Drago and others like him lived their lives outside of the council's purview. That made him a danger to them, since he wouldn't obey their commands like the rest of us.

There were some noises I interpreted as kissing sounds, and then Hedyle sighed.

"What have we done, Drago? What have we done?"

CHAPTER 22

It was difficult to stand there with a hundred questions in my brain. Were they responsible for Makaleigh's death? I wanted to know, but I also wanted to stay alive. Both Drago and Hedyle were very powerful witches. My amulet might have no defense against them, although Hedyle seemed impressed by it.

"Dearest heart." His voice was tender as he tried to soothe her. "We've done nothing wrong. There can be nothing wrong done in the name of love."

"But if we're discovered, it could mean an end to us both." She wept softly.

I could imagine him holding her in his arms. I couldn't see them—didn't dare try to peek around the velvet drape.

"I won't let anything happen to you. What we've done has been necessary. There was no other way."

They had to be talking about Makaleigh's death. What else could this pertain to?

Elsie pinched her nose closed so she wouldn't sneeze.

"I fear some of them, particularly Abdon, already know the truth. We shall be found out, Drago. There will be nowhere to hide from their punishment."

"There will always be a place to hide," he assured her. "What about the witch, Molly, who was with Makaleigh when she passed? Does she know?"

"She would not allow the discovery spell, and I believe her magic comes from a greater source than a witch's magic. I don't think we can force her to tell us."

Drago made a hissing noise like a cat. "It doesn't matter. She obviously doesn't plan to tell anyone what she heard, or she really doesn't know what it is. When the castle doors open, we shall be free."

There was more kissing and cooing before they parted.

Elsie and I waited soundlessly behind the curtain, not moving. I helped her keep from sneezing with my hand over hers at her nose. I wasn't sure when we'd decide it was safe to emerge.

"Do you think we can get out of here now?" she barely whispered.

"I don't know."

"I have to go, Molly. You know? Too much champagne. I can't wait any longer." She threw open the curtain, and I followed her lead.

The hall had changed. The real stairs were still there but farther away. The magic that had created the short, intimate space where the lovers met was gone.

"Good thing we didn't disappear with it," Elsie said, sneezing. "Come on. Let's go."

Brian and Dorothy were in the room when we got back. Elsie made a beeline for the bathroom.

"No luck finding Kalyna," Dorothy said. "And I wish you'd back me up on what happened with her and Brian, Molly. He doesn't believe me about her mesmerizing him and getting to be the size of a panther."

"It's not that I don't believe you," Brian defended. "It's just that it's hard to imagine. Back me up here, Molly—witches see shifters. It would be impossible not to have noticed that Kalyna was more than a house cat."

"Witches do see shifters, in most cases," I replied, hoping I wasn't adding fuel to their disagreement. "The whole situation is odd. Even Elsie and I noticed something off about the cat but couldn't say what. You didn't know either, Brian. I think someone spelled the cat so we wouldn't know it was a shifter."

"But why?" he asked. "It doesn't make any sense. Why bother?"

"Because whoever did it knew we were going to be here at the castle," Dorothy guessed. "They knew we could sneak Kalyna in as your birthday present."

"That's possible," I agreed. "It's even conceivable that Kalyna shifted into her human form, killed Makaleigh and then shifted back into a cat. No one would know."

"That's a lot of ifs," Brian replied. "And who'd do such a thing? Why not just kill her themselves?"

Olivia nodded, agreeing with Molly as she was floating near the ceiling. "I've heard odder things in my time."

"Elsie and I might have something even stranger to add to it," I told them.

The toilet flushed, and Elsie ran out of the bathroom. "You didn't tell them yet, did you?"

"What?" Olivia came down to be sure to hear what was going on.

Elsie and I glanced at her and shrugged. There was no way to keep this from her. Hopefully she was over Drago.

"We overheard Drago meeting with Hedyle." The words burst out of Elsie. "And not just any meeting. This was passionate."

"Passionate?" Olivia frowned. "What does that mean?"

"You haven't been dead that long," Elsie countered. "You

know—smooch, smooch, smooch—'Oh, Hedyle. Oh, Drago.'
You get it."

Dorothy and I sat on the bed together while Brian leaned
against the wall.

"You mean the two of them are lovers?" Olivia queried.
"But she's so old. Ancient Greece, ladies. Thousands of
years. What can the attraction be?"

"How old is Drago, Mom?" Dorothy asked. "You said he
was really old too."

"But not that old," Olivia quipped. "I mean, I was with
him. And look at him. He's just a perfect male specimen."

"But how much of that is magic?" Brian asked. "With
enough magic, anyone could look young forever."

"Anyway," I continued, "the story isn't really about their
ages." I repeated what we'd heard from behind the velvet
drapes. "It sounded like they could be guilty of killing
Makaleigh."

"It's true." Elsie backed me up. "I'm sure they were talking about Makaleigh, and about Molly hearing her last
words."

"So you think Makaleigh found out about Hedyle and
Drago?" Brian summed up. "There's no doubt the council
would be furious if they knew she was dating someone considered beyond their reach. We all know that he's a renegade.
The council hates renegades."

"She might have been asked to leave the council," Olivia
added. "Maybe Makaleigh found out somehow and threatened to tell."

"People in control always hate renegades," Elsie said.
"Trust me. I taught history for many years."

"That would mean Drago and Hedyle murdered Makaleigh to keep her quiet, not to keep her from changing poli-
cies on the council," Dorothy said. "This is big. But how are
we going to prove it to the council? The two of them could
kill us if they knew that we knew."

"Just like they did Makaleigh," Olivia repeated.

I hated to agree with her, because I would have liked nothing better than to turn over the whole mess to Abdon and the council and let them deal with it. I didn't want to be in the middle of this feud, if that's what it was, and I didn't want my friends there either. It was a risky place to be.

"You're right," I finally said. "We're going to have to keep this to ourselves. At least until we can find something to corroborate our information. Maybe it's in the three words Makaleigh whispered. It makes sense now why Hedyle was so intent on getting them from me. She had a lot to lose."

"Good thing you didn't let her do the discovery spell on you," Elsie said. "You could be floating around on the ceiling with Olivia right now. I'm sure Hedyle and Drago wouldn't let you live once they had the words."

Brian put his hand on my shoulder. "Don't worry, Molly. We won't let that happen to you."

"That's fine," Olivia whined. "Where were you when I was killed?"

"I'm sorry, but we didn't know each other that well," Brian said. "We're family now. We have to look after one another."

"Which is why we have to find that cat," Dorothy reiterated. "I know proving who killed Makaleigh is important too. But I don't want to ever see Brian looking like a zombie has eaten his brain again either. Besides, we don't know for sure that she didn't shift from cat to human and kill Makaleigh. If that was the case, we'd probably have to take the blame for that too, since we brought the cat here and Abdon saw her here. Anybody have any ideas on how we can find a woman who can become any size cat she wants in this huge placc?"

"I don't know about the rest of you," Elsie said, "but I was thinking that Molly could do some scrying. She's very good at it, being a water witch and all."

"But her magic is limited," Olivia argued. "How is she supposed to manage it?"

"As much as I hate to admit it, she's got that amulet that is nothing but water magic," Elsie continued. "She should be able to skirt the castle's magic, at least in this case, since she'd be using water directly. It's worth a try anyway."

"Scrying, huh?" Brian grinned. "I love the old-fashioned magic. I've never done it, but I have an uncle who used to find water with a willow wand."

"Oh, the dark sheep in the family." Elsie laughed.

"That's true," he agreed. "My parents never wanted him to visit. They were afraid I'd grow up like him. He wasn't exactly a renegade, but he never went along with the council's edicts either. I'm not really sure what happened to him. It's been years since I saw him."

"I suppose we could do some scrying," I said. "It is old-fashioned but also doesn't take as much magic as creating something out of nothing. And Elsie's right about the water magic." I didn't go into how right she was. "We'll need a large bowl—silver would be nice. And some water. The purer the better."

"There's a well right outside the castle," Brian said. "I can draw it from there. It's supposed to be very pure."

"You must have forgotten that you can't leave the castle." Olivia giggled. "Glad I'm not the only one with a bad memory."

"Sorry." He laughed. "I guess we might as well get water from the bathroom. I'll go to the kitchen and get a big silver bowl and be right back."

When Brian was gone we talked about his affinity for the missing cat.

"I guess they really meshed," Dorothy mourned. "I hate that she's evil. She should have been the perfect birthday gift."

"She's probably not evil. Someone may have put her into this position, and she might have had no choice. We don't know yet what the situation was. She certainly didn't cloak herself from witches seeing her as a shifter," Elsie told her. "But she's definitely not familiar material. Shifters are a whole other thing. They don't hang around with witches much."

"It wasn't your fault, sweetie." Olivia patted Dorothy's back the best she could, being a non-corporeal entity. "There was no way to know—at least not without magic recognition."

"Something we were all lacking in this case," I said again. "The man at the library could have been someone who wanted Dorothy and Brian to get the cat in here just to kill Makaleigh. If so, it was a brilliant plan."

"Could it have been Drago?" Elsie asked, eyes narrowed. "Could he have used his own daughter to help him get rid of Makaleigh? He had to know that if she was caught, it would look like she was part of the conspiracy."

"I've been telling you the whole time that Drago was evil and would hurt Dorothy if he knew about her," Oliva said. "I'm sure that's the only reason he came to find her in the first place. I'm sorry, honey. I didn't choose to have you in the Paris sewers for nothing, you know."

"Maybe it's just because I've never seen a shifter before," Dorothy suggested. "Maybe it didn't have anything to do with the cat being protected by magic. I am still new at this."

We considered the idea, and the three of us rejected it with a resounding no.

"I'm sure if you think back to when you met Larry for the first time, you'll remember that you felt something," Elsie said. "Maybe a tingling and something didn't feel exactly right about him."

Dorothy nodded. "Yes. I remember that feeling. I felt the same way with the sea witch. Is that magic recognition?"

"Yes." I got up from the bed and wandered around the room. "I'm sure none of us—including you—felt it, because she was disguised. Whoever did this didn't want us to know. Maybe it was Drago, if he and Hedyle killed Makaleigh."

"If?" Olivia demanded. "It seems to me that we have all but their fingerprints on the knife! I still don't know what he sees in Hedyle."

"Maybe it's her power," Elsie suggested. "Or her place on the council. Drago seems like he might be the kind of man who'd be thrilled to mock the council this way."

"That's very true." Olivia sighed. "I wish I'd known then what I know now."

"But you wouldn't have Dorothy if you did," I reminded her.

"That's so true!"

Brian came back with the silver bowl. It was two feet across and a few inches deep. "Will this work?"

"Perfect," I told him.

"I brought a pitcher to fill it with." He produced the pitcher as well. "Now what?"

"Now we use it to find that pesky cat."

CHAPTER 23

The first thing we did was to find some sage and smudge both rooms to clear them of any bad influences. After that, we blessed everything we were about to use. Knowing we'd been tricked by the shifter, we were extra careful. We didn't want to miss anything important that could cause the scrying magic to backfire on us.

We stood together holding hands. Dorothy declared her earth magic with the power of flowers, trees and all living things that drew life from the soil. Elsie called on her power from the fire that was part of the sun and brought life. My magic was of the water—the rivers and the seas—without which none would survive. Brian took his magic from the very air we breathe, that gave us life, and gave it back to us, blessed and potent.

We drew our power and combined it. It shimmered around us like an enchanted bubble, a sheen of magic and life essences, surrounding us. It felt warm and comforting as well as strong and protecting.

Our coven was more powerful than it had ever been when it was me, Elsie and Olivia. Or we'd never called magic to us this way. I wasn't sure which.

I invoked the power of sight as I first cleansed my hands and splashed water into my face. Elsie and Dorothy made the bowl even shinier by rubbing it with a smooth cloth and adding our intentions to see what we could not see with our eyes. As Brian poured the water into the silver bowl, we chanted and invoked that sight to be used for good.

The water in the bowl was on a nightstand we'd moved to the center of the room. I blessed it again, and holding my amulet with one hand, I plunged the other hand into the cool water as I murmured the spell.

"Water, stuff of life, give us sight.

Water, without there can be no life, give us sight.

Water, building block of the universe, give us sight."

Immediately images began to form. I could see witches, servants, everyone and everything trapped in the castle while we waited for the spell to end. I could see them laughing, dancing, crying. I could see their faults and their fears. Nothing was hidden from the scrying bowl.

"I see her." I finally saw the cat. "Kalyna is hiding in the north end of the castle. She is in human form to blend better with the guests. Take a cup of water from this bowl and bless it as you approach her. Throw it on her, and she won't be able to change back to the cat."

Dorothy drew water carefully into the pitcher Brain had brought with him. "I want to bring her back, since I was responsible for her being here."

"Not alone," Brian said. "I'll go with you."

That met with a resounding no from all of us.

"Hey. Just because she spelled me once doesn't mean she can do it again," he protested. "I'm not stupid. I won't fall for whatever it was again."

"You can't help yourself," Elsie concluded. "It's like the

sea witch. Once they put the come-hither on you, it's twice as hard to get away from them the next time."

"I think we all agree," I told him. "Elsie can go with Dorothy. That way we don't have to worry about what could happen when you come face-to-face with Kalyna again."

"Well, I feel stupid," Brain protested as he sat on the chair by the desk.

"Don't feel stupid," Elsie told him, pinching his cheek. "Sometimes a female witch is just better with things."

Olivia giggled. "Especially anything that has to do with S-E-X!"

We all laughed at that. Brian groaned and put his head in his hands.

"It's okay." Dorothy hugged him. "They're just teasing you."

When Dorothy and Elsie were gone, I had Brian draw more water to put in the bowl. We threw away what was already in there, blessed new water and put the bowl back on the table.

"What are you doing now?" Olivia asked.

"Trying to discover why we didn't recognize the cat as a shifter." I plunged my hand in the water. Images floated through it.

"See the moment when she got the cat." I held my amulet as Olivia and Brian peered into the water.

"There's the man outside the library," Brian said. "Hey. This is great. I wish I'd learned to do it. It's like watching TV."

"Oh, you can still learn, although you won't be as good at it as Molly is, since she's a water witch. I know, since I was an air witch like you."

"I can see something wrong with him right now." I nodded at the image. "His face is wrong. It's not what it should be. Do you see it?"

"I do." Brian leaned closer. "It's obvious like this. He

almost looks like a ghost. See how his face is shimmering. He's masking himself."

"You're right, Brian," Olivia said. "It looks like mine, but it shouldn't be that way. I can see—oh my lord—it's Drago. He did give her the cat. Elsie was right. He piggy-backed on the shifter to get in the castle."

"If I see him again, I'm going to rip his head off," Brian growled. "He shouldn't have used her that way."

"Take it easy," I warned. "He's got magic we don't under-stand and more of it than all of us together. You don't want to try to rip anything off him or it might be you that's dead."

As we watched, Dorothy came out of the library with a big smile on her pretty face and approached him. As soon as she picked up the cat, Drago began the spell.

"He spelled her not to recognize him or the magic in the cat," Brian said. "That SOB. He's as bad as my family. He used her to get into the castle. He didn't care what happened to her because of it."

"I know." I gently put my hand on his shoulder, feeling the tense muscles there.

"I guess that answers that question," Olivia said. "I just can't believe Drago would do such a thing. Oh wait. I've seen him do much worse. I wish he'd never found Dorothy."

"Can you find Makaleigh's killer while you've got your hand in the scrying bowl, Molly? I'd like to get out of here and find Drago." Brian's hands clenched on the silver.

Olivia and I exchanged warning glances. We both knew how dangerous it could be for Brian to attempt any kind of revenge on Drago.

"I'm afraid it doesn't work like that." I withdrew my magic and my hand from the water and used a towel to dry my hand. "I have to know what I'm looking for."

"It's pretty obvious that Hedyle and Drago killed her." Brian watched as the images disappeared from the water. "All we have to do is find them and get them to confess."

"I don't think even the witchfinder would take on one of those interrogations," I told him. "If they don't confess on their own, we might never really know the truth."

"You can't let Drago drag you into this, Brian," Olivia added. "He'll ruin your life."

"I don't care right now," he said.

Dorothy and Elsie returned with a surprisingly compliant shifter held between them. Kalyna was shaking and trying to dry off as though she were still a cat, but she was in her human form.

"She tried to get away, but we were on it," Elsie said with a laugh. "I felt like I was on *Starsky and Hutch*. Remember that old show?"

"Which one were you?" Olivia laughed with her.

"Definitely Hutch. Dorothy would make a much better Starsky." Elsie made the cat girl sit in a chair with her hand on the girl's slender shoulder.

Brian spelled a sash from his robe so it would hold her and tied her to the chair. "I think we deserve some answers, Kalyna."

"Is it okay if he's that close to her?" Dorothy whispered. "I don't want him to get all crazy again."

"It should be fine now," Elsie said. "Now that we've discovered her secret, she's lost a lot of her magic."

"Probably as okay as you being close to her," I told her. "Drago was definitely the one who gave you the cat at the library. He immediately put a spell on you not to recognize him or sense the magic in her."

"What?" Dorothy's dark eyes were huge in her face. "Why would he do such a thing? I thought he came to see me."

"Apparently not," Elsie said. "Not surprising, I guess. He's a bad guy. We all knew he was a bad guy. He just didn't act like one, so we got confused."

"So yeah." Dorothy channeled her anger and betrayal at

Kalyna. "You better start talking, cat girl. We want to know what's going on."

"I don't know anything," Kalyna said. "Drago asked me to do him a favor. He wanted to visit his lover, but the wards on the castle were too strong. He sneaked in with me. That's all."

"Except for you enchanting Brian," Dorothy accused. "I don't think that was part of Drago's plan."

"No." Kalyna smiled slyly as she peeked at Brian from beneath her thick lashes. "You gave me to him. That made him mine. I just wanted him to like me."

"Ha! Not that you have to worry about it now," Dorothy raged. "As soon as the castle doors are open, you are so out of here and out of our lives."

Kalyna shrugged and continued to gaze longingly at Brian.

"We know this now, but is there anything we can do about it?" Elsie asked. "We still can't prove anything if she won't cooperate."

"Did you kill Makaleigh Veazy?" Brian asked Kalyna.

"I haven't killed anyone," she smiled slyly. "Not lately."

"I think we should bring the witchfinder and Oscar up here. She can tell them what she knows. There's no point is us being involved anymore. Once they know about Hedyle and Drago, that's it," Brian said.

None of us, except for Brian, were sure if this was a good plan. I was afraid he was biased by feeling foolish at what happened between him and Kalyna, not to mention wanting to get back at Drago.

"Whatever Drago and Hedyle did, it should be up to the witchfinder and Oscar to figure it out now." He was adamant. "We've done more than our share to help out."

We argued with him, but he insisted on calling them. There wasn't much else we could do. And who knew if he wasn't right? I wasn't willing to bet our lives on it. We weren't police officers. The tale seemed to have wrapped itself up to a disagreeable end. What else was there to say?

With a little over ten hours to go until the spell was lifted from the castle, the witchfinder and the castle manager were packed into our room to hear what the shifter had to say. Elsie and I added to her testimony our own report from what we had heard behind the velvet drape.

Oscar seemed impressed by what we had to say, but Antonio was doubtful.

"They could've been talking about their forbidden relationship," he said. "What they had to say hardly amounts to enough proof that they killed Makaleigh. What was their motive? Why would they do such a thing?"

"We thought that Makaleigh found out somehow about their relationship and threatened to tell the rest of the council," Elsie suggested. "That would be enough to kill her. Relationships can be more than you can stand."

There was a noise from the closet where we'd hidden Olivia while the two men were there. With what Cassandra had said to us about Olivia, we didn't want to take any chances. It was the typical bump in the night that gave ghosts away and frightened little children.

Brian kicked his foot against the wall. That seemed to explain the mystery noise.

"I still think we should take this to Abdon," Oscar said. "It's the best lead we've had on Makaleigh's death so far. I know it will be hard to catch or contain Hedyle or Drago, but the council should be able to come up with something."

The witchfinder was still skeptical about Hedyle and Drago being responsible for Makaleigh's death. He also didn't seem convinced that the council could come up with a way to imprison two of the most powerful witches in the world.

But Oscar seemed to be on the same page with Brian, and he thought his job could be on the line if he didn't tell Abdon what he knew. He left right away, leaving Antonio in charge of Kalyna. We all stared at the thin, rather pathetic shifter. It was hard to imagine that at any moment she could turn into a huge black killing machine.

"I do not like it." Antonio finally turned away from her. "Drago and Hedyle do not need to meet here. They could be anywhere in the world before and after this ball. Why decide to be here now?"

"Wouldn't that go along with them killing Makaleigh?" Dorothy wondered. "They had to be here to kill her. They knew she'd be at the party with a lot of other witches. It was a good opportunity."

He considered her words. "Bah. I still do not like it. I do not believe these two powerful witches chose to kill Makaleigh with a dagger, of all things. I am sorry. I just do not see it. There is something more that we are missing. Our haste to locate a killer and resolve the issue blinds us to the truth."

I considered that Antonio might not be eager to return to his prison. That could color his view on whether or not the killers had been found. I didn't blame him. The longer it went on, the longer he was free. I couldn't imagine what it was like for him to live in that hellish prison.

"Maybe the council will take into consideration the work you've done for centuries and free you." I tried to comfort him. "It's been a long time. Everyone deserves forgiveness."

His eyes were hungry for resolution behind his mask. "That may not be true for me, Molly. You are a kind soul. Not all are willing to release their hatred."

Oscar returned with two security guards. They took Kalyna with them. She hung compliantly between them as though drained of all energy and hope. Antonio went too, with a beautiful bow in my direction.

"I hope that was the right thing to do." Elsie chewed on her bottom lip as she worried.

"I hope so too." I dumped the water from the bowl but couldn't empty my thoughts as easily.

CHAPTER 24

There was a party organized in the ballroom for grumbling witches who were bored and looking for something to do. The Fuller family was trying to show sympathy for the rest of us.

Abdon, Yuriza and Schadt went all out with multicolored fountains where partygoers could dip their cups for various types of drinks. A dozen tables held elaborate foods and desserts with ice sculptures on each table. Every food imaginable was available for even the most sophisticated palates. A lot of it I didn't recognize. Stone potatoes?

For entertainment, games of magic were organized. Some were simple gambling competitions, while others were games of flying. A few younger witches were throwing a magic football that returned when it was thrown. There were also magic light shows for the rest of us who didn't want to participate.

Laughter greeted us as we got downstairs. We were bored

and grumbling witches too. It had been a few hours since Oscar had taken Kalyna. We'd spent time in the rooms talking and playing cards, worrying if we'd done the right thing or the best thing. Dorothy and Brian had found other ways to occupy themselves with the adjoining door closed and locked between the rooms.

"This really stinks that I have to wait up here while you get to go to a party." Olivia stamped her ghost foot before we left, but without physical substance, it wasn't much of a protest.

"We just can't figure out any way to safely hide you," Elsie told her. "We have to be careful, since everyone is on high alert after Makaleigh's death. You wouldn't want to be exorcised by the council."

"No. I wouldn't," Olivia agreed. "Being a ghost isn't much fun. I thought it might be—going through things other people couldn't go through and such—but it sucks."

"I'm sorry," I told her. "We probably won't be gone long. Try not to get into trouble. Elsie is right. No one is in a forgiving mood right now. Cassandra has given us a distinct warning."

"All right, Molly. I'll just be here, flying around the room, bored out of my skull. If Brian and Dorothy don't go with you, I might just sneak a little peek in there."

"Don't you dare." Elsie's voice was stern. "You had your turn at that kind of thing. Use your imagination. I'm sure you can recall how it went."

Olivia sighed, making anything made of cloth ripple around the room.

"Nice ghost trick," I commended. "You're coming right along with your ghostly powers."

"Thank you. I just wish there was a school or something you could go to and take classes. I need someone to train me like you all are training Dorothy."

"Let's go, Molly," Elsie urged. "I'm starving."

We left Olivia on her own. I didn't blame her for being upset and a little depressed.

"I wish we could help her," I said to Elsie as we went downstairs.

"She'll figure it out. Ghosts have been haunting people for thousands of years. She's just feeling sorry for herself and whining about it." Her eyes flashed. "Is that spumoni?"

Elsie went to get a crystal goblet full of spumoni. I dipped my cup into the chocolate-flavored champagne. It was bitter, so I handed it off to one of the servants and tried the strawberry champagne. It was much better.

It seemed as though we'd been locked in the castle for centuries instead of hours. No wonder everyone was bored and grumpy. I noticed the remaining council members mingling with the "ordinary" witches.

Only Abdon wasn't present. I knew where he was and tried not to think what they might be doing. I hoped Kalyna would be all right. Not everyone was as fortunate as I was to have a protector. Joe always told me that I had a soft heart for the underdog.

"Hello, Molly." It was Hedyle in a beautiful gown that seemed to be made of pale green sea foam. "Are you enjoying the party?"

"I'd rather be home," I told her honestly. "I'm not really much of a partygoer."

"Neither am I." She watched several couples float by during a magic waltz, their feet never touching the floor. "The island I live on is very remote. I share it with only a few goats and the families who tend them. I do some healing for them, and they give me milk and cheese. I've lived many years this way and seen a hundred generations born on my island."

"That sounds very peaceful." I glanced at her. "And lonely."

"Sometimes," she agreed. "But mostly I am happy with my own company."

I nodded, wondering if she was going to ask me about Makaleigh's last words again. I was even more set to deny her now than I had been when she'd first approached me.

"What about you?" she asked, turning to gaze at me with her pale blue eyes. "Is there someone in your life?"

"Yes." I sipped my strawberry champagne. "My husband and my son." I didn't feel threatened telling her. It was common knowledge that I was married to someone who wasn't a witch and that my son had no magic.

"How wonderful. It is one of the few things I regret, not having children. They are a blessing to be cherished and protected."

Was that a hidden warning about Mike? I hoped not, because his safety from the council would always be top priority for me. I would protect him with my last breath if necessary.

"I don't know a mother alive who wouldn't be willing to show her fangs at the idea that her child might be harmed." I hoped that was clear enough for her.

How long was she going to stand there before she badgered me about Makaleigh's last words? It seemed like I could feel her intent without her voicing it.

"I hear you had a surprise visitor when you came to the castle. A shifter, I believe."

"Yes." Were we finally getting to the heart of the matter? "Brian's girlfriend wanted to surprise him with a familiar for his birthday. She didn't realize it was a shifter."

"Odd, that, since she is a witch."

"Yes, except that she's still in training. She was raised in a family without magic. She didn't realize she was a witch until recently." I didn't go into the fact that none of us knew about the shifter. She knew the truth too. I was sure Drago revealed his plot for sneaking into the castle to her.

"Olivia Dunst's daughter, yes?" Hedyle smiled at me. "I was dismayed to learn that Olivia had chosen to stay here after her death. It's not something I would have expected from a witch of her lineage. And who is the girl's father? Is he a witch?"

I turned to stare at her. Surely she knew the truth of the matter. What game was she playing?

I was getting tired of playing. "Her father is Drago Rasmun, as I'm sure you know. Olivia gave her up at birth to protect her from Drago. I believe he is still considered a renegade outside of the council, isn't he?"

"Drago is a renegade, but a very powerful one," she said. "He has lived almost as long as I. No doubt he could have found his daughter at any time if he'd really tried."

"What are you trying to tell me?" Yes, she was a member of the Grand Council of Witches and as such deserved my respect, but I felt that she was toying with me. What response was she looking for?

"I was only making small talk, Molly. I believe that's what you call it. I don't concern myself with renegades or their daughters. But I would like to know what Makaleigh said to you as she lay dying. That is important to me."

"It comes back to that."

"Yes. What she said may have been very important. I would hate for that information to fall into the wrong hands." Her gentle eyes skewered me like a shish kebab. "I won't wait much longer for your response. Then I suppose it will be you and your amulet against me and my magic, hmm? Good evening, Molly. Enjoy the festivities."

I watched her leave, angry and scared. Her threat had been plain against me and Mike as well as Olivia.

Elsie joined me there with a full plate of food. "I saw her. What did she want? The words again, I guess."

"You would too if you were afraid you were going to be

Brian and Dorothy were finally moving around outside their bedroom when we went back upstairs. Olivia was talking to them about her pregnancy—mostly spent under the city streets of Paris hiding from Drago. She'd given up so much to keep her daughter safe. I knew she considered him to be a real threat.

"How was the party, girls?" Olivia asked when she saw us.

"It was okay, if you like that kind of thing," Elsie answered. "The food was good. And Hedyle was threatening Molly again."

"She still wants those mixed-up words that you got from Makaleigh?" Dorothy asked, her pretty face a rosy shade that matched Brian's.

"Hedyle also wanted to talk about you, Olivia," I said. "And Drago and Dorothy. She was threatening everyone who matters to me if I don't give her Makaleigh's last words."

"What did she say about me?" Olivia demanded, coming

found out." I took a sweet pickle from Elsie's plate. "I guess that means we're not done. We have to figure out what those words mean, even if it's only Makaleigh telling everyone about Drago and Hedyle's relationship."

"Let's do it."

close enough that I could almost see through her to the wall behind.

"She was upset about you being a ghost," I told her. "She also said Drago could have found Dorothy anytime he wanted."

"What's that supposed to mean?" Dorothy wondered.

"I think the whole conversation was just to see if she could get me to tell her what I knew. She said I could pit my amulet against her magic."

"I'd like to pit my baseball bat against the side of her head," Elsie muttered angrily. "The nerve of her!"

"Secrets travel fast in the council," Brian said. "You can't tell anyone those words if you don't want them to get back to her, Molly."

"Maybe," I agreed. "I still think that the best thing we can do is to find out what the words mean. That way, no surprises from Hedyle or the council. We can take matters into our own hands."

Elsie groaned. "I hate code stuff. We already know that Hedyle and Drago killed Makaleigh because she found out about their love affair and that Drago smuggled himself into the castle using Brian's shape-shifting cat. Why do we need any more information?"

"There is probably more to the story than what we know," I said. "And I can't stand Hedyle threatening me every few minutes. I have to know what those words mean so I can deal with her on my level. She threatened Mike, Elsie. I can't let that go."

"You're right, Molly." She took my hand. "I'm sorry. We should figure out those words if for nothing else than to get her off your back."

Dorothy sat at the desk again. "I'm ready. Let's do this."

"You mind if I go get something to eat?" Brian dropped a kiss on Dorothy's neck. "I'm starving. I promise to come right back up and help out."

"I'll come with you," Elsie said. "I'm not good with rid-dles. We can let them figure it out. I can show you where the best food is too."

"Sounds good to me." Brian held out his arm for her. "Let's go."

"Elsie?" I questioned.

"Like he said, we'll be right back up. I can't let him go alone, since the killer might be looking for him."

"All right. But don't waste time down there, please," I capitulated.

"So what were these words again?" Olivia asked.

"Aba. Mho. Ord." I repeated the words that felt seared in my brain. It was hard to imagine now that we had to do a discovery spell to find them. I felt like they'd been inside of me for an eternity.

"Those aren't really words." Olivia flitted around the room. "Words don't sound like that."

"Old words did," Dorothy said. "It wasn't until later that words got so fancy. People didn't have huge vocabularies before the sixteenth century. They only used words they needed. But these could also be mixed-up letters. If Maka-leigh knew Hedyle might try to take them from you, Molly, she might have mixed them up on purpose."

Dorothy, Olivia and I tried variations of the letters in different orders. Nothing seemed to work in a magic or a normal way. We switched them back and forth until I was actually dizzy from looking at them. Nothing.

"What if the letters are actually related to numbers?" Dorothy suggested.

We tried changing the letters to numbers, but that didn't seem to work either. An hour later, Elsie and Brian came back, and we were still hard at work at determining the meaning of the words.

"I guess we got back too soon." Elsie sank down on the bed.

I lifted a brow in her direction.

"Just kidding, Molly. Of course I'm glad to help. I just don't know what to say."

Brian and Elsie added their ideas to the mix. Nothing we came up with seemed to be the prize we were looking for.

"Maybe it's really not anything," Brian said. "Just because Hedyle thinks it means something doesn't mean it does, right? She's having an affair with Drago. That's enough to make anybody paranoid. I don't know what would happen if Abdon found out."

"I don't know." Dorothy got up from the chair and stretched her long, lean body. "He might be right. Maybe it is just gibberish, Molly, like we thought to begin with. Just because we found it with the discovery spell doesn't make it important, does it? You heard what you heard. People say weird stuff when they're dying."

"Maybe she meant to say something but just wasn't able to," Brian added.

"Anyway," Dorothy said as she put on her shoes, "since no one brought me any food back, I'm starving. I'm going to get something to eat before it's all gone."

"I'll come with you," Brian offered.

"I don't know." She pretended to be angry. "You didn't bring any food back. Maybe you should stay here."

"I'm sorry." He kissed her hand. "Really sorry. I could hold your plate and you could just walk around and eat. How does that sound?"

She smiled at him. "That sounds pretty good. You can come." She glanced at me. "I think Elsie is asleep. You want to come too, Molly?"

"I'm not hungry." I took her place at the desk. "You two go on. I'll stay up here and keep looking at this."

"It's nice that someone is going to keep me company for a while. I wish I had a big glass of that pink champagne," Olivia said wistfully.

"Okay. We'll be back in a while," Brian said.

Elsie had begun to snore softly. I smiled at her smooth face. She was so much happier since she'd met Larry the werewolf. How could anyone think that was a bad thing? And yet I knew there were witches who would scorn her, as they did Olivia, if she married him.

I looked at the paper with Dorothy's neat handwriting on it. I'd never asked, but I was willing to bet she was very good in school. She wanted to please everyone. I'd always found that quality in my best students. They were in for a few rough patches—no one could please everyone all the time—but they were driven to accomplish what they saw as their personal goals.

Olivia came down from the ceiling like a shower of stardust and draped herself artfully on the desk. "This is all happening so fast, Molly. I expect Brian to ask Dorothy to marry him in the not-too-distant future. I could be a grandmother. You know how I always said how much I hated that idea of being someone's grandmother when I was still alive?"

"I know."

"Well, I lied. I'm excited about the idea. I just wasn't happy about getting old. Now I don't have to worry about that part of it, do I?"

"I guess there are good things about being a ghost."

"There are. And look what I can do." She stared at the closet door. It took a few moments, but it slowly opened with an unnerving creak.

"Olivia!" I applauded. "That's wonderful. You've been practicing."

"I have. I just have to get some of my old mojo back." She smiled. "And I can levitate things. I can also do this."

I stared at her, and she appeared completely solid. "You don't even look like a ghost. How are you doing that?"

Her image changed immediately, becoming more like a

movie projection of herself again. "I can only do it for a moment or two right now, but I'm getting stronger. I know I won't ever be a witch again, but I want to be the best ghost I can."

Sitting back in the chair, I congratulated my friend. We'd grown up together with Elsie, who took babysitting duties for our parents when we were very young.

"I was just thinking about Dorothy and how sweet and pleasant she is. She reminds me so much of you. You were always driven to please people and do the right thing. Even though you weren't in her life when she was a child, it was a trait she picked up from you."

Olivia cried ectoplasm tears that ran down her face. "Why thank you, Molly. You know I've always loved and respected you too. I think you should consider coming back as a ghost when you pass. The world will still need you for another hundred years."

"I wish I'd known you two were going to spend the whole time telling each other how wonderful you are." Elsie yawned as she sat up. "I would've gone down with the children for more champagne."

"Well, don't let that stop you," Olivia told her. "I think alcohol makes you a better person, Elsie Blair Langston!"

"Thank you." Elsie frowned when she saw me still sitting at the desk. "Haven't you deciphered those words yet, Molly?"

"No." I put down the pen that I'd picked up. "We've looked at them from every direction. I don't know what to say."

There was a discreet knock at the door. "Molly? Are you in there?" It was Antonio.

"Hide," I whispered to Olivia. She flew into the closet, closing the door behind her.

"Help me get off the bed." Elsie threw her feet over the side. "I think this must be a feather bed. It's like sinking into a cloud. But it's hard to get out."

I helped her, and we made ourselves presentable before I answered the door. The witchfinder stood at the threshold, the white mask covering his face, black hair spilling on his shoulders.

"Something has happened. I wish I did not have to be the one to tell you. Please hear me out before you pass judgment."

"What is it?" I asked him, alarmed by the tone of his voice.

"The shape-shifter is dead."

CHAPTER 26

"You killed her," Elsie accused. "I knew we shouldn't have let you take her. What was her crime? Helping that rogue, Drago, who got her in here? I can't believe it."

"Please." Antonio took my hand. "It was not I. I did not kill the cat woman, Molly. You must believe me."

Too stunned to do anything else, I invited him into the room and closed the door. "Sit down. Tell us what happened."

He sat on the embroidered seat of one of the hard-backed chairs. His face registered no emotion, but his voice was anguished. "I did not touch the girl," he said. "Oscar had her taken to a room for interrogation. I thought about what you said—that using pain accomplishes little when questioning a suspect. I had determined that I would simply talk to her and find out what her role was in Makaleigh's murder, if any."

"And what happened?" I asked.

"She was dead when I got there. Oscar said the door was

locked and spelled. No other beside myself should have been able to enter. And yet someone did. The girl had the same ceremonial knife in her heart as Makaleigh. I swear to you that it was not me. Look at her. There are no marks of torture on her. Yet was she in my charge and lies dead still. I have failed to reciprocate your kindness."

Elsie was softly crying. I wiped a few tears from my eyes. This was a needless death and clearly seemed to be Drago and Hedyle acting to tie up their loose ends. "You should have questioned Hedyle and Drago instead," I remarked in a bitter tone.

"It would be difficult to demand anything of Hedyle. She commands a position of extreme power and influence on the council as one of the founding members. As to questioning Drago Rasmun—we have yet to find him. Even then, though I possess magic greater than many witches, it is doubtful that I could hold him for interrogation."

"I don't know what to say."

"I do." Elsie's voice was angry. "We shouldn't have let them take her. We should've known better."

I sank down at the desk again, staring at the words that seemed to have no meaning. "What now?" I asked the witchfinder.

"We start anew." He shrugged his lanky form. "We search all avenues until the spell is lifted from the castle. If I have failed to perform my duty, Abdon has promised me a painful death."

"More painful than living in a wall for hundreds of years?" I asked.

"Just so." He bowed his head.

"Well, we have to gird our loins and ask Hedyle directly about her involvement," Elsie decided. "What's the worst she could do?"

"Kill us," I replied. "Turn us into slime. Make us a septic

tank for the rest of eternity. Hundreds of things. Whatever she can think of."

Antonio agreed. "I have seen such punishments with my own eyes. You cannot imagine what it is like to be still living, still thinking, for hundreds of years with no reprieve. To feel the ache of hunger and the pangs of pain. Not ever able to stretch one's self, relieve one's self or even to scratch an itch."

"It was just a rhetorical question," Elsie replied. "I know they can do terrible things. I know Hedyle is one of the most powerful witches in the world. But there has to be something we can do to prove she and Drago killed Makaleigh and now Kalyna. This can't go unanswered."

Elsie's voice kept getting louder as she spoke. Antonio and I said nothing while she ranted. No one really needed to be reminded that this was a difficult position. I was getting worried that someone from the council might hear her outside the room. I started to shush her, but that was when it happened.

The closet doors blew off. They shot across the room, barely missing Elsie, coming to rest against the wall on the other side. Olivia followed behind them with a low moan that slowly became one of the most horrendous noises I'd ever heard. It was something between the squealing of brakes on a car and a hurricane.

"*Madre de Dios!*" The witchfinder leapt to his feet and ran to the door to get out of the room.

Olivia's eyes were glowing circles as she followed him. Her ghostly raiment seemed to grow in size around her as though the winds of hell were beating against it. "Leave now while you still can."

"It's okay, Antonio," I told him. "This is Olivia. She's a friend of ours."

"A friend? She must certainly be a demon. I will banish her for you." He drew his sword.

"I don't think so!" Elsie said, holding the tiny sword that represented her power around her neck.

"She's not a threat," I said. "She won't hurt you."

Elsie and I stood between him and Olivia's new, frightening presence.

To make matters more unsettling, Dorothy and Brian came back from their snack. Dorothy took one look at her mother and started screaming. Not just any screams—but long, noisy ones that had to be heard up and down the halls and around the castle.

"What in the world is that thing?" Brian demanded, his arms around Dorothy.

Olivia resumed her normal ghostly form. "It's just me, Dorothy. It's just your mother. I was trying to frighten the witchfinder and get him out of here so I could tell Molly something really important that I just realized."

"How the heck did you get yourself to look like that?" Brian asked. "You even scared the crap out of me."

Olivia smiled and patted her hair, an old habit from when she was living and her hair got out of place. It hadn't moved since she'd died. "That's high praise indeed. Thank you, Brian. I've been working on it for weeks. I knew it would come in handy sometime. I can do so many things now. You won't believe it."

"I was not frightened by your charade, undead one." The witchfinder dismissed her new appearance. "I have faced the demons of the night that fly through the air and dig beneath the earth. I fear nothing."

"Then why were you running?" Elsie laughed.

He held his head high and shoulders straight. "I was leaving to bring help, attempting to protect you and Molly."

Even I had to smile at that.

The room was tight with all of us in it, but Olivia clearly had something important to say to make such a dramatic entrance.

"I think I figured out one of those crazy words Makaleigh said to you, Molly. It came to me while I was in the closet hearing about the terrible news."

"What terrible news?" Dorothy asked. "What happened now?"

We had to go through the explanation of Kalyna's death again, including our personal recriminations and guilt.

"How could something like this happen?" Brian demanded. He glared at the witchfinder. "Oscar should be held responsible. I'm going to talk to Abdon and my parents. This has gone too far."

Before we could stop him, Brian was gone, the door closing behind him.

"Should I go after him?" Dorothy asked. "I mean, I don't want Brian's parents to really notice me. I sure don't want Abdon to decide he should talk to me or something. What should I do?"

"Stay right here," Olivia said. "Let Brian deal with his parents. He knows them and knows how far he can push them. Everyone is stressed right now. You shouldn't get in the middle of it."

Dorothy sighed and sat down on the chair. "So what did you realize while you were in the closet, Mom?"

"I realized that I knew one of those words—and it truly is a word, not just gibberish as we kept thinking."

"Maybe we should wait until Brian gets back," I said, giving her the hand slicing across the throat sign.

I tried to get her to back away from whatever she was planning to say. Antonio was there. Anything she said might be something he'd take back to the council. I wasn't sure if that was the best idea. Hedyle could finally know what she couldn't get me to tell her. It may be nothing, but it could also mean the key to her and Drago getting out of this without any consequences.

"Don't keep us waiting for the punch line, Olivia," Elsie

said. "Does everything have to be a dramatic entrance for you?"

Dorothy picked up on my cue, but Elsie and Olivia were still falling behind. "I think we should wait for Brian," she said. "He'll be angry if we say it before he gets back."

"Make fun if you want to." Olivia frowned at Elsie, ignoring me and Dorothy. "None of you could figure out what those words meant. You're just jealous that I could."

"That's right." I glanced significantly at the witchfinder. "We've all worked on it together. That's why we should wait for Brian!"

"Olivia," Elsie blurted out. "Just tell us what you know."

"What is this you are speaking of?" Antonio finally asked. "Are you referring to Makaleigh Veazy's last words?" He stared at me. "Molly? Did you realize what she told you but did not tell me?"

Too late, Olivia and Elsie figured out what Dorothy and I had been trying to tell them. No one said a word. We stared at one another, waiting to see what would happen next.

"Oh, we might as well tell him now. What harm can it do?" Olivia was proud that she was the one who'd discovered the secret. "I recognized this word from an ancient text I'd seen years ago while I was shopping for new runes for my staff." She floated to the desk beside me and pointed a spectral finger at the paper where I had written the words.

The witchfinder moved with her. I didn't even have time to cover the words. He peered down at them. "Mho," he said aloud. "What does it mean?"

"It means to shed or molt. You know, like a snake," Olivia revealed. "Some have used it to mean change. That's what I took the rune to be."

"Really?" Dorothy came to look too, as did Elsie.

"Are you sure?" Antonio pondered the words.

"Quite sure," Olivia replied. She appeared to be very well pleased with herself.

I wish I could have said the same.

"If that is true," he said, "then these other words must have meaning. We must concentrate on them. They could hold the key."

CHAPTER 27

"I don't see how they can hold anything," Elsie said. "They don't make any sense."

Better late than never, Elsie's gaze told me as she tried to get rid of the witchfinder's attention.

"Witches today have beautiful, poetic spells," Antonio said. "Not so witches from the past. The fewer the words, the better. Some words were found to have power in simply saying them. Mho is one of them."

"He's right," Olivia agreed. "Just like the rune symbols. Mho has a vibrant power that can be used for good or evil magic."

"Look at the other words again," Antonio urged. "Perhaps you can understand what they are too, undead one."

I tried to think of any way to get Antonio's attention away from Olivia and her explanation of the words. I even hoped she'd end up being wrong. It was too late to take back what he'd already heard. Our magic wasn't strong enough to stop him.

"Wait!" Olivia shouted. "Aba. To make amends or atone. I know that one too. I have that rune on my staff. It's an important one."

"Indeed it is," Antonio agreed. "Few know that better than I."

Dorothy sank to the floor. "It's very warm in here, isn't it? I'm feeling faint. Maybe we should all go to the main hall and get something to drink. If these words have any power, I can't tell it. Anyone else?"

"You go." The witchfinder stared at her. "I shall stay here with the ghost. She can explain the other rune to me. Once we have these meanings, we may well understand why Makaleigh was killed."

"I don't feel any power from the words," Elsie said. "I think we're grasping at straws here. Dorothy's suggestion is excellent. We should go downstairs for a while and look at them later."

Antonio shook his head. "I stay. The words have meaning. These are not random words or gibberish. They are the most powerful of runes arranged in a certain order to enhance their magic. We must surely decipher the last word."

There was a brisk knock at the door, and we all jumped at the sound.

"Now what?" Elsie asked. "I'm exhausted. I thought this was supposed to be a party."

"Witchfinder! Are you in there?" Abdon yelled through the closed portal. "Get out here now!"

"What's happening?" Elsie whispered. "What can we do?"

"We could all disappear into the closet like Mom," Dorothy suggested.

Antonio bowed to us, said, "Allow me, ladies," and opened the door.

Abdon looked at the group assembled in our room. "What's going on in here?"

We all looked at one another. It wouldn't have been possible to look any guiltier.

I replied, "We're trying to figure out what happened to Makaleigh. And it would be nice to know what happened to Kalyna."

"I don't care what the rest of you do. I didn't summon the witchfinder to play games in your room. There's been an attack on Hedyle." He scowled at Antonio. "Either get out here and find the person doing this or I'll put you back in the wall where you belong—maybe permanently this time."

Antonio was immediately contrite. "I believe we are doing that, sir. Take a look at the ancient words that Makaleigh spoke to Molly as she perished."

"No!" I called out. "No, Antonio."

But it was too late. Abdon pushed his way to the desk and snatched up the paper where Dorothy had written the words.

His cold eyes turned on the list. "I see." He flicked that glance on me. "I thought you couldn't remember, Molly? I thought the words were too difficult for you to understand? What happened to your pitiful excuses?"

"I couldn't remember or understand them." I defended what I'd said. "My friends helped me with a discovery spell as Hedyle threatened to use."

"Perhaps this could be useful." He put the paper in his jacket pocket. "I'll take it with me. The three of you, stay out of it." He shot a look at Olivia floating on the ceiling. "And get that thing out of here. Come with me, witchfinder."

Brian showed up at the door as he was leaving. "What's going on?"

"Come along, Brian." Abdon led the way out of the room.

Antonio went without another word. Brian shrugged and followed them.

Elsie and I fell back on the bed. Dorothy slumped.

"I guess we were wrong about Hedyle," Elsie said. "Someone has gone after her too now."

"Not necessarily," I said. "She may have done this to throw us off. Obviously everything is pointing to her and Drago as Makaleigh's killers. Even though she is powerful, she probably doesn't want everyone looking at her and making accusations. This was probably an act of desperation."

"That could make sense," Dorothy added. "All she and Drago have to do is stall for time until the castle doors open again. The council probably can't do anything to them after that. They'll never find them."

"There's no doubt about it, baby girl," Olivia agreed. "But there's one more thing—I recognized that last word before Abdon took the paper. It was ord. It's the old word for either the point of a weapon or a beginning. Now what do you all think Makaleigh was trying to say with that?"

None of us had any idea. I kept repeating the words and their meanings in my head as we agreed to go downstairs and find out what happened to Kalyna. We all felt guilty over our part in her death. The least we could do is demand some answers on her behalf.

The ballroom was strangely empty as we got there. The food, music and games were gone. No one lingered in the hall talking or making demands on the council. It may have been due to the attack on Hedyle.

"I think we should ask around about what happened to her too," I whispered.

"Good idea," Elsie muttered back, her eyes darting quickly around the room. "Maybe we should split up."

"No way," Dorothy decided. "Brian's gone. I'm not walking around here by myself. If we don't stick together, I'm locking myself in the bedroom until the castle doors open. There are too many strange things going on, even for a bunch of witches. Haven't you two ever watched a horror movie? Everyone always splits up, and it makes them easy targets for the killer."

Elsie frowned. "I haven't watched many horror movies, but I guess you're right. It might be better if we stay together. Safety in numbers and all that."

"Look. There's Oscar. Let's ask him," I suggested.

I didn't think Oscar looked happy to see us. He had a tea service on a silver tray and was about to rush up the stairs.

"What can I do for you, ladies?" he asked impatiently.

We told him our predicament and what we needed to know.

"I'm on my way to Hedyle's room right now. I'm sure she won't mind if you accompany me." He started back on his way up, leaving us to follow or not.

"He's probably wrong. I wouldn't want to see us," Elsie said in a low voice. "But what the heck. It might be the only way we're going to hear about her being attacked that isn't gossip."

"What about Kalyna?" Dorothy asked. "Are we just going to forget about her?"

"Unless you want to split up," I reminded her. "One thing at a time."

"I don't want to be alone. You're right, Molly." She smiled nervously, tugging at the bracelet she wore even though Olivia wasn't inside of it. "One thing at a time."

We followed Oscar up two flights of stone stairs until he reached a door and quietly tapped on it. The whole way there, the halls were empty and quiet. Was everyone afraid to come out after hearing the news that Hedyle had been hurt? After all, if she could be attacked, with her strong magic, the rest of us might as easily be killed.

"Why don't these people get elevators?" Elsie struggled to catch her breath. "They have magic galore and plenty of money. I'd get an elevator if it were me."

"Abby's daughter, Sunshine, has an elevator in her home office in Norfolk," I said by way of conversation. "She's doing very well there."

"Is she a witch?" Dorothy asked. "What does she do?"

"She's a private investigator and a witch," I told her. "She mostly deals with magical creatures but not always. She has a *bean sidhe* working with her now."

"Wow." Dorothy smiled. "I'd like to meet her."

"No doubt she'll be down for Mabon or one of the other festivals," Elsie replied. "That's when all the witches go back home."

The part of the castle we were in looked older than the areas we'd been so far. There was brown and green lichen on some of the damp stones where water leaked from the roof or walls. The substance that held the stones together, some kind of older mortar, was brown. In the other parts of the castle it had been bleached white. The windows were smaller too and covered with bars as though to protect from arrows. The doors were rounded at the tops and made with coarser wood.

"I guess Hedyle doesn't like her comforts, does she?" Elsie whispered.

"I told you what she said about living on her island with more goats than people," I responded.

"You think she's really gonna be okay with us popping in like this?" Dorothy asked.

The door to Hedyle's room swung open with a grating sound as Oscar pushed it. He had to bow his head to get into the room.

"I don't think I'd be," I answered. "But maybe she's used to it. She is a member of the council. Maybe they get callers at all times of the day and night."

"Another reason I wouldn't want to be on the council," Dorothy replied. "And I hope Brian isn't going to be either."

"But surely that's the least of your worries," Elsie suggested.

"You also get people trying to kill you, and you make unpopular decisions. Not to mention that everything you do could put in jeopardy the entire fate of all witches."

"*Shh*," I warned. "She can probably hear us."

There was another man there as well who seemed to have actually opened the door for Oscar. He had masses of thick white hair and a long, scraggly white beard. He was dressed in a plain gray robe and held a gnarled staff in his hands. He reminded me more of Gandalf in the *Lord of the Rings* movie than of Santa Claus.

It was unusual to see a witch dressed like this—as people without magic would expect us to look. It would be a little like Elsie, Dorothy and me wearing black dresses and pointy hats. Those same people would call Brian a warlock, even though that was actually a slur against a male witch.

There was something about the healer that teased my senses. I couldn't put my finger on what it was exactly. It was one of those things like the stairs and hall where Hedyle and Drago had met. Something was just not as it should be.

As if the man in the gray robe sensed my question about him, he nodded and smiled amiably. "I am a council healer," he said. "I was attending Hedyle after the attack against her."

"That's very nice of you," Dorothy said. "I'm Dorothy Dunst Lane. I work at the library in Wilmington, North Carolina. I'm not sure if you know where that is, but nice to meet you."

Elsie and I followed Oscar to Hedyle's simple bedside. Her headboard was made of plain wood, possibly a plank that had washed up on her island. There were insect holes in it, and it was chipped and worn. No paint or stain covered it. Her mattress was thin, barely more than a rag, and it was on the rough floor. There were paintings of the sea around her as well as stones and shells I thought she might have collected from the beach to make this place feel more like her home.

"Your tea, madam," Oscar said, putting a tray on the table beside her. "Shall I pour?"

"Yes, please." Her pleasant voice sounded rough and hoarse. There were bruises on her throat. "Molly. I'm so happy you came to call. No one likes to visit a sick friend. I do hope we can be friends. I see you've brought some people with you."

"Yes. I'm sorry you were attacked," I commiserated. But inside I was scrutinizing the way she looked and sounded. It was difficult to imagine someone sneaking up on this highly powerful witch and trying to choke her. I was still very much of the belief that this was a ruse to keep the council away from her and Drago. If she had been attacked too, how could anyone suspect her?

I introduced Elsie and Dorothy. They each said a few words to her and then backed away from the bedside. No matter how any of us thought about the council, there was always a part of us that revered them, I supposed.

I was quickly learning to feel different through and through from my experiences with them. They were older, more powerful than us, but in the end, they were no better or wiser. I thought we were all learning that lesson.

"It's very kind of you to come." She delicately coughed and rearranged the yellowed lace at the top of the sleeping gown she wore. "I've heard you gave Makaleigh's last words to Abdon and the witchfinder. A good decision. I would hate to see you hurt over this nonsense. I'm glad you've come to your senses."

Dorothy and Elsie stood still and stared at her. Oscar poured tea for her, but the rest of us shook our heads when he asked if we wanted cups. The fragrant brew smelled like a summer meadow. I could swear its scent nearly transported me there. Magic tea? Anything could weave a spell if used properly.

I couldn't hold my suspicions in any longer. I knew there

might be a price to pay but believed my family and I were protected from her. At least I hoped so. "I don't know how else to say this—Elsie and I heard you speaking to Drago. I've mentioned to Abdon that the two of you might be lovers and that you may have plotted Makaleigh's death because she knew your secret. A love affair with someone considered a renegade and an outsider by the council might make the other members turn against you."

Hedyle laughed feebly, the sound ending in a pretty but false cough. How many mornings had Mike wanted to skip school and manufactured such a cough or a stomachache so he could stay home?

"How dare you?" She gathered her strength as she pushed herself up on the coarse bed. "How dare you suggest I would have anything to do with that outlaw? I have been the most powerful member of the Grand Council of Witches for five centuries. I helped create it. It was my decision to cast out Drago Rasmun. I would never consort with him."

I didn't flinch from her tirade. Mike used to get angry when I called him out on his fake sicknesses too. What else could she say?

What Elsie and I had heard was still valid in my mind. "We all make mistakes, Hedyle. I'm not saying that I think you should be punished for it or even lose your place on the council. I'm sure you knew that you would get caught with him at some point. It doesn't matter how powerful you are. Love drives us all mad."

"But we'd all like some of that absolution," Elsie chimed in. "If you love Drago, I'm not judging you. But I love Larry, and I'd be judged for it. Things need to change."

Hedyle didn't back down, her sharp eyes boring into my soul. "Leave me now, all of you. How dare you bring them to me this way, Oscar? I am ill. Is there no respect left in the world?"

Oscar bowed his head, and Dorothy, Elsie and I were quickly shown the door.

Just before it closed on us, Dorothy stopped it, putting her hand on the rough wood. "Dad?" She stared at the white-haired healer. "Is that *you*?"

CHAPTER 28

Dorothy had managed to put her finger on what had bothered me about the healer. It had been a nice disguise, but it was hard for a witch not to see magic. It was almost an insult that Drago had thought he could hide that way and we wouldn't notice. But he'd almost been right.

The heavy portal slammed with unnecessary force. We heard a scuffle behind the door. Someone cried out. But by the time we managed to get the door open again, Oscar lay on the stone floor, unconscious. Hedyle and the healer had vanished.

"They have to be in the castle," Elsie cried out. "We should alert Brian, Abdon and the witchfinder. They can still catch them."

"Go on," I said. "Dorothy and I will stay and help Oscar."

The pair had laid the castle manager low with a simple but powerful spell. Oscar was a witch but not a powerful one. As he came around with our healing spell, he told us what had happened.

"The healer changed, it was a disguise," he said. "I've never seen Drago Rasmun in person, but the healer was a powerful man—tall and lean with short white hair, wearing leather."

"I knew it was him," Dorothy said, supporting Oscar's head. "Maybe it was because he's my father. For one instant when our eyes met, I could see behind his illusion."

"He's kidnapped Hedyle," Oscar raged, trying hard to get to his feet, but the spell had left him weak.

"I believe that's what she wants us to think." I tried to calm him. "Hedyle is as involved in this as Drago."

"She would never stoop so low to be with that renegade. You're wrong about her." Oscar angrily shoved himself away from our ministrations and staggered to a standing position with one hand on the wall to support him. "We should inform Abdon and the rest of the council before she's hurt."

"I am here," Abdon said to him as he walked into the room. "Never fear, my faithful friend. Go to your room and rest. We'll find Hedyle and learn the truth of what happened."

"I want to help, sir. I can't bear the idea that she's out there in his power."

It was the only time I heard Oscar argue with anything Abdon said.

"I know you do." Abdon put his hand on Oscar's shoulder, and I felt magic pour from him. It was obviously going to take more than logic and reason to convince Oscar that Hedyle wasn't herself and that he needed his rest. "But I swear we'll find her and the renegade. Things will be made right. Now rest."

Oscar bowed his head and disappeared from the room.

Brian and the witchfinder had come in with Abdon. Antonio used his special gift to check for magic. "The magic that spirited Hedyle away was strong, but I cannot say whose magic was used. Hedyle's magic is entwined with Drago's. It could as easily be hers as his."

"Never refer to that man by his name here," Abdon decreed. "He is the renegade, the outsider. When I find him, I will flail the skin from him for this disgrace!"

"My apologies, lord." Antonio bowed his head.

Abdon glanced at the pallet where Hedyle had been. "Summon the security staff, Brian. While Oscar is unable to function, you will take his place. You know the castle better than anyone else here."

"Of course, grandfather." Brian left the room quickly with a curt nod in Dorothy's direction.

We waited, but it was plain to see Abdon and Antonio had no idea what they were looking for, or what to do next, since they couldn't ascertain a specific magic signature that had been left behind. They were clearly almost too amazed by Drago and Hedyle's actions to function.

What they really needed was a witch police force to come in and handle it. I shuddered at the thought of a police force for witches who all had superpowers like Antonio to control and see magic. I was so glad Joe wasn't here, because he would have stepped right in and taken over. It was his nature.

I finally whispered to Dorothy and Elsie that we should leave. There was no point in us remaining there when there was nothing we could do.

"What now?" Elsie asked as we went back to our rooms. "We think Drago killed Makaleigh because she could cause trouble for him and Hedyle. Now he's taken Hedyle. They can't catch Drago, much less hold him. As far as I can tell he's probably the strongest of us."

"With the exception of Hedyle," I half agreed. "With the two of them working together, I don't know if they can be stopped."

"Are you sure about that?" Dorothy asked. "Hedyle seemed very sincere about not having anything to do with Drago. We could be wrong about her."

"I think she's just an excellent liar," I replied. "There's

no doubting what she and Drago were talking about when Elsie and I saw them together."

"I'm too afraid that's true, dear." Elsie hugged her. "Just be glad Olivia isn't still with him."

Dorothy cringed. "How many people know he's my father? This doesn't seem to be a good way to get started in the witch world."

"I think it's only us, Abdon, Drago and probably everyone on the council." I smiled and hugged her too. "Don't worry about it. Almost every witch has someone evil lurking in their family tree."

"That's true." Elsie opened the door to our room. "I have a famous evil witch in my family tree. The Wicked Witch of the West."

Dorothy wrinkled her nose. "No. Not really, right?" She glanced at me. "That's just a story, isn't it?"

As soon as the door was closed behind us, Olivia appeared. "Ignore her, Dorothy. *The Wizard of Oz* is just fiction, and so is Elsie's evil witch."

"My great-grandmother told me that we were related to her," Elsie said. "She wouldn't have lied."

"That's crazy talk," Olivia argued. "Next you'll be telling us that your great-grandmother went to Oz too."

"As a matter of fact," Elsie continued.

"Ladies!" I interrupted. "We have bigger fish to fry. We need to figure out what those words mean together."

"They mean Drago and Hedyle, or maybe just Drago, killed Makaleigh." Elsie sat down on the big bed. "Where's the mystery in that? I wished they'd do another buffet. I'm hungry again. All of this stress has taken a lot out of me."

"We know that Drago and Hedyle are lovers, forbidden to be together by the council and Hedyle's own rules," I corrected. "That doesn't necessarily make either one of them Makaleigh's killer."

"What about Drago using Kalyna to sneak into the ball?" Olivia demanded. "Are those the actions of an innocent man? He had something nasty in mind, like always."

"It could be the actions of a desperate, lovesick man," I said.

"Lovesick?" Olivia's entire body wrinkled. "Drago has never been lovesick a day in his long life. Remember? I was with him for months. He never acted lovesick with me."

"Maybe he didn't love you like he loves Hedyle," Elsie suggested. "Maybe you were just handy to have around. I doubt if he meant to get you pregnant, like most men don't."

"Why you—" Olivia flew at Elsie, who simply stepped aside.

"Really," Dorothy implored. "We should try to figure this thing out in case Drago isn't the killer. Otherwise, when the castle doors open, the real killer is gone. If it's possible, I need to clear my father's name. Maybe someday he won't be a renegade."

"Well." Elsie sniffed. "Maybe Drago isn't the killer, but he certainly took Hedyle. I doubt any of us can argue that fact. That might be because he's lovesick. Or maybe it's because he's afraid she'll tell the truth. Or it could even be that he wants to keep her safe. Someone did try to kill her."

"The only thing that bothers me is who attacked Hedyle." I considered the issue. "I don't think Drago is lovesick over her *and* attacked her."

"It happens." Dorothy shrugged. "Shall we take another look at the words?"

Elsie flopped back on the bed. "Jiminy Cricket! Haven't we looked at those enough already?"

"No," I said, resuming my seat at the desk. "We basically know what they mean now at least individually. But what do they mean together?"

"Molly's right," Dorothy said, joining me. "Let's put our heads together and see what we can do. If it turns out to be my father, no one will be surprised."

"All right." Olivia hovered close to us at the desk. "We've got aba—meaning to make amends or atone. Atone for what? Who needs to make amends?"

"Maybe Makaleigh needed to make amends," Elsie said from the bed. "Maybe she did something to the killer that she wished she could atone for."

"That's possible," I agreed, writing down what she said.

"And mho—to shed or molt." Olivia studied the word. "Maybe to change."

"She was planning on changing the rules about punishment for non–magic users in families," Dorothy snapped back.

"Maybe that was what she wanted to make amends for," Olivia said. "Girls, maybe all we have to do is figure out who Makaleigh wronged with her harsh rules about taking the memories of non–magic users in our families."

"That sounds easy enough," Dorothy agreed. "But where would we find that kind of information?"

Elsie giggled. "You know she's gonna freak out when she sees it."

I smiled and got to my feet. "I think it's time we showed her."

"Oh yes!" Olivia agreed. "Why didn't I think about it sooner? Oh, you have to take me along so I can see the look on her face when she sees it."

"We can't take you, Olivia," Elsie said with a yawn. "We've been through this. Everyone on the council has threatened you. You can't leave this room."

"What?" Dorothy demanded. "Quit talking about me like I'm not here. What am I going to see?"

"The Grand Council of Witches' library," I told her. "I think you'll be impressed."

"Oh, girls," Olivia sighed. "I must go with you. If you don't try to hide me, then I'll just float out there by myself."

She appeared so pathetic that we were all moved to take

her with us. It couldn't be easy being left out of everything that was once part of her life right as she had finally found the daughter she'd never known.

And that was the problem. Feeling sorry for Olivia because she was dead. There was no way around it. We loved her and wanted her to be with us—even if it did mean trouble for us all.

"Have you ever actually been to the library?" Elsie asked after we put Olivia back into Dorothy's bracelet.

"I've been there many times," I admitted. "But never actually here at the castle." The library moved from place to place on a regular basis to protect it. With the wisdom of the ages stored in it, no one wanted to take any chances.

"How exciting." Olivia's voice was strange from inside the metal around Dorothy's wrist.

"*Shh!*" we all said at once as we passed a group of witches in the hall outside our rooms.

They stared us at for a moment but then kept walking.

"Don't say another word," Elsie reminded her. "I like having you around, and I believe Abdon will exorcise you if he catches us smuggling you around the castle again."

We all nodded and smiled to another group of witches, who looked angry and ready to cause problems. We got past them quickly without saying a word.

"How are we going to find the library if none of you have been to it when it was here?" Dorothy asked. "It's a big castle, and I think some of it might be magical, so you can't tell if it's real or not."

"Once you know the spell, you can see the golden glow," Elsie said as we slipped into an alcove and recited the spell together. "That's what my mother always said."

"Mine too. And look—I think we may have found the witches' library—where all the knowledge of the world is kept." I opened the huge wood door, and the golden light spilled out on us. "Dorothy, welcome to the biggest library in the world."

"Oh. My. Gosh!" Dorothy's jaw dropped and her eyes grew wide.

"I think she likes it," Olivia said.

"*Shh!*"

CHAPTER 29

"Why didn't you tell me?" Dorothy's voice was barely above a whisper. "It's—it's beautiful. Awesome. Spectacular. I wish I could live here."

"Don't get carried away," Olivia said.

"If we have to tell you to be quiet again," Elsie threatened, "I'll put you in my pocketbook. Now pipe down before we get caught with you."

I ignored them as I urged Dorothy into the library. "There are books here from the library at Alexandria."

"Really? I thought it burned."

"It did, but magic saved the books. Don't forget the ancient past was the domain of today's witches," I said. "Before the goddess's temples were destroyed, women took care of the world."

"I can't believe it. Can I touch them?"

"Of course you can touch them." A woman with bright red hair appeared from behind a tall desk. "It wouldn't make much sense if you couldn't."

"But they're so old," Dorothy marveled. "Aren't you worried about them falling apart?"

"These books have all been preserved by a powerful spell." The librarian stared at me. "What's wrong with her? Every young witch knows about the library and the books."

"Dorothy Dunst Lane, meet Sylvia Rose Gold," I introduced the two women. "Dorothy was raised without magic but has since joined our coven. Sylvia has been the librarian here for hundreds of years."

"It's wonderful to meet you." Dorothy cautiously reached her hand toward Sylvia, who looked at it as though Dorothy was offering her a poisonous snake.

"I said you could touch the books, dear." Sylvia took a step back. "I am obviously not a book."

"Oh. I'm so sorry." Dorothy drew back her hand. "How do I get a library card?"

"She really doesn't know anything, does she?" Sylvia asked me.

"Every witch has a library card," I explained. "It's part of your magic heritage."

Dorothy laughed. "I might never leave this place." She started down an aisle of books that was twenty feet tall and went on farther than I could see.

"That's the wonderful thing about the witches' library," Sylvia told her. "You can look at the books whenever you like. You don't have to be here."

"We'll show you how later," I told Dorothy. "Let's not forget why we're here now."

"Sure." Dorothy's brown eyes gazed longingly at the books. "You're right, Molly. Let's find what we came for."

We went to the aisle that held the histories of witches.

"Every witch ever born has a history here," I told her. "Here's your great-great-grandmother's. You'll have a book here too."

"Where is Makaleigh's book?" Elsie glanced through the tomes.

"I see it." Dorothy stood on the tips of her toes to grab the book.

Sylvia Rose Gold laughed as she watched her.

"You just bring it down to you, dear." Elsie pointed at the book, and it came to her.

"Wow." Dorothy grinned. "That's awesome."

"It's big." I helped Elsie with the book. "Let's take it over there and sit down."

Dorothy started toward the table but was soon lost in the rows of ancient texts. Elsie and I were left on our own to go through more than three hundred years of Makaleigh's life.

"I don't see anything she'd have to make amends for," Elsie said as we searched. "At least not anything that stands out."

"She hadn't been on the council for three hundred years," I said. "Maybe we should concentrate on that time before she was a member."

"What about the third word she said to you," Elsie added. "What was it—ord—the point of a weapon or a beginning?"

"That's what she said." I didn't look up from the book, which had been penned in gold ink.

"So she did something terrible that she needed to make amends for and she wanted to change that and start again," Elsie interpreted. "I don't think that would be in this book."

"Maybe it is." I pointed to a spot that had happened during the witch trials in our country. "Look. She turned in another witch to save her life. That could be something that would fit that description."

"Yes. But I've never heard of this witch before, have you? Let's look for her name in the histories."

We searched, but there was no history for the witch that Makaleigh had handed over to the madness of the Salem witch trials. We asked Sylvia Rose Gold if she'd ever heard of the witch. She searched through the histories as well.

"I don't think there was a witch by that name," she finally

decided. "Maybe it wasn't a witch at all. Most of those killed in the Salem fires weren't witches, you know. They were healers and midwives mistaken for witches. People lumped them all together at the time."

Elsie and I thanked her, even though it wasn't the answer we were looking for.

"So that was nothing," Elsie said. "Do we have to look through Makaleigh's whole life to see who she wronged? The castle doors will be open by then."

"You're right. We need a better way to do this."

"Try using magic inquiry," Sylvia suggested. "No one reads the whole book. Just tell it what you need. The book should be able to do the rest."

This was an improvement that we'd never heard of. To our embarrassment, it had been some time since Elsie or I had used the library. We probably had the magic for it but just didn't have the time.

"Aba. Mho. Ord," Elsie said to the book.

The book pages fluttered back and forth for a moment before finally settling on one page.

"Words of power," I whispered as I read from the book.

"So Makaleigh was trying to save herself?" Elsie observed.

"She was invoking magic when she died. These weren't her last words, not exactly."

"Why didn't the spell work?"

I looked into Elsie's eyes. "Maybe she didn't have time to finish it."

"Hey, guys!" Dorothy called from what seemed like miles away in the shelves. "You have to see this."

"We found something," I said to her. "You should see this."

"No, Molly. If I leave, I'm not sure if we can find this again. and you really need to see *this*."

"I'll wait here," Elsie said. "Go see what she found. Maybe it's something that will get us out of here."

I left Elsie with the book of Makaleigh's life and followed the sound of Dorothy's voice until she became clear to me. "How did you get so far away?"

"I don't know," she said, her voice full of youthful excitement. "But you won't believe this. And I can't tell you why. I have to show you."

Finally reaching her, I saw that Dorothy had her hand on a book but hadn't taken it down from the shelf.

"Guess what's up here?" She nearly squeaked with delight. "We looked up my mother and found a reference to this book."

"For goodness' sake." Olivia's voice slid out of the bracelet. "Tell her."

Olivia was excited about the find too. That made me curious as I helped Dorothy move the book. It took both our magic to get it from the shelf.

"It's our old spell book! I can't believe it."

CHAPTER 30

"How did it get here?" I examined it carefully.

There was the last spell we'd written in it a few months before Olivia's death. The book had disappeared the same night that she'd died. We had been given to understand that Olivia's killer had sold it to someone. None of us ever expected to see it again.

"I don't know." Dorothy shrugged. "And why did it take extra magic to get it off the shelf?"

"Not extra magic," Olivia added in a tinny voice. "It took magic from one of the three of us. Even though you're my daughter, your magic is different. We haven't imprinted it to the book, since it was missing. But how did it get here, Molly?"

"I think we should ask Sylvia Rose Gold," I decided. "I've always heard nothing goes in or out of here without her knowing."

With the spell book firmly in my hands, Dorothy and I marched to the tall desk at the front of the library.

Sylvia, back at her desk, glared at us. "What do you want now?"

"This is our missing spell book that was stolen two years ago," I said. "We haven't been able to find it. How did it get here?"

She looked at us over the top of her very large dark-rimmed glasses. "It was probably somewhere it shouldn't have been. Spell books and other magic items that fall into the hands of non–magic users frequently turn up here— especially spell books, for obvious reasons. Centuries ago, the council put a covering spell that accomplishes keeping magic for witches. They don't call this the witches' circulating library for nothing."

"We'll take it with us," I told her. "It can't stay here."

"Sorry." She lifted a finger, and the book quickly flew out of my hands and back down the aisle where it had come from. "You were careless with it. Once it ends up here, it becomes property of the Grand Council of Witches."

"You can't keep it from us." I lifted my hand, and the book returned to me. "My family, and those of my coven, wrote our spells and preserved this book for several past generations. We aren't leaving it here."

This time when she tried to re-shelve it, I was ready for her. The book trembled a little in my arms but didn't move.

"No one leaves here with one of my books," she said in a voice of quiet thunder, her eyes glowing behind her glasses. "You know the rules."

"In this case, the rules don't apply." I stared back at her, my amulet beginning to glow as it perceived a threat.

Sylvia took a step back. "We'll just see about that. The council shall hear of this."

When she said the council would hear of it, I thought she meant she'd call for a hearing or file a complaint. Instead Cassandra—herald of the council and sometimes liaison between witches and the council—instantly appeared there with us.

"What?" Cassandra was covered in bubbles, apparently from the bath she'd been snatched from, and her long raven tresses but nothing else.

"I have a complaint against this woman," Sylvia told her. "She's trying to steal a book from the library."

Cassandra's eyes swiveled from Sylvia to me and Dorothy, who stood close by. Elsie was behind us. "Molly? What's the problem?"

"This is our spell book." I almost held it out to her but remembered that Sylvia could command it and kept it close to me. "It was on a shelf in the library. You know we've searched for it everywhere and finally decided to start a new one."

"Yes, but—"

"But nothing," I objected. "This belongs to us—Elsie, Dorothy and me." There was no point in using Olivia's name. That would bring up a whole other issue. "We're not leaving the library without it, Cassandra."

"You know books can't leave here or thousands would have been lost through the generations." Sylvia made her point. "She can't take the book."

"It doesn't belong to you or the library," I argued. "Obviously we couldn't find it because it was cloaked here. But now that we know, it's going home with us."

Sylvia lifted her hand to try to take it again. I held my amulet, ready for her with a good grip on the book.

"Ladies!" Cassandra inserted herself between us, bubbles and all—though the bubbles were quickly fading. "This will have to be decided by the council. I can't make this decision. As you are both aware, the council is short two members and unlikely to take up this matter immediately. The library has a claim to it, Molly. I can't negate that without permission from the council."

Before I could speak, the book disappeared.

"Nooo!" Olivia wailed, emerging from the bracelet. "You don't know how I've suffered believing it was my fault our spell book was stolen. You can't take that away too."

She flew at Cassandra, arms outstretched, screeching in the most terrible way.

Cassandra stepped aside, and a door opened in the air. Olivia continued into the opening and disappeared when it closed.

"No!" It was Dorothy's turn to screech. "Where did she go? What did you do with her?"

"She's had plenty of warnings. So have the rest of you," Cassandra told her. "You shouldn't have had her here. She should have moved on after she died. I'm sorry, Dorothy. She's gone."

"What? You can't do that. What gives you the right?" Without another thought, Dorothy used her very emotional magic to strike down the herald of the council.

"Dorothy!" I pulled her back. "What are you doing?"

"I was giving her a taste of her own magic." She stared at the floor.

A black snake was slithering across the ancient wood and slid behind the desk with Sylvia Rose Gold. The librarian let out a shriek and jumped on the desk, losing her huge glasses. The snake went across them and continued toward the shelves.

"Change her back, Dorothy," I implored. "Right now."

"No. Not unless she brings my mother back."

"Well, she can hardly do it as a snake," Elsie said.

"Then I guess she'll be a snake for a while," Dorothy replied. "I'm tired of her constant threats and stupid proclamations. She's not all that much anyway."

"No, but the council is," I reminded her. "Where do you think she's slithering off to right now?"

"I don't care, Molly." Dorothy was defiant. "Everyone is

so prejudiced against my mother. They all need to get over it. I'm not hiding her anymore. At least not once I find her."

Dorothy stormed out of the library. Sylvia Rose Gold was yelling for help.

I glanced back to see how Elsie was taking it—laughing no doubt. She wasn't there. She must have gone back to where we'd left Makaleigh's book. But there was no one there. The table was empty. Makaleigh's book was gone too.

"Elsie?" I looked around me. There was no sign of her.

Even though my magic was at half strength, I grasped my amulet. "Take me to Elsie."

I had never tried doing anything like that before. It was a far cry from fixing the car or running a load of laundry for my son. It involved magic I wasn't even sure was available to me. But the circumstances were so traumatic that I spoke and acted without thought.

And yet, it worked.

There was Elsie, lying on a small bed in a part of the castle that had seen better days a thousand years before. I tried to wake her, but she was under a powerful spell. Her breathing was shallow but regular. She seemed safe for the moment.

I wasn't leaving her there.

Grabbing the amulet again, I took her hand. "Back to our room," I said. When I opened my eyes, we were back in our room in the castle. I went one step further, since I seemed to be on a roll, and tried to leave the castle, but nothing happened when I told the amulet I wanted to go home.

"Better than nothing," I said as I carefully arranged Elsie on the big bed. "What did you find? Who did this to you?"

Brian burst into the room. "Where's Dorothy?"

"I don't know."

"Did you know she turned Cassandra into a snake?" He ran his hand through his hair in frustration. "What's left of the council wants her put in prison. The herald is protected by the council."

"Did you know that our spell book was confiscated by the library and Cassandra wouldn't let us take it with us without a hearing from the council?" I asked him. "Cassandra also sent Olivia somewhere. I don't know where or if she can get back. That's why Dorothy changed her. And then someone put a spell on Elsie and moved her from the library to some shabby tower room. I brought her here, but I can't wake her."

"Is everyone going crazy?" he asked. "I have to find Dorothy before anyone else does."

"I understand. But Brian, we found something when we were looking through Makaleigh's life history. I think that's why someone took Elsie away. It's about the words that Makaleigh said to me before she died."

"Okay." He put his hands on my shoulders and stared into my eyes. "Let me find Dorothy and we'll get on that and then wake Elsie. Just stay here, Molly. Let's not lose anyone else."

"All right. Be careful. You're right. Everyone is crazy after being locked in here."

He surprised me by giving me a quick hug before he left the room. I heard him use a magic key on the outside of the door, probably hoping to keep anyone from getting inside.

I sat next to Elsie on the bed and tried every spell I knew to wake her. Nothing happened. I went back to the desk and rewrote the three words on another sheet of paper. What was it about those words that had made someone spirit Elsie away before she could find any further answers?

It was hard sitting there and waiting for Brian to return. I wasn't even sure he could find Dorothy in the state she was in. I tried calling to her, but she didn't answer. I hoped she wasn't in danger. It was going to be hard enough to get the council to overlook her emotional outburst.

Something of the same nature had happened between Cassandra and Dorothy once before. Dorothy's magic was only strong enough to do anything to Cassandra when she was upset. I didn't know if the council would be willing to take that into consideration.

I was worried about Olivia too. Had she been completely exorcised and couldn't be brought back? I'd heard of it happening before. If she was entirely gone, there might be nothing we could do to help her.

Closing my eyes, I wished I was home with Joe and Mike, away from this place. I knew it couldn't happen. I'd already tried to get Elsie and me out of there.

And then I opened my eyes to find myself in my kitchen.

CHAPTER 31

A cup of coffee crashed to the tile floor, spilling brown liquid all over the blue tile.

"Molly! When did you get back?" Joe's startled tone greeted me.

"I don't know." I looked around the room and down at myself. "I mean, I just wished to be home and here I am."

"Are you saying you can wish things to come true and it happens now?"

"I'm not sure. Magic doesn't work that way. Not my magic anyway." I hugged him. "I don't know how I got here, but I'm glad to be home."

"What's going on in here?" Mike joined us, rubbing his eyes, half awake. "Mom? I thought you were out of town?"

"I was. I am." I went to him and hugged him tightly too.

He squirmed. "Are you guys fighting or something? What's with the coffee cup on the floor?"

"We're not fighting." Joe grabbed a bunch of paper towels

and started cleaning up the mess. "Go back to bed. I'm sure we'll all understand what's happening later."

Mike yawned. "Sure. Okay. See you later, Mom."

I helped Joe finish cleaning the broken cup and coffee from the floor.

"So what happened?" he asked. "You got away? Everything is fine now?"

"I don't know. Someone put a spell on Elsie, and I couldn't wake her. We were trying to figure out who killed Makaleigh—she's a member of the witches' council. Cassandra took away our spell book and banished Olivia into another world or something. Dorothy got angry and turned Cassandra into a snake. Of course they can't keep our spell book, Joe. It belongs to us."

"Yeah. That sounds bad," he agreed. "I'm surprised with all that going on that you wished yourself home. Did Elsie, Dorothy and Brian come with you? Did you get Olivia back?"

"No. I didn't do anything. Wishing myself home shouldn't have worked. I can't even do things like that outside of the castle, never mind inside, which drains half a witch's magic. I don't know how or why it happened."

"At least you're okay." He put down the last broken piece of cup and hugged me.

"But I'm not. Not really." I wished I was as I stared into his eyes. "I have to go back and help them. I got out of the spell that's keeping the castle closed. I guess I can get back in too."

"I know they're your friends, Molly, but maybe you should just wait for them to un-spell themselves or whatever. I don't like the idea that you're going back in there with people being killed."

"Thanks." I kissed him. "I don't have any choice. It's not just Elsie and Dorothy. If the council finds out that I got out of the castle, it could be very bad for me too. I could be branded a renegade or an outsider like Drago."

"Who?"

"Dorothy's father." I smiled at him. "I'm sorry you don't understand, and I wish I could explain, but I have to get back."

"Okay. But take me with you. I can help solve the murder."

I smiled and kissed him again, loving him more now than I had thirty years before when we'd first married. "Believe me, I wish I could. You might be the only one who can figure out what's going on." I glanced at my watch. "We've got another eight hours until the spell falls away from the castle. We have to catch the killer before that happens."

"Molly, if you could get out of the castle, what's stopping the killer from doing the same?"

Thinking of Drago Rasmun, I shook my head. "I don't know. Probably nothing. But I have to go back. I love you."

"I love you too. Be careful!" He kissed me fiercely and stepped back.

Holding the glowing amulet, I closed my eyes and wished myself back into the castle again.

But when I opened my eyes again, I wasn't at the castle. The sharp tang of sea air was in my nose. I could hear gulls crying and the lapping of the ocean at the shore. There was the lighthouse and the ferry, trees jutting out from the old gravestones.

"Oak Island?"

"And what did you expect, Molly Renard?" the Bone Man demanded. "Why are you flitting around from place to place using your magic? I think your council would find this highly irregular."

He laughed boldly. The sound scared a group of birds in the trees around us. It shook the dried bones that hung around his neck.

"Why am I here? Did you bring me here?"

"Yes. I thought you might be in need of assistance. How goes the murder hunt at the castle?"

"I don't know. I wished to go home and ended up there. I wished to go back and ended up here instead. Did you have something to do with it?"

My question amused him so much that he had to drop his thin, seven-foot-tall frame to the damp cemetery beneath his feet. He put one large, bony hand to his corpse-like head and then stared at me with his empty black eyes.

"Did you think you did this on your own? Council magic sealed the castle. Even though the magic in your amulet is not of their magic. It couldn't have overcome it alone. Of course I brought you here after I helped you get home. Why do you want to go back?"

"My friends are still trapped there. I have to go back and help them."

"Oh, Molly. Witches are so amusing with their spells and magics. I quite enjoyed my time at the castle, but I wouldn't want to return anytime soon. Neither should you."

"I don't care what you think about this, MacLir. I'm going back." I used his real name to let him know that I meant business. He might be an ancient sea god, but he couldn't tell me what to do. I kept his secrets for both our sakes, but this was different.

He got up from the damp sand, not bothering to brush it from his black suit. "Things may get very ugly there before they get better, my dear. Please reconsider. I am saying this to spare you any harm or ill."

Straightening my shoulders and ignoring the strong wind blowing through my hair, I faced him. "Thank you. But I have to go."

He sighed, the sound like the sea. "Your choice, of course."

I didn't have to use the amulet to get back to the castle. In an instant, I was there in the hallway outside the room I shared with Elsie, as though I had never left. It was very disconcerting and made me feel the need to straighten my clothes and hair, though neither were out of place.

Drago was watching me.

"And where have you been, Molly?" There was a sly smile on his face. "Does the council know you wield outsider magic? I don't think they'd approve, do you? What were you doing?"

I already felt like a Ping-Pong ball being bounced around the ether. I faced Drago angrily. "What about you? I know that you and Hedyle are involved in a forbidden relationship."

"Quite the pair of rogues, aren't we?" He grinned. "I never knew Olivia's friends were so outside the norm."

"Speaking of Olivia, she's been banished somewhere by the council. Can you help me find her?"

"Where did you get your magic?" His gaze narrowed on my face. "I've never felt anything like it."

"Will you help me find her or not?"

"You have plenty of magic for the job," he said. "Why do you need my help?"

"Do it for your daughter, Drago. Do it for the woman you once cared for. Help me find Olivia and bring her back."

He nodded slowly. "I could do that. No matter what the council says, no ghost is ever permanently banished. They've just sent her to a nether realm. She doesn't have the power to get back through their magic."

"But you have the power to bring her back," I coaxed. Let him think what he would about why I chose not to use the magic in the amulet.

"Yes." He looked down his aquiline nose at me. "But I want something in return."

What could he possibly want from me? "Yes?"

"Help me find Hedyle."

CHAPTER 32

"I assumed you took her somewhere. You were in the room when she vanished." Was it really true that he didn't know where she was? It was hard for me to believe.

"I was there, but I didn't take her anywhere. I've looked everywhere I can think to look. I can't find her."

I was contemplating his words—was he setting me up for something, maybe taking the fall for Makaleigh's death or Hedyle's kidnapping?

"That doesn't make any sense." I wouldn't be his patsy for whatever game he was playing. "I know that you and Hedyle are lovers. Did you attack her?"

"No. Of course not. The deed was done, and I found her injured. Just as you found Makaleigh. That makes you guilty in some people's eyes. But we both know simply being there isn't a crime. Now she's gone, vanished right before my eyes. I suppose I was hoping your *unusual* magic could locate her."

I thought about what he was asking. Drago was dangerous. He was outside of the council. We all knew what that meant. And yet if the council suspected I was using borrowed magic from an ancient sea god, I would be considered an outsider too. I wondered if Drago had received magic from a nontraditional way, possibly passed down through his family line.

But how could I deny him when I needed him to find Olivia? Contrary to what he thought, I had no idea how to find her. Even the best magic in the world doesn't work if you don't know where to look or how to find what you're looking for.

"I'll assume that you're telling me the truth, Drago, and that you don't know where Hedyle is. I'll help you find her, if you bring Olivia back."

"Good." He offered me his hand. "Then we have an understanding. You will keep my secrets, and I will keep yours. We'll help each other through this without telling anyone else."

I put my hand in his. His hand was hot to the touch. It suddenly occurred to me that we were looking at him the wrong way. He wasn't an ancient witch. And Drago wasn't his first name—it was his family name.

"Drago. The dragon." I smiled. "Dragon magic is rare."

"So is an amulet full of sea god magic." He turned to go. "I'll bring Olivia to your room. Be careful that you hide her better in the future. You can return a ghost to our world, but if it happens too many times, there will be nothing left of the woman you knew."

He walked away, to my surprise. He could have vanished if he'd wanted to. I started into the room and remembered that Brian had spelled the lock from the outside. I had to remove his spell to get back in.

Elsie was still asleep on the bed—but this was not a natural sleep. She was growing colder, and the color was leaving her face. Her body was stiffening as though she were dead. I knew she was still alive, but how could we bring her back? I wished I could ask Drago for help with that too, but I didn't want to get any further enmeshed with him. Brian, Dorothy and I had to take care of her first before I honored my pledge to Drago.

I was thinking about a removal spell and wishing I'd been able to bring our spell book out of the library, when Brian and Dorothy came in. Dorothy paled when she saw Elsie and rushed to the bed. Brian spelled the door closed behind him.

"Did someone take my spell off the door?" he asked angrily. "No one has any respect for privacy."

I smiled as the words came out of his young mouth. He sounded just like Abdon.

"It was a mistake," I said. "I was trying to use a spell to unlock the spell on Elsie and the door unlocked. I'm sorry. You know how it is sometimes."

My spells very rarely went wrong anymore, not since I started wearing the amulet, but it was a good excuse. I didn't want to tell my friends what had happened either. They were already suspicious of the Bone Man and the gift he'd given my family.

We lit some candles. Brian found a sage smudge stick and cleared the air. We joined hands around Elsie and agreed on a spell Brian knew to release her from the enchantment she was under. We closed our eyes and repeated the spell together until it had become a chant.

Elsie didn't move. She didn't seem to change at all. After about thirty minutes, we released hands and blew out the candles.

"What else can we do?" Dorothy asked with tears in her eyes. "This is terrible—they have Mom somewhere, won't let you take the spell book and now something's wrong with Elsie."

"We keep trying different spells," Brian concluded. "That was only one spell. It's not helping that we're all on half power until the doors open. We may not be able to help her until then."

"I don't know if she'll last that long." I was holding Elsie's cold hand. It felt as though she was drifting farther away from us. "Who would've done such a thing?"

"Someone who didn't want you to continue reading Makaleigh's story," Dorothy replied. "And how could that book vanish? It still has to be in the library, right? Isn't that what Sylvia said? That's why you can't take the spell book out."

"I didn't even think of it. So much has been happening," I said without discussing the part where I went back home and then to Oak Island. "But you're right. Maybe one of us should stay with Elsie and the other two go back to the library and keep researching those words of power. Things seem to be tied to them."

"Brian and I will go," Dorothy decided. "You've already been through enough. Plus, everyone seems to be more willing to take Brian's word for everything than ours."

I had been about to suggest the same thing but for different reasons. I didn't know if Drago would come here with Olivia when he released her, and I didn't want them to know about my deal with him.

"That sounds like a wonderful idea." I heartily endorsed it. "And I think Elsie will feel more comfortable with me here if she wakes up."

Dorothy hugged me tightly. "Don't worry, Molly. We'll figure this out. We'll get Mom and Elsie back—and the spell book too."

"I'll have a word with my grandfather about the spell book issue," Brian promised.

"Thank you. But you have to tread very carefully here," I warned. "If you don't want to be leveraged into being part of the council, don't owe them too many favors."

He nodded. "I know what you mean. And in normal circumstances, I'd figure this stuff out by myself. But these aren't exactly normal circumstances. We don't know if we can wait until those doors open."

I watched them leave. They were not only the hope of our coven but the hope of witchcraft for the future. I knew Brian didn't want to sit on the council, but I couldn't think of anyone who'd be better than him. He might still be subverted by the power the witches on the council had given to them. I could only hope it wouldn't be so if he decided to take up his grandfather's offer.

Sitting in the quiet room with only Elsie, I knew how Brian felt about getting out of the castle. Still, I was filled with wonder and amazement that I'd escaped even for a short time. The Bone Man had helped me. I realized that. The amulet had turned out to be so much more than I'd ever thought. My mother had never worn it, calling it ugly. I wasn't sure if she would have worn it if she'd known about the magic it contained. She wasn't exactly an adventurous witch.

But then neither was I. The same was true for Elsie, though her life had changed as well. Olivia had always been the traveler, the witch who did it all. Now she was dead, and I only had it on Drago's word that she could come back at all.

I wished I was home with Joe and Mike, eating cold pizza and watching some sports event on TV. I was careful not to touch my amulet as I wished it. Things here had to be resolved first.

When Drago didn't show up with Olivia and Elsie stayed asleep, I finally drifted back to the desk and stared at the three words of power. It would've been nice if I could have willed them to make sense. Things didn't work that way.

I put them in different order, changed the letters. Even made crossword puzzle–type pictures of them. Was Makaleigh trying to create her final spell, or was she muttering the words so I'd understand what she was talking about?

But if she'd wanted me to know, why hide them? Why make me dig them out of my head with another spell?

Perhaps it was impossible for me to understand a witch that old and powerful. I had only lived one normal human lifetime, as had my mother and my grandmother. Our witch-craft had been simple—that of the moon, the water, the earth and fire. This more complicated magic, such as the one contained in my amulet, seemed unnatural to me.

Makaleigh and Hedyle had no doubt started their lives the same way. Something had happened to them that made things different too. They'd joined the council to wield more of their power and created rules that governed and protected witches' lives, though some of them were bad for us all.

And yet I had liked and admired Makaleigh. All witches believed that things happen with a purpose. That meant there was a reason that I had found her before she died.

The question would be: Why? Why had I found her? Why had she given me her secret before dying? And how was I ever going to figure it out, much less on a timetable in less than eight hours?

CHAPTER 33

I felt Olivia enter the room before I saw her.

She breezed in with a laugh and the aura of someone who'd been trapped and was happy to be free. Ghosts are primarily only what's left of our auras, so it was a strong presence.

"Oh, Molly! I'm so glad to be back from that awful place." She swooped around the room a few times and then came close enough to plant a static kiss on my cheek.

We'd given up hugging because it felt more like suffocating when she came too near.

"I'm so glad you're here." I wiped tears from my eyes. "I thought you might not be able to come back."

She stopped swooping and stared at me. "You know, it was the strangest thing. I was in this place. I'm not sure where it was, but I tried to get out and couldn't."

"Were there other ghosts too?"

"If there were, I couldn't see them. It was so lonely and empty. I thought I might truly die there." She smiled and swooped a few more times. "Then suddenly it was like the sun came out in one direction and I followed the light. Maybe that sounds cliché, like when they say don't go into the light. Only this was a good light that led me back to you."

Drago had taken care of the problem, good to his word, but hadn't involved himself. I wanted to tell her—maybe later when this was over and we were back in Smuggler's Arcane trading stories about Brian's never-to-be-forgotten birthday party. It was certainly bound to be something we all remembered.

"I'm just really happy you're back. We have a problem. After you were sent away, someone sent Elsie to another part of the castle and put a sleeping spell on her. Brian, Dorothy and I tried to break it. We couldn't do it, and she's wasting away."

Olivia came close to Elsie's face. "Oh no. She can't die like this. It's not her time. We have to figure something out, Molly. We always do. We have to bring her back."

"I've been looking at these words again, hoping if we could figure out the answer, it would lead us to whoever did this to Elsie. Without knowing the spell, you know how hard it can be to break it."

"But honey, if that person isn't feeling charitable today, he or she might not want to help anyway. The answer for that could be in our spell book. We have to get it out of the library." She frowned, a thousand lines dragging her uncertain face down. "You know I always supported our library back home. I can't believe I'm advocating taking something from the best library in the world."

"I know what you mean. But they had no right to confiscate it. With Sylvia Rose Gold keeping it in her hoard, I don't know what we can do besides appealing to the board. You know how long that could take."

"I do indeed. But we have to stay positive, Molly. We'll get it back and we'll save Elsie. You look so distressed. I can see a lot of darkness around you. You have to cheer up. I mean, I thought when I was killed, it was over. And yet here I am. Nothing is ever truly final. We have to remember that."

"You're right." I wiped the tears from my face. "We have to focus and figure this out."

"I know we do."

"Olivia, did you know that Drago has dragon magic? That's why he's a renegade. The council is probably afraid of him. Dragon magic is very strong."

She twisted her hands together. "Why do you think I was so afraid for Dorothy? She has that in her too, Molly. I can feel it every time she gets angry."

I told her about what had happened to Cassandra after she'd banished Olivia.

"Oh no! My poor little girl." She thought about it. "We have to get her trained better, Molly, so she can learn to conceal it. I don't want her to be an outsider. That's awful."

"We have to help her learn control," I agreed. "It won't be easy."

There was a discreet knock at the door. I knew before I answered that it was Antonio. The witchfinder had his own unique presence that was very strong.

"If I may come in?" He bowed his head. "I feel we are walking in circles, accomplishing nothing. Time is fleeting. We need the answers to the riddle of the words."

"Come in." I glanced up and down the long hall outside before closing the door behind him. He was alone.

He nodded to Olivia and stared for a moment at Elsie's prone figure on the bed. "This one does not sleep naturally, I think. She has a powerful spell on her."

"Yes. I know. We've tried breaking it but without luck so far. Brian and Dorothy have gone to plead our case to have our spell book returned from the library. Otherwise, I don't know what to do."

He went near her and closed his eyes. It was only a moment when he opened them again. "I'm so sorry. I do not

know this spell, though I can tell you it is very old and unlikely to be in your spell book."

That riled Olivia. "Our spell book is several generations
old, witchfinder. Our great-great-grandparents wrote in it.
It may well be older than you. So if you recognize the spell,
we might also find it in our book."

"My apologies for making light of your dilemma. Perhaps it is only my mind stuck on the problems of not only
finding Makaleigh's killer but also Hedyle's kidnapper,
Drago, who I begin to think might be the same person."

I wanted to tell him that wasn't true, but I knew he
wouldn't believe me, and I couldn't validate the statement
without giving away my bargain with Dorothy's father. I
kept silent, agreeing without words that it was a shattering
problem.

"Our friend is dying," Olivia pointed out. "Makaleigh is
already dead, and there isn't much you can do for her.
Hedyle can take care of herself. I think Elsie should come
first in this situation."

"You're right," I agreed with her. "But without knowing
the spell or having our book, I don't know what else to do."

We pondered the question for a few minutes. Antonio
asked to see the words again, complaining of a pesky
memory problem. I could relate to that. No doubt being more
than five hundred years old and sealed most of that time in
a wall made it far worse.

"I understand the point of the weapon, ord." Antonio
embellished his words with flourishes of his hands as he
walked about the room. "This is obvious. She was killed
with a blade."

"Although that word also means beginning," Olivia
added. "She could have been talking about a new beginning,
which there will certainly be with her death."

"True." He continued to contemplate the words. "Have
you tried using the words in a spell?"

"Yes. And they led us to Makaleigh's book in the library. Elsie and I were looking at it when Dorothy found our spell book. But I have to tell you that there didn't seem to be anything in there. Makaleigh led a long life. The book meticulously notated everything she did. It might take years to find an answer in there."

"It might still be worth the effort, Molly," he said.

"It might," I agreed. "But it vanished with Elsie. I found her in one of the other rooms, but the book wasn't with her."

"Aha!" He held one finger in the air. "You see? The book was important, else why steal it? It may even be that your sleeping friend saw the answer and was spelled for it. It is imperative that we wake her."

I sighed, feeling a headache coming on. "Which brings us back to our problem—we can't wake her."

He frowned. "Yes. There is that."

"Maybe we need the runes for those words of power," Olivia suggested. "That's how I knew about them."

"That might work, madam," he said. "Where are the runes to be found?"

"I'm not sure. I might have them in a book at my house." She glanced at me. "Maybe the library has the book."

"That's possible." I got to my feet. "Antonio and I will go back to the library. You stay with Elsie. Don't let anyone in until I get back."

Olivia nodded. "I can do that. How will I know it's you?"

"We could use a secret knock," Antonio suggested. "We used them regularly when we were running from the witches after the Inquisition. We just agree that the knocks will come in a certain manner." He demonstrated. "One knock. Silence. And then two knocks. Are we clear?"

"Perfectly," Olivia said. "Be careful out there, Molly. Who knows what's going on now."

I promised her that I would be careful. Antonio and I left the room.

"It is this way," he said. "It seems you were right about these new times, Molly."

"In what way?"

"Things are different. Had I tortured you for answers, which was my wont, I might have killed you and lost the words you had in you. Makaleigh chose a strong champion. She was right to give you the words."

"I think even the Inquisition could have used a lot more persuasion and less torture," I said as we passed several witches in elaborate clothes. "They must be having another party downstairs. I think we'd all be better off with some sleep."

"Persuasion." He rolled the word around in his mouth a bit. "It is my new philosophy. Thank you, dear lady. I have learned much from you."

Oscar was at the library when we reached its doors. "Molly. Witchfinder. May I be of some assistance?"

"Is there a problem with the library?" I asked, since the room behind him was dark.

"The council has decided to close the library for now. There have been a few incidents recently that they aren't happy about." His eyes found mine. "I think you know what I mean."

I thought about the incident between Dorothy and Cassandra. "Yes, I think I know. It was regrettable but so was Cassandra's decision to withhold our spell book and shove Olivia into some nether realm."

He shrugged. "I'm not saying mistakes weren't made. But the council feels they involve the library, so they're closing it until further notice."

"I am the council's witchfinder," Antonio blustered as he raised his chin to stare at Oscar. "I have special privilege. Let me through at once."

"Suit yourself. If you can get in there, I guess you can do what you want. It's not my magic that closed it. All I did was put up the sign. If you'll excuse me, I have to get a room ready for what's left of the council to meet shortly."

"That man is insufferable," Antonio declared. "Of course I can enter the library."

He tried both physically and using his magic. The door wouldn't open.

"How can this be? I am empowered to enter all domains in my pursuit of justice. I cannot be stopped."

I watched him again as he tried to walk through the sealed door. He bounced back from it, even angrier than he had been.

"The council shall hear of this at once," he shouted passionately. "I must leave you now to find Abdon and demand entrance to the library. I shall find you when I do this. Do not worry. We shall prevail."

He stormed down the hall. Several other witches came up to use the library. All of them read Oscar's sign and went away. Only Antonio believed he should be able to enter no matter what.

I went back to my room, surprised to find that I was actually beginning to learn the halls and rooms of the castle. It was poorly laid out, and more maze-like than I would have built it, but it was possible to learn its secrets.

When I reached the room, I used Antonio's secret knocking code, but Olivia didn't answer the door. Frustrated, I called out, "It's me, Olivia. Open the door."

"But how can I tell it's you, Molly? You said not to let anyone in."

"For goodness' sake, Olivia. You know my voice. And I used the witchfinder's secret knock. Open the door."

Instead of answering, Olivia stuck her head through the portal. "Oh, it *is* you, Molly. I just wanted to make sure."

She opened the door, and I laughed at her. "Who else did you expect to find out there?"

"I don't know. Who else did you think would try to come in?"

"Good point."

I didn't have time to tell her about the library being closed before Brian and Dorothy returned. Dorothy's eyes were red, as though she'd been crying. Brian's mouth was tight. I could tell they'd been arguing. A glance from Olivia said she knew too.

"Abdon agreed to a hearing about your spell book with what remains of the council," Brian said.

"But he made Brian promise to take Makaleigh's seat to get the hearing," Dorothy said in a voice that quavered. "They want to take him away from us."

CHAPTER 34

I moved closer to them. "We can't let you go against everything you believe in to get the spell book, Brian. We'll find another way."

"There isn't time to find another way." He glanced at Elsie. "She could die before we find another way. I don't have a spell book. Nothing like that was ever handed down to me. Let me do this for you—for the coven. You've been more like my family than my parents or Abdon have ever been. I want to do this, Molly."

"Once you take the council seat, you'll never be able to give it up," Olivia said. "Dorothy is right. You'll be lost to us."

Brian stalked across the floor to Elsie. "I'm not going to be lost. Just because everyone else takes the oath to stay on the council forever doesn't mean I have to."

"It goes with being sworn in," I told him. "It's an unbreakable oath, not some casual promise. No one who's sworn that oath has ever left the council."

"That's one reason it's way past time for a change," he

said. "Makaleigh knew that, and she was probably killed for it. No one likes change. I get that. But I'm not letting Elsie die because I have to do something I don't want to do. I've lived that way my whole life. It wasn't until I met the four of you that I understood making sacrifices. You could've died taking me away from the sea witch. You didn't even blink. Let me do this and handle the fallout later."

Olivia and I were silent on the matter. I was sure both of us felt this was more Dorothy's decision than ours. I knew that a relationship between her and a member of the council would be almost impossible. Those marriages were specifically designed to empower the witch on the council. Dorothy would never have that kind of standing in the witch community.

She was crying again, taking out a mottled tissue and trying to stop the tears. "I just found you, Brian. I can't lose you already."

He went back to her and took her in his arms. "You won't lose me, Dorothy. I swear it right now on a more powerful witch's oath than even the Grand Council requires. I'll still be me, and I'll still love you. But Elsie will be alive, and we'll all leave here when the castle doors open. I need you to tell me it's okay. I need your strength behind me when I go up there and pervert everything I've ever thought was true."

"Oh, Brian!" She hugged him tightly, crying into his shoulder.

Olivia and I were crying too—Olivia's tears were great drops of ectoplasm sliding down her face.

"All right," Dorothy finally relented. "But you better be prepared. If you turn into one of those council zombies, I'll turn you into an orange tree or something equally as terrible."

I mouthed, *Orange tree?* at Olivia, wondering why Dorothy had chosen that form of revenge.

"Oh, she hates oranges," Olivia whispered.

At least that made sense.

The couple continued to embrace until a knock on the door made them part.

It struck me that we should have simply stayed in the main hall to save everyone the effort of knocking at our door so frequently. Was this what it felt like to be a member of the council with people demanding your time?

Oscar was there. "The council awaits you, sir."

"Okay." Brian took a deep breath. "Let's do this thing, ladies."

Olivia was halfway out the door before I reminded her that she couldn't go to the council meeting. "You don't want to end up in that other place," I said. "I hear it's bad."

"Bad?" Olivia demanded. "Yes, it was bad. But I don't want to miss Brian taking his oath on the council."

"Listen, I've heard that ghosts who are sent to that place can't always come back," I told her. "You have to stay here with Elsie. We can't take any more chances that we might lose you."

"Besides," Dorothy said, taking out her phone. "We can take a video. That's what normal people use when they want to see something over and over again."

"Like your wedding to Brian?" Olivia smiled.

"Just like that," Dorothy promised. "But even if we have to get married in the cave under Smuggler's Arcane, you're going to be there."

"Oh, honey." Olivia started crying again. "You make me so proud to be your mother."

"We have to go," Brian said.

Oscar led the way down the old stone halls. I followed him while Dorothy was at Brian's side, holding his hand. It felt like we were saying good-bye to him forever. I kept telling myself that he was right. It didn't have to be the way it had always been. Brian could escape his oath and come back to us, come back to Dorothy.

We were led into a large, stark stone room where each of the remaining council members was seated behind a long table. It was nothing as elaborate as their usual meeting place, but the rough stone and rustic furniture made me more fearful than grand elegance would have.

Members of this council had ruled witches around the world for hundreds of years—through the dark times of the Inquisition when admitting that you were a witch could be a painful death sentence. It made me understand why Maka-leigh had insisted on protecting us from anything like it happening again. There was tradition here—and respect for magic—even if not always for those of us who practiced it.

We stood before them silently. Brian was glaring defiantly at his grandfather even though he planned to take him up on his offer. Dorothy kept her gaze on the stones at her feet. I studied each of the council members, wondering how they'd all come together. I wasn't as afraid of them as I had once been with the outsider magic I carried.

A large gavel came down on the table—and I realized it was a stone table. There appeared to be red stains on it, possibly from a less civilized time when sacrifices were made to accomplish magic. Realizing what I was looking at made me shiver. Intuition surged through me. There was more to this than simply Brian taking his place among them, and something bad was going to happen.

Defining bad is always difficult. Was it the kind of bad that we should run from now or that we could get through—like a dental appointment?

Oscar was wearing a black robe and standing alongside the council table with a runed staff that would have fascinated Olivia. There were many intricate carvings, paintings and stones set in it, up and down the wood.

"The Grand Council of Witches is in session!" He brought the staff down hard on the stone. It reverberated through the room.

"Why have you come before us this day?" Abdon asked.

Brian stepped forward. "To request the return of my coven's spell book, which is in the witches' library."

"We do not send out books from the library," council member Owen Graybeard reminded him.

Joshua Bartleson agreed. "This is not a lending library but a research tool for witches."

"Request denied." Zuleyma Castanada put it quickly behind them.

Dorothy looked up. "What? I thought we had an understanding. This might be the only way we can save our sister."

Brian laid his hand on her arm and addressed the council again. "I am Brian Fuller, son of Schadt and Yuriza Fuller. Grandson of Abdon Fuller. I request a putting aside of the law."

"And why do you ask this of us?" Abdon said.

Of course, I realized. There had to be some showmanship and bartering for the spell book. It was, after all, our governing body. Strange how much the ancient council was like modern-day politics.

"I request Makaleigh Veazy's vacant seat on the council, which gives me the right to change the rules in this instance." Brian's voice was fierce. It echoed around the chamber with his strength as a man and as a witch.

"We acknowledge your request." Abdon looked so relieved that he almost smiled. "The sitting members of the council will vote on your appeal."

"No!" a surprised voice called out from the back of the room.

We turned to look, as did everyone else. Schadt and Yuriza—Brian's parents—were standing behind us. They were both dressed in gorgeous robes and carried their tools of witchcraft. Schadt had a wand, which meant he was an air witch, like Brian and Olivia. Yuriza carried the thinnest sword I'd ever seen. It was marked with inscriptions up and down the blade, making her a fire witch, like Elsie.

Abdon stared at his son. "You plan to challenge Maka-leigh's successor, your own son?"

As was usual in the case of back-and-forth confrontation, even in a good tennis match, heads swiveled between Schadt and Abdon.

"Yes, Father," Schadt said. "It should be *my* seat on the council. I have waited patiently for this moment. I won't see it given away to a young man who is fickle and doesn't care about our traditions."

I wished that Elsie could have been there. I was sure she would have had some appropriate response to Schadt's sudden claim to Makaleigh's chair. Some of her past remarks came to mind and brought a smile to my lips—hardly appropriate in the tense moment, and yet they made me feel better.

"I'm not fickle, Dad," Brian responded. "And I have as much respect for our traditions as I need to have to get the job done. When did you get so ambitious?"

"Silence, both of you!" Abdon's voice thundered toward us.

"This is highly irregular," council member Erinna Cop-tus protested. "I thought it was all decided but for the vote."

Bairne Caelius stood. He was a large, burly man who al-ways wore the clothing from his time, which included dozens of animal skins. He had a full beard and a rough manner that no witchcraft or years on the council had changed.

"Is it to be a challenge, then? I believe Schadt has a right to physically challenge Brian for the seat."

He said it in a way that made me think he'd known this was going to happen. A friend of Schadt's, no doubt.

"It has been a very long time since a new member of the council was seated," Larissa Lonescue said. "We are in mourning for our past member. Perhaps this is not the ap-propriate time for either a challenge or a new member."

"And yet, Sister," Rhianna Black added, "not only is Makaleigh gone but also Hedyle, though she may not be dead. The council needs a new member. It has been a long time, but surely new blood is appropriate."

"Get on with it," Sarif Patel ventured. "We all know that there are rules that govern this situation. Schadt and Brian must duel to decide the victor and a new member of our council."

Bairne laughed heartily. "That's right. To the victor go the spoils. A battle to the death."

CHAPTER 35

"What?" Dorothy yelled. "That's crazy. No one does that kind of stuff anymore. They can't fight each other for the seat. Let's vote or something. This isn't the Dark Ages."

"Quiet, girl," Bairne said. "I'll have you removed."

"I don't care," she shouted back. "This can't happen. Brian isn't going to fight his father for a place on the council."

Brian took her hand, a grim expression on his face. "I have to go through with this. I can't let him mess things up."

Her dark eyes drenched with tears, Dorothy said, "This is what we were talking about. This is how you become a different person—the kind they want you to be, not the kind you want to be. You can't do this."

He smiled sadly. "It's for the best."

"I'm not going to stand here and watch you. If you want to do this, count me out." Dorothy stormed away from him and out the thick wood door.

Bairne guffawed. "Anyone else with a tender heart or a queasy stomach?"

I didn't want to see Brian killed or watch him kill his father. Frankly, I didn't believe it would come to that. This was a drama for the sake of the witches watching and the council's honor. But no matter what, I wasn't leaving Brian by himself.

"We are speaking of a duel of magic, are we not?" Arleigh Burke questioned.

"Of course," Joshua Bartleson replied. "We aren't barbarians as were our ancestors who used the sacrificial table."

That relieved me. They could say to the death, but really they meant until one of the men gave up. Schadt was older and more experienced than Brian, but Brian was powerful. He was also more aggressive. He'd stood up to Abdon his whole life. His mother and father were like ghosts in the background.

Had Bairne put Schadt up to this? It seemed odd Abdon's only son hadn't shown any interest in the council until now.

"So what do we do?" Brian asked. "Do I hit him with my wand or try to shoot sparks from it?"

Always the joker, I mused. Brian rarely took anything seriously. Even now he was laughing at the council and his father.

"Whatever suits you," Sarif Patel said. "Let's see what happens."

"I agree with the young witch who left," Owen Graybeard said. "This is not what Makaleigh or Hedyle would want."

I had been watching Schadt. Yuriza had stepped away from him. He was using his wand and a spell to gather power. He obviously took it very seriously.

When he stood and held his wand toward Brian, I shouted out a warning, "Look out!"

Brian ducked his head as an enchantment passed over him. It was so strong that it hit the wall behind him and broke a piece of the old stone.

Larissa Lonescue glanced at me. "No warnings from those not participating or we shall clear the room."

"Thanks, Molly." Brian grinned at me, but the laughter was gone from his eyes. "I guess that's how we do it, huh?"

He didn't pause to gather his forces. He took out his wand and barely muttered an incantation before the force of it knocked his father to the floor. There were gasps from those around me. Bairne frowned. It seemed he hadn't anticipated Brian's strength.

"I can't believe you did that!" Brian's mother shouted at him. "Just give up your claim to the seat. It means nothing to you but everything to your father. Are you really prepared to kill him to claim Makaleigh's place?"

Brian shook his head. "This wasn't my idea. None of it was my idea. I'm following your weird rules to get what I want. Change the rules. Tell Dad to forget about it."

She turned her slender back to him. Schadt was still getting off the floor.

"Is that it?" Brian asked. "Can we move on now?"

With his mother in the way, he couldn't see that his father was preparing another salvo against him. It happened faster this time. As he got up, Schadt flung his wand at Brian. It took form and substance, becoming one of the large rocks from around him.

Brian didn't move in time. The rock creased his forehead, drawing blood. He staggered but didn't fall. His bright blue eyes were angry. He paused for only a moment before he lifted his wand and subjected the chandelier above his father to his will.

The large metal fixture dropped to the floor, taking Schadt with it.

Everyone, including me, was beyond gasps. Schadt didn't move. Yuriza rushed to his side and tried to move the elaborate candlelit chandelier off her husband. She called on the magic of her sword for help. Alone, she managed to free Schadt, but he wasn't moving.

Without a word of warning, she turned on her son and threw her sword straight at his chest.

With barely an inch to spare, Brian deflected it with his wand.

The crowded room was completely silent.

Abdon slowly got to his feet and began applauding. The rest of the council—except for Bairne—joined him.

"Well done," Abdon said to Brian. "Well done, my boy."

"You mean I don't actually have to kill him?" Brian's voice was laced with sarcasm.

"Of course not," Zuleyma Castanada replied. "Death isn't the only way to win a battle. And your girlfriend was right. This is not the Dark Ages. Welcome to the council, Brian Fuller. Blessings on you and your lineage."

"We'll take an hour break to seat our new council member and rule on the placement of the spell book." Abdon hit his gavel on the stone again. Oscar followed by bringing down his staff.

CHAPTER 36

I ran through the departing crowd to Brian's side. The cut on his head was dripping blood down the side of his face. He was just standing there, not moving, looking dazed as he stared at his parents. There was a pitcher of water and a few napkins on the stone council table. I poured some water on the napkins and held one of them to his head.

"Brian?" I tried to get his attention.

"Molly." He shook his head and finally held the napkin. "Thanks."

"This was too much to go through, even for our spell book."

"It wasn't just about the spell book," he admitted. "I talked to my father about this before I agreed to accept Abdon's proposal. He wasn't interested in the politics of the council, he said. He'd never wanted any part of it."

"What do you think happened?"

"I think one or two members of the council didn't want me to have Makaleigh's seat and got him to challenge me for it."

"That's what I thought about Bairne from the look on his face." We both watched Bairne and Sarif try to help Yuriza get Schadt to his feet.

"Let's get out of here," Brian said. "I need to talk to Dorothy."

I walked back to the room with him. Dorothy was there. There had been no change in Elsie's condition. Brian got Dorothy to go in the other room with him and closed the door. Olivia and I waited to see what would happen next.

"Well, I'm glad I wasn't able to go after all," she said. "I'm assuming Brian won the challenge. I've never heard of such a thing. I thought maybe Dorothy had a fever or something when she came back here crying."

"I don't understand it either." I told her what Brian said about talking to his father. "Maybe that was just what Schadt needed to determine that he really wanted to be on the council."

"I'll be so glad when we're out of here," she sighed. "How much longer now?"

"Six hours." It seemed like forever at that point. "Remind me not to come back for Brian and Dorothy's wedding, or any other function. I never want to go through this again."

"Well, Dorothy said she wouldn't have the wedding here if it meant I couldn't come. I believe her, don't you?"

I paced around the room. "Yes, but you didn't see the look on Brian's face when he brought the chandelier down on his father. I'm afraid he's already changing."

"For goodness' sake, Molly. What did you expect him to do? Even if it is his father, he had to defend himself. And he was trying to get the spell book back so we could help Elsie. I think that's different."

"I hope so."

Elsie's hand was stiff and icy. There was no color in her face. We had to do something to bring her back right away.

"I don't know if we should wait for the council," I said. "We have to break Elsie free from this spell."

"But you all tried and it didn't work. You need the spells from the book."

"Or the witch who did this to her."

"But how are you going to do that, Molly? With everyone at half magic, there's barely enough to make a wand work."

"I know."

Dorothy and Brian seemed to have patched up their differences, at least temporarily, as they came back into the room. I told them my fears about Elsie.

"Let's go get the spell book now," Brian said. "No more games."

"I didn't want to say anything before," I added, "but I had a feeling there was more to you taking the council seat.

He looked into my eyes. "We've put up with their crap, Molly. Let's go kick some butt."

I agreed, though I had misgivings. I didn't know what else to do. We needed a strong healing spell created by another fire witch like Elsie. There was bound to be one from someone in her family—her grandmother and great-grandmother were both witches of the fire.

We left Olivia with Elsie again and returned to the stone council chamber. Brian was right about the council. They were all in the meeting room drinking tea as they discussed their newest member and the challenge.

Oscar met us before we could get in. "They aren't ready for you yet. I'll come get you when they are."

Brian pushed past him and approached the ten remaining members. "My friend is dying, probably as part of Makaleigh's death. We need a healing spell from her family's spell book that shouldn't have been in the library to start with. I want it back now."

Dorothy held my hand so tightly that I was afraid she might break it.

"You little whelp." Bairne got to his feet and stared at Brian. "We give you the opportunity of a lifetime and all you can think about is the death of one witch. If we thought in such small scale, there would be no witches left in the world."

"All that matters is one witch," Brian debated. "That's what you've forgotten. Maybe you do have to make decisions for a world of witches, but each of them are distinctive and make us strong. Elsie Langston was only trying to do her part in solving Makaleigh's death. We can't abandon her now because the library made a mistake in taking her spell book."

"It's not only the spell book involved in all this." Arleigh Burke stared at Dorothy. "There's the matter of your girlfriend using her magic against our herald."

I hadn't noticed before, but the black snake that was Cassandra was slithering around on the stones at our feet. She immediately went closer to Arleigh and hissed at Dorothy from a safe distance.

"Is that it?" Dorothy demanded. "I take full responsibility. She shouldn't have sent my mother off that way and decided not to give us our spell book."

"We do not attack each other out of anger," Rhianna said. "You need to learn control, young witch. Your magic is obviously powerful. But you lack patience and understanding. Something your coven members should be teaching you!"

Rhianna glared at me. I raised my chin and glared back. Dorothy was a good witch who'd been pushed to her limits by the things that had happened in the last twenty hours or so. Yes, she was impetuous and her magic was strong. But she was also good-hearted and learning control.

I was about to state the obvious when Dorothy put her hand on mine.

"I'm sorry about what happened to Cassandra," she said. "I'll be glad to change her back for you."

Erinna Coptus nodded. "Please do so that we may get on with other important issues."

Dorothy closed her eyes and summoned up the only transformation spell that she knew. It was a very basic spell—something a young child would use—and yet she was able to accomplish changing the thousand-year-old council herald into a snake. It shouldn't have been possible with her limited experience.

The black snake convulsed, writhing on the stone floor, before splitting open to have Cassandra emerge. She was naked, no bubbles, and covered with slime.

"Well!" she said in an angry voice.

"That's enough, Cassandra," her mother, Rhianna, said in a stunned voice.

The council had begun whispering among themselves with fearful eyes glued on Dorothy.

The thick door to the council chamber burst open to reveal Hedyle on her knees. Her gown was torn and dirty. Her long white hair was pulled out of its usual neat style.

"Stop her!" Hedyle, the head of the council, had a hard time getting her voice above a whisper. "She killed Makaleigh!"

CHAPTER 37

"What?" Dorothy's stare went sharply to the council and over to Brian. "That's ridiculous."

Brian took her hand and glared fiercely at the council members, who'd all come to their feet.

Oscar and Abdon had run to aid Hedyle, helping her up and allowing her to rest against them.

"What are you saying?" I demanded. Not even the Council of Witches was going to accuse Dorothy without a fight. "She had nothing to do with Makaleigh's death."

"She had everything to do with it—her and her outsider magic." Hedyle raised her arm weakly to point at Dorothy. "She is Drago Rasmun's daughter. They killed Makaleigh and kidnapped me, wanting me to dissolve the council. I escaped when they left me alone. But they both wield dragon magic. They will destroy us all if we allow it."

The remainder of the council was shouting angrily at her words. They began moving toward Dorothy as Brian urged her to leave the room.

Dragon magic. It wasn't hard for them to see that she was too powerful for a witch with no training. Dorothy had been born with it. It wasn't like my amulet that the council had tried to take away from me, although at that time I had no idea why. Once I'd accepted it, it was impossible to remove. But dragon magic was part of Dorothy, impossible to remove.

"Seize them," Hedyle weakly urged.

"No," Abdon said. "Brian has nothing to do with this. It was her father and the young witch. Leave my grandson out of it."

Hedyle looked as though she wanted to rip him apart for questioning her. "Regardless of who he is, he is no doubt in league with Drago and his daughter. Their outsider magic will destroy the council."

Abdon stared at her with wild eyes. "No." He turned to Brian and Dorothy. "Leave. Get out of here until we can sort this out. Go now!"

Dorothy glanced at me, but Brian reacted, getting both of them out of the room immediately.

I stood there, not knowing what to do, shocked by the turn of events.

Hedyle gave a large sigh and collapsed into Oscar's arms. As the council moved toward her, the witchfinder grabbed my arm and led me quickly through a side door in the stone wall.

"I don't understand. How could she accuse Dorothy of killing Makaleigh and kidnapping her? Dorothy was with us the whole time."

"Can you prove that?" Antonio demanded. "Can you show them where she was every moment before Makaleigh's death? If not, the council will take Hedyle's word for what happened. Why else would Drago take her? And the daughter shares his magic. The council will want to banish her as they have her father."

"Where are we going?" I asked as we ran through what looked like identical hallways.

"We are going to get your spell book from the library so you can help your friend and get out of the castle. Things are going to get very ugly now, Molly. The council fears magic stronger than theirs, especially magic out of their control."

"But I can't just leave Dorothy and Brian here. They won't be safe."

"Dragon magic keeps the girl safe," he said. "Abdon will allow nothing to happen to his grandson."

We were finally outside the closed library again. The magic bonds were strong, keeping everyone out.

"Do not worry," Antonio told me. "Abdon gave me power to reopen the library and retrieve your book."

"Really?" My mind was whirling with everything that had happened and wondering why Abdon would want to help us.

"Stand back." Antonio spoke an incantation aloud that immediately began to remove the spell away from the door. The powerful closure was lifted, and we walked into the library.

"Find your book," he said. "I shall guard the door against intruders."

"Thanks. I'll hurry."

My mind was so full of—everything—that I didn't even realize I was running around in the dark library with hundreds of thousands of books until I'd run up and down the same aisle three times.

"You'll never find it this way," I reminded myself, trying to pull my thoughts together. I grabbed my amulet. *"Light my way, bright as day."*

My amulet glowed, directing its light down the aisles until it landed on a single spot. It was our spell book. I hugged it to me and closed my eyes. "Blessed Be."

One more thing. I didn't want to leave without Makaleigh's book too. Whatever Elsie had seen in there had been
enough to put her under this powerful spell. There was
something in it we needed. Makaleigh's book was there. I
guess the library put it back. I grabbed it too and clutched
both books tightly.

"Are you ready?" Beads of sweat had formed on Antonio's
brow. He was having a hard time keeping the library open
as he stared hard at the closed door to keep it unlocked.

"Yes, but how are you going to get the books past the
library spell?"

"Abdon gave me the incantation to free the books." He
glanced at me and smiled. "I hope I only free these two. I
might release all of them. A crime to be sure, but perhaps
necessary."

I looked back at the huge library behind us containing
books that most people didn't even know existed. I hoped
he could keep most of the books here too. It would be a
terrible loss to the world if the books were gone. If Elsie's
life wasn't at stake, I would never have considered helping
him. But as far as I could see, it was the only way.

Antonio continued to stare hard at the door but directed
his magic toward the books in my arms. I felt a tingling
sensation and hoped his magic wasn't affecting me too. A
moment later I had my answer. I was back at our room with
the purloined books.

The witchfinder wasn't with me. I assumed he could take
care of himself and went inside.

"Oh, Molly, I'm so glad to see you," Olivia said. "What
happened? Is Brian on the council now? Oh my gosh—you
have our spell book. I've never seen anything so beautiful.
I guess that means everything went all right."

I sat at the desk chair. "No. Everything is far from all
right." I told her what had happened. Her face grew less
distinct as I spoke, her eyes worried.

"Outsider magic? I never thought about Drago passing that to Dorothy. I knew he'd been banned by the council for it—which was why I was so worried about you with that amulet even though it *is* water magic. How was she able to keep it under control with no training? My poor baby."

"It's a bad situation," I agreed. "I couldn't believe when Hedyle accused Dorothy of murdering Makaleigh and her own kidnapping."

"Well, we know my angel had nothing to do with it."

"We do. But the council doesn't. They'll hunt her and Brian down. I don't know what else will happen. I'm afraid to think about it."

"Oh, that Drago!" Olivia flew across the room, dragging a few items from the tops of the dressers and shelves with her. They crashed to the floor when she stopped. "I'd like to kill him for doing this. I'm sure it has something to do with him coming back. Huh! I knew he didn't just want to meet his daughter."

"You're wrong." Drago appeared in the room with us. "And don't blame me because Dorothy wasn't adequately trained to handle this situation. You were the one who took her away and hid her from me."

Olivia flew back into his face. "I wanted her to lead a good life, not be banned and hunted by the council because she was the daughter of an evil witch who uses dragon magic."

He stared right through her. I could see his eyes going through the opaque form. "Olivia, I didn't want that for her either. I thought your way was best. I've known where Dorothy was for years. She's my flesh and blood. You couldn't actually hide her from me."

"Well, now what?" Olivia backed away from him with tears flowing down her face. "The council thinks she killed Makaleigh. They think she kidnapped Hedyle. What now?"

"It seems to me that you need help bringing your friend

back to life." He bowed his head. "Which is why I've sought you out. We can discuss the rest after. Don't you agree?"

I got to my feet quickly. I had been asking myself how I was going to revive Elsie alone since I'd returned from the library. "Yes! Thank you, Drago. I have our spell book with a spell that should work on her. Will you help us?"

"Yes. Let's save your friend."

Looking through our old spell book was like going home again. There was my mother's handwriting and my grandmother's spells—the same for Olivia's and Elsie's. There were our spells that we had collected and painstakingly added to the book from the time we had reached adulthood. Holding the book I thought we'd never see again was a wonderful balm for my fractured energy.

I found Elsie's grandmother's spell. I could still see her grandmother writing in the book as we played with our wands and other magic accessories in her basement. "This is it," I told Drago.

He nodded. "Repeat it and I shall follow."

Together we chanted the spell to free Elsie. She was completely stiff, no color to her lips or cheeks. Fear clutched at my heart, but I pushed it away to concentrate on the spell to free her. I wished Dorothy and Brian were there too, but I was going to have to be happy and grateful to have Drago's help.

We chanted holding hands with candles lit above Elsie's head. I could feel the pull on my strength and energy. I hoped I wouldn't let her down by collapsing on the floor before she was awake again.

I saw her hand twitch, and faint color returned to her face in a slowly blossoming pink. She moved and opened her eyes. I collapsed on the bed beside her.

"Welcome back."

CHAPTER 38

Olivia and I took turns filling Elsie in on everything that had happened. Drago sat silently in a chair by the door, looking faintly amused. I supposed that he was thinking how silly we were and so much less sophisticated than him.

She glanced at Drago. "So we're friends with him now?"

"He's helping us," I told her. "I probably couldn't have wakened you without his help."

She was sitting on the edge of the bed sipping water—I figured she must be dehydrated. She was right. We were an odd group.

"What are we going to do to help Dorothy?" Elsie wondered. "How did you manage to mess things up so badly without me?"

I laughed. "I'm just very good at it. I'm so glad you're back to help me."

"As you ladies have guessed," Drago said, "we have to find the killer. We know Dorothy didn't do this. She's just a convenient scapegoat."

"For you?" I asked. "I think it's time that we came clean on some things."

He shrugged, his tight leather making a creaking sound. "Everyone *knows* I'm the bad guy, Molly. I'm game if you are."

"I'm not worried about it." I squared my shoulders and held his gaze. I was a little worried about what I'd done to help him, but there was no reason to give it away.

"What are we talking about?" Olivia asked. "All this is making me feel dizzy."

"Drago has been having an affair with Hedyle," I revealed. "Elsie and I saw them together."

Olivia's eyes widened dramatically as she confronted Drago. "Hedyle? I can't believe it. Why would she want to do such a thing?" She smiled at Drago and shook her head. "Silly me. I know why. But I'm still surprised."

He chuckled and glanced away.

"Yes. Well," I began again. "Drago and Hedyle have been lovers outside the knowledge of the council. She was attacked and then kidnapped. Now Hedyle is accusing Dorothy and Drago of those crimes along with killing Makaleigh."

We all stared at him, waiting for answers.

"I don't know what to tell you." He wasn't a bit remorseful. "Sometimes people have bad breakups. I thought things were going well for us. That's why I tricked Dorothy into helping me sneak into the castle. Hedyle said she wanted me here."

"That's another nail in Dorothy's coffin," Elsie said. "Between having outsider magic, helping Drago sneak in and Hedyle accusing her, Dorothy is in a bad way."

"Oh, my poor baby," Olivia mourned. "We have to help her, girls. You too, Drago, since this is partly your fault."

"Only by birth, I assure you." Drago got to his feet. "Now, I believe that Hedyle invited me here to pin Makaleigh's death on me. It may have been the motive for our love affair from the beginning. I think Hedyle killed Makaleigh."

"No way!" Elsie said. "How could something like that happen?"

"Maybe she was completely against the changes Makaleigh wanted to see," I guessed. "Maybe she knew she couldn't change Makaleigh's mind and that she would sway the council in her favor. There was only one way to deal with the problem."

"Oh my stars!" Elsie bolted to her feet, almost falling, before I helped her to the chair at the desk. "I just remembered what I saw in Makaleigh's book before I was so rudely snatched away."

"I hope it's something that's going to help Dorothy," Olivia said.

"I have the book." I pointed it out on the desk. "Antonio helped me get it and our spell book out of the library."

"I thought Brian was going to take care of it," Olivia said.

"He didn't have time. Everything happened with Dorothy before he could get the council to agree. Antonio said Abdon had given him special powers to get in the library and retrieve the spell book."

"I wonder why he'd do something so generous," Olivia demanded. "It's not exactly his style, is it?"

"Maybe he knows what we suspect," Elsie added.

"He gave Antonio the privilege before Hedyle reappeared and accused Dorothy," I explained. "He may feel differently now."

"Let's get back to the book," Drago said. "What was it that made you suspect Hedyle for Makaleigh's murder?"

Elsie started flipping through the pages of the big book. "I was looking for the words of power and how they might pertain to what had happened. Ah! Here it is. It seems that Hedyle and Makaleigh were rivals and fierce enemies for hundreds of years. They fought bloody wars against each other for power before Makaleigh started the Council of

Witches. She offered a truce to Hedyle as well as a place on the council. That was the end of their fighting."

Drago considered what she told him. "I vaguely remember that time. Thousands of non–magic users died in their wars. I was surprised when Hedyle agreed to join the council and help Makaleigh begin recruiting witches to it. I was one of the first they asked to join."

"You?" Olivia laughed. "But you've been considered an outsider for a hundred years. You told me so yourself."

"The council was different when it was first started just after the Inquisition. The witches were looking for protection from persecution. The more power the better. After a while, they began to refine the council. They changed it so that they were the rulers, lording it over the witches they considered to be of lesser power. They were afraid of outsider magic. I wasn't the only one excused by them and then banned."

"So it probably was a setup," Elsie considered. "Hedyle didn't want Makaleigh on the council anymore. You were a good way to get rid of her."

"Precisely." He nodded. "Although I confess to being completely unprepared for this betrayal. I love Hedyle. I would never hurt her."

I didn't doubt his sincerity. He was there with us, after all. I couldn't speak to his relationship with Olivia. Maybe he loved her too. That was a long time ago. It was possible they wouldn't have broken up if Olivia hadn't found out that she was pregnant and left him.

"I'm still having problems with the idea that Hedyle would kill Makaleigh." Elsie interrupted my thoughts. "I'm not saying you did, Drago. And I certainly don't believe Dorothy killed anyone. But how do we prove it anyway? If I'm having trouble believing it, so will everyone else. We need better proof than an old book that says the two women were enemies before Christopher Columbus sailed to the New World."

"Yes." Drago frowned and stared off blankly.

"So we're right back where we started from," Olivia said, "except now the council thinks Dorothy killed Makaleigh."

"We have to think of some way to make everyone understand what happened," Elsie said. "Surely with all the magic in this room we can think of something."

I was feeling drained and uninspired. How could we prove our theories about Hedyle?

"There is only one way," Drago said. "I must go to her. She will no doubt want to banish or imprison me."

"She may want to kill you to keep you from talking," Olivia said. "I don't think that's the answer."

"There is no other," he continued. "I shall go to Hedyle and get her to confess her deed. You will hear what she has to say and speak up against her no matter what happens to me. It is the only way we can free Dorothy."

"Hedyle is too smart for that," Elsie said. "She's been planning this for a while if what you're saying is true. Don't you think she's considered everything that could happen, including you putting your life in her hands to try to protect Dorothy?"

"Elsie's right," I agreed with her. "But Drago is too. Hedyle is smart and powerful. She manipulated you and will try to do it again if she gets the chance. We need a better plan. Something she won't expect."

"Let's just scrap that idea and go back to the words of power and the fingerprinting," Olivia suggested. "If Hedyle killed Makaleigh, she probably hasn't even thought about leaving fingerprints on the knife. All we have to do is take care of that. No one gets hurt."

"We never got her fingerprints," I told her. "Maybe she did consider it."

"Or it was just bad luck and then we were sidetracked," Elsie said. "Maybe we can get her fingerprints now and can compare them to the ones on the knife."

I shrugged. "So much has happened. The same knife killed Kalyna. And that's to say everything is still in the kitchen where we left it."

"Do you think Oscar, the faithful servant to the Fuller family, could be involved?" Drago wondered. "He seems to be about quite a bit. It would be easy for him to be part of Hedyle's plan."

"I agree. I don't know. All the people I thought I could trust have let me down, and those I didn't trust have been friends. Anything is possible at this point."

"What about the witchfinder, Molly? The two of you seem close."

The door to our room burst open. Antonio, followed by a group of security guards, came in with hard looks on their faces.

"I am sorry, Molly, but the council requests your presence in the matter of finding Dorothy Dunst Lane." His eyes narrowed as he saw Drago with us. "And you, sir. You will come with us. You have been accused of murdering Makaleigh Veazy."

CHAPTER 39

The council was at the table in the stone room. Hedyle had cleaned up and taken her rightful place among them. There was an empty chair where Makaleigh, or Brian, would have been for the meeting.

The guards were rough getting us there. I was sure my arms would be black-and-blue the next day. Every instinct told me to flee, but I went with them to hear what the council had to say.

Drago went too, although he could surely have escaped. I wasn't sure what his motivation was. There was no way of knowing what was going through his mind or hid behind his gloating smile.

Cassandra was back to her normal self—dressed to kill in sparkling silk, her black hair clean now and flowing down her back. Oscar stood on the other end of the table. I thought he looked bemused, as though he was having a hard time taking it all in too. I could only guess by his expression. No doubt he would be forbidden to say anything.

"I see you have been harboring this fugitive," Hedyle said in her normal tone. With a change of clothes and her hair back in order, she looked and sounded tough. She seemed completely recovered from her ordeal. It was a little quick to me for someone who could barely stand when she'd returned to accuse Dorothy.

The witchfinder had not been able to spare bringing Olivia along with us to the council. I had no doubt they would want to send her back to that realm Drago had warned me about. I also had to wonder if he would unmask me as having outsider magic now as a way to deflect the anger of the council.

"They were not harboring me, my love." Drago bowed deeply to Hedyle as he smiled and flirted with her. "I helped them bring their friend back to life. That is all."

Her eyes were hard when she looked at him. If there had ever truly been love between them, it seemed to be gone.

"Drago Rasmun. You have corrupted your daughter and led her into murder. We should have killed you instead of banishing you. What have you to say on your behalf?"

"Nothing the council would like to hear," he said. "But I will tell you, if you agree to a private audience with me now."

"No," Hedyle said quickly. "You won't have another chance to hurt me or anyone else on this council."

"We do want to know where Brian and Dorothy are," Abdon said. "They don't have the magic to leave the castle, which means they're here somewhere."

"You might as well tell them to come out of hiding," Owen Graybeard said. "Brian has forfeited his right to be on the council. But he won't miss his chance to be in prison."

As he was laughing heartily over his own sarcastic joke, I stared at him and at the other members of the Council of Witches. They were every bit as bad as politicians in the non-magic world. They did what they wanted to do, not what the rest of us needed them to do.

"What now?" Elsie whispered, her gaze not leaving the council.

"I have something in mind," I told her. "I hope it will work."

"You *hope* it will work?" Olivia murmured.

"Yes. But I'm up for anything else you have in mind."

"Just do it," Drago urged.

"Oh, why don't you just go ahead and disappear now," Olivia said. "I know you aren't sticking around to help us out of trouble."

"You're wrong," he said. "I'm here for the whole thing."

By that time the one person on the council not laughing— Hedyle—brought the gavel down. "Why is there such frivolity regarding the death of our sister? It could have been one of you. It almost was me. I'll hear no more laughter from the council this day."

My plan was roughly based on the fact that a large group of witches were also in the stone chamber. I didn't know any of them, but they weren't on the council, which meant they weren't that different from me, Elsie, Dorothy and even Olivia. They lived their lives with help from the magic they were born with, but not for it. It enhanced their lives, but they still had children, families, probably jobs and mortgages. Being a witch was more a choice of philosophy than whether or not they could fly across the moon.

What I had in mind was more for them than for the council. Maybe Hedyle had too strong a hold on the council for it to work, but no one else had any other ideas.

"Where are the other traitors?" Hedyle demanded. "This will go much easier on you if you tell us."

"I can't tell you that because I don't know," I said to her in clear, ringing schoolteacher tones. "What I can tell you is who killed Makaleigh Veazy. Any interest in that discussion?"

The council members muttered among themselves. It was clear to see that they weren't entirely convinced it was

Dorothy and Drago. The witches in attendance were even more interested in what I had to say.

Again Hedyle brought the hammer down on the stone table. "What proof have you of what has taken place?"

"This is Molly Addison Renard," Abdon introduced me. "She was the last person to speak with Makaleigh while she was still with us."

There were lots of whispers and muttering between the crowd and the council at the table.

"Addison," Arleigh Burke said, letting the word roll around in her mouth. "I knew your great-grandmother. She was a wonderful witch. How came you to us this day, Molly?"

"There is no secret to how she came to be here," Hedyle snarled. "She's part of the group of terrorists who killed Makaleigh and tried to kill me."

"Ah!" The witchfinder stepped forward. "She did not kill Makaleigh. I can swear to that. Makaleigh died after she had imparted secrets to Molly. As for kidnapping, she was definitely not part of that, as she was with me."

I could see Hedyle was getting angrier. Could she let it stand that I wasn't to be lumped with Drago and Dorothy?

"Very well." Her teeth were on edge when she said the words. "But I hope you don't mean to question me about my own kidnapping, witchfinder."

"Not at all, madam." He deeply bowed his head in respect. "These are only facts that I know."

"Continue, Molly," Arleigh invited. "Tell us what you know of Makaleigh's murder."

I glanced at my friends, and Drago. I hoped they were ready.

I'd taken drama in high school and college. So had Olivia. She didn't want to be a teacher like I did, but she enjoyed going to school because she was always popular. Elsie was already teaching, since she was twelve years older than us. Her mother had been very strict. There had been no drama, music or anything not pertaining to teaching while she was in college.

Since I was about to give a performance that might save all our lives, I hoped I was ready for it.

I bowed deeply and considered the part I was playing, just as our old drama teacher had instructed. "Council members and fellow witches, let me assure you that not only did I hear Makaleigh Veazy's last words, I took her spirit into my body to protect and shield her from the rest of the world."

That started a much louder buzz around me. Hedyle had to bring down the gavel several times, struggling to keep control of the council. The witches around us were amazed and appalled. Taking a spirit into the body was not a witch practice. It ranked right up there with letting a ghost hang around.

As people's voices began to get lower, I raised my hands in an elaborate fashion. What they didn't notice was that Olivia had leveraged herself against me so that her ectoplasm appeared to be part of every move I made. I wasn't sure how far we'd get with it, but it was a wonderful idea.

"I was despicably murdered!" Olivia's voice joined mine, making it unforgettable.

CHAPTER 40

People pushed their hands to their ears so as not to hear the horrible caterwauling. Several women fainted, and others screamed.

"We should take this on the road, Molly," Olivia said right beside my ear. "This is good stuff."

I didn't respond as I cast suspicious glances around the room. Olivia actually put one hand over my face to give it a shocking appearance. I couldn't see it, but I could imagine it was ghastly from the way people reacted around us.

"What do you want from us? Why are you here?" Erinna Coptus demanded, though her voice shook.

"Is that really you, Makaleigh?" Bairne asked. "Are you really with us?"

"Are they really falling for this?" Olivia whispered. "Is it just me or did everyone think they were smarter than that?"

"It is I, Bairne," I returned. "I am here within Molly Renard to renounce this council and the one who killed me."

Several witches screamed, but Oscar had bolted the

heavy wood door from the inside and would let no one pass. He nodded at me as though he knew what I was trying to do.

"If you are who you say you are," Hedyle said as she struggled to take charge again, "tell me something only you and I would know."

I thought back to everything I'd read of her, as well as the things I'd heard and Drago had intimated. What could I say that would continue the masquerade?

It suddenly hit me. What makes two people angrier than anything else? What makes two women difficult to reconcile?

"There are many things only we know," I told her in a moaning voice. "There are the things only known to the heart, Hedyle. The wars we fought because we both loved the same man."

I waited for a sign that I'd hit the mark. Already the loud buzz around the room believed it. That left Hedyle's judgment of my claim. I hoped that had been a problem between them with Drago. If that was possible then so was their previous relationship.

Hedyle's face turned pasty white. She forgot to pick up her gavel and instead got slowly to her feet. "What do you want, Makaleigh? You have no right here now. You are no longer a witch but a thing that we abhor. Leave now or be sent to that place."

She bought it! I almost couldn't believe it.

"You got her," Olivia said. "Let's really hook her."

In full view of everyone, I slowly began to rise—with Olivia lifting me. We kept going up as people cried and hugged one another.

"I didn't know you could do this," I said when we'd reached the ceiling. "Don't drop me."

"Don't worry. I've been practicing."

She brought me slowly back to the stone floor.

I glared at Hedyle, who had resumed her seat behind the table.

"You murdered me," I said. "You couldn't stand the changes I wanted to make, and you plunged the knife into my back."

"No!" Hedyle stood again on shaky legs. "No. I didn't kill you. I arranged it, but I could never put the knife in you. You have to believe me. You weren't able to see. It was Bairne who killed you. He said we were doing it for the good of the council."

Bairne started to his feet, but Oscar and Abdon pushed him back into his chair.

"I only served Hedyle in this. I would never have done it alone," he claimed. "She was the one who made it happen. She set up Drago and his daughter so they would look guilty. She changed the fingerprints. She had everything planned perfectly."

"You killed Makaleigh?" Owen Graybeard's roar echoed in the chamber as he leapt across the table and threw himself bodily on Bairne. "I'll kill you myself."

Oscar had left his position by the door. He and Abdon were able to keep the two men apart. But that had left the door out of the chamber unguarded. A few witches pushed it open and ran into the hallway. It only took a few minutes before the entire audience was gone.

All that remained was the brawling council. Elsie, Olivia and I stayed where we were.

"What's going to become of us now?" Elsie wondered. "There's not enough left of the council to keep going."

"You heard Drago," Olivia said. "There wasn't always a council."

"Speaking of Drago," I added. "Where did he get off to?"

"I'm afraid I might know the answer to that." Olivia pointed toward the stone table. There was a large knife, the same knife that had killed Makaleigh and Kalyna, in Hedyle's throat. In all the confusion, someone had killed her.

"How could this happen?" Elsie shook her head. "I'm leaving too. There's only an hour before the doors open. I need something to drink."

I waited long enough to see the look on Abdon's face when he realized that Hedyle was dead too. There were only ten of them up there. None of the witches had run that way. The suspect pool, as Joe liked to call it, was very small.

"Wait for me," I called to Elsie. "I think I need a drink too."

We walked to the main hall down several flights of stone stairs. Halfway down, we met Dorothy and Brian. They'd been hiding in the castle, unable to leave.

"I'm so glad to see you, honey." Olivia hugged her daughter even though she was still working on her hugs not feeling so suffocating.

"Hi Mom. Elsie. Molly." Dorothy waved to us. "Oscar let Brian know that things were even worse than before. We thought we might as well come back."

We continued to the main hall and easily found drinks and places to sit. The place was a ghost town, presumably with witches cowering in their room until it was time for them to leave.

"I don't understand what happened," Brian said. "Who killed Makaleigh?"

"Apparently it was Bairne and Hedyle. She got Drago to sneak in with Dorothy's cat under the guise of a lover's tryst so she could blame him for it," I explained again. "They killed Makaleigh because she wanted to make too many changes to the council."

"And now Hedyle is dead?" Brian said.

"I think Drago did it," Olivia said. "He was angry with Hedyle and probably felt like a fool because she'd used him."

"We don't know that," Elsie said. "He was there right before the fight broke out and gone right after. But I can't swear that I saw him kill anybody."

I agreed with her as I sipped my pink champagne. "I didn't see him kill Hedyle. I suppose his actions—leaving right after it was over—make him look guilty. But I don't think Drago would kill her that way. He doesn't need a knife."

Dorothy shivered. "What does that mean?"

"It means that your father has powerful outsider magic. Dragon magic. So do you." I smiled at her. "It means that he could have killed Hedyle with just his magic. Someday you might be that powerful. That's why it's important for you to learn control now."

"I'm sorry about Hedyle," Dorothy said. "But I didn't kill her. I would never kill someone."

"The only way you know that, honey," Olivia said, "is if you steel yourself not to let it happen. That's why I wanted you to grow up away from your father. I didn't want that life for you."

"So he's killed people before," Dorothy surmised. "And he probably killed Hedyle."

"We don't know that," Brian added. "Let's not put the blame on someone else the way they tried to put it on us."

She smiled and kissed his cheek. "You're right. Maybe I'll see him again and ask."

"But if you don't think Drago killed Hedyle," Elsie said, "who else could've done it?"

"I hope we don't have enough time to find out." I grinned at my friends. "I can't wait to get out of here."

CHAPTER 41

We only had about twenty minutes to go before the doors would open. We'd gone back to our rooms and picked up what few things of our own were there.

"Can we keep the spell book?" Elsie asked.

"We can," I said. "Even though the council didn't officially rule on whether or not it could stay out of the library, it's out now with Abdon's help. I think I should return Makaleigh's book. It's not ours. I'll be right back."

"Do you think you should go alone?" Elsie asked.

"I'll be fine. Not even Drago wants to mess around with the Bone Man."

Elsie giggled. "I'd like to see that fight actually—Drago vs. the Bone Man. Sounds like a thriller, doesn't it?"

"Oh, go on, Molly," Olivia said. "I want to be out that door the minute it opens."

I smiled and left Olivia and Elsie together as they argued the merits of a fight between the Bone Man of Oak Island and Drago. I followed the hall and came to the outside of the library. There was so much in there yet that I would have loved to explore. The chances were they'd never invite me back again, and if they did, I wasn't sure I'd go.

Sylvia Rose Gold was at the front desk. She glared at me when I gave her Makaleigh's book. "And the spell book? Where is that?"

"The spell book belongs to us and our families. It's not coming back here again. And I hope if I find out you were to blame for it being here in the first place that I won't hurt you. I can't think why anyone took it from us."

"It was stolen." She sniffed. "You said so yourself. Books that contain witchcraft will always find their way back to the library where they belong. What would've happened if a non–magic user had found it and tried some of the spells? Disaster. That's what would have happened."

I leaned closer to her and felt my amulet glowing. "Times are changing. Be sure that you don't get rolled over by them."

She sniffed again, trying to appear as though what I'd said didn't matter. But her glasses fell on the floor and she hit her head on the desk getting them. I added a few dozen books that had been on the desk to the pile on the floor. She got a few good lumps before it was all over.

Leaving with a satisfied smile on my face, I nearly ran into the witchfinder as I went out the door. "Antonio."

"Molly." He took my hand and kissed it. "I was hoping to see you before Abdon put me back in the wall. I still have a few precious moments while the remaining council bickers and fights about what happened and what they should do."

"What will they do?" I asked, sitting beside him in a shadowed window seat.

"Find new members to keep the council going." He shrugged. "This has happened before and doubtless will happen again."

"Maybe you should leave now before they notice," I

suggested. "In my eyes you've paid your dues. When the door opens, leave the castle before they trap you again."

"You are a dear, kindhearted woman." He smiled and took my hand again. "They have given me part of each of their magic. They did this with the idea that I could do what needed to be done without their interference or possible hope of stopping me."

His hands were cold, and that shouldn't have impacted me. Yet I shivered near him when I looked into his icy dead eyes. Suddenly, I knew the truth. "You killed Hedyle, didn't you?"

A pause. Maybe a minute or two in the quiet hall. No one was interested in the library when it was so close to escaping from the castle. We were completely alone.

"Yes. I killed her." He bent his head but not before I saw the triumph in his eyes. "It was the only way I could be truly free. As long as she held the council magic and could decide my fate, there was no way out of the castle for me."

"So you decided to take advantage of the situation."

There was no response, but I had my answer.

He got slowly to his feet, joints cracking. "I am fortunate to have met you, Molly Renard. I shall always cherish that memory."

"The words of power." I stopped him. "What did they really mean?"

"They were words for the runes that trapped me in the castle wall. They are no longer viable with Hedyle's death. Only she and Makaleigh had worked them through."

"So it was a call for help from her." I stared up at him. "She wanted to make sure we knew to summon you to solve the murder and then put you back again."

"Yes. And that idea was done intentionally by Hedyle herself." He smiled at me grimly. "Now I take my leave. I wonder what the world is like now."

I tasted the three words on my lips. With Hedyle and Makaleigh gone, they had no power. They were only three simple words. At one time they had held a killer in the castle so that the council could use him however they saw fit as punishment for his terrible crimes.

A loud chime from the inner workings of the castle told me the magic that had held us all there was over. We could leave anytime—and so could Antonio.

He was already gone as I got to my feet. Should I bother telling Abdon or someone else on the council? There was nothing they could do to get him back. Someday when things had calmed down, they'd recall that they hadn't put their genie back where he belonged.

Dozens of excited witches came toward me. I made room for them to escape the prison that had been created for us. I made my way back to our room and joined my friends to go.

But there was another surprise waiting for me before we could depart.

Abdon was joined by Arleigh Burke at the bottom of the stone stairs. I saw them there as we left the upper floors accompanied by dozens more witches who were eager to reach the front door.

"If we might have a moment," Abdon said in a polite voice. He almost had a smile on his face.

"Please," Arleigh added. "You are free to leave when we're finished."

We stepped off the stairs and followed them to an empty alcove. Things looked dingy and empty now that the party was over. Brian's large pile of gifts was still in one corner, never opened.

"I'm not leaving here without you," Elsie said, sticking close to me as we walked toward the council members.

"Me either." Olivia's voice was mostly captured by the silver in Dorothy's bracelet again. We were trying not to make a fuss on our way out.

"That's it for us too," Brian added with Dorothy's hand in his.

"All right." I smiled at them. "Let's see what they want."

Arleigh broke the silence once we were all gathered around. "Molly, because you have shown to be a witch worth remembering, and because of the excellent family line you come from, on behalf of the Grand Council of Witches, I ask that you take Hedyle's seat at the council table."

Elsie's mouth dropped open. "Oh my stars!"

"Oh, Molly!" Dorothy said.

Abdon smiled in a way people do when they know they are offering you something extraordinary that you can't possibly pass up. It's a mixture of pride and sure knowledge that this is what you will do.

"Of course you'll be joining Brian on the council with the rest of us. We haven't yet decided on someone to take Bairne's place for his part in this plot, but that will be one of the first things up for discussion at the next council meeting," he said.

"Think of all the good you can do on the council," Arleigh added. "You and Brian can make a big difference in every witch's life."

"You have only to accept for now," Abdon said. "The rest will come later after we've all had a chance to grieve and catch up with ourselves again."

Everyone was staring at me. My heart was pounding and my hands shook. I knew what my answer was, but I was dreading saying it aloud.

"I appreciate the offer," I said, "but I'm truly not council material."

Brian grinned at Elsie, and they slapped hands.

"What are you talking about?" Arleigh demanded. "You come from a wonderful family of witches. You are young compared to most of us. You're exactly what we need."

"I'm not convinced witches need a council at all." I spoke

my mind. When would there be a better time? "People fear you and hide their lives from you. I can't think of a single thing that the council has done to make my life better."

"You're at least safer," Abdon snarled. "Who do you think protects witches from the dangers around them?"

"We protect ourselves. I'm sorry, but I don't want to be part of a group that isn't needed." I glanced at Brian. "I'm sure he'll do more than enough for both of us."

"Wait." He glanced around. "What? I'm not going to be on the council. I was only going along with all that until we could get out of the castle. You guys know me. Am I a council person?"

"Brian!" Abdon yelled, making departing guests look back at us.

"Sorry. But my dad would really enjoy being part of the council," Brian told them. "I'm with Molly. The council has never done a thing for me. Maybe you need to take stock and revamp what the council actually is. Until then, I don't want anything to do with it."

"I think that means we can go," Elsie said triumphantly. "I need to see my honey-bunny. And we have witches to train."

Arleigh appeared angry and uncertain. Abdon was just angry as we gathered ourselves and our spell book and left the castle.

"Oscar," Brian said to him as we walked by him on the castle steps. "Can you send those birthday presents to my apartment?"

"Of course." The manager smiled as he held the door for me and Elsie. "I hope you enjoyed your party."

"Yeah. About that—let's plan something small next year, huh?" Brian grinned as he got in the car.

"With pleasure."

CHAPTER 42

We were in the cave beneath Smuggler's Arcane the next day. We'd all gone home and changed clothes then tried to put our lives back in order after the long party.

I was showing Brian and Dorothy how to use scrying as a way of looking for things and people. They would always be handicapped by not being water witches, but they both had strong magic and would do well at anything they decided to accomplish.

"What about accusing Hedyle of fighting with Makaleigh over a man?" Elsie demanded as we continued going over everything that had happened to us.

"It was just a guess," I replied. "What else could happen between two women that couldn't be forgiven? And Drago had told us that he'd been asked to join the witches' council before being tossed aside as they grew in strength. It just made sense to me."

"Lucky guess!" Elsie slapped her thigh. "And good

theater with Olivia! I think we could have figured it all out if we'd been able to get Bairne's real fingerprints."

"I don't know if it would have mattered, but I agree."

The water in the crystal bowl I used for scrying began to form images. Brian and Dorothy glanced into it.

"What's that?" Brian asked.

"It looks like a cat to me," Elsie said. Olivia agreed with her.

"You didn't get me another cat, did you?" Brian asked Dorothy.

"I did," she admitted. "But this one is different. Now that I know about shifters pretending to be cats, that won't happen to me again."

She brought a small carrier down from the shop and handed it to him. "Happy birthday. Don't ever ask me to your party again."

He laughed. "I won't. So what is this one's name?"

"You'll have to hold her and find out."

Brian took the small black-and-white cat out of the carrier and stared into her pretty blue eyes. "Hey! She says her name is Laue. Awesome! Is she going to try to kill me now?"

Dorothy tried to take the cat from him, but she scratched her just like Kalyna had.

"Oh no. I think this is where I came in," Elsie complained. "I'm going upstairs for tea, and maybe a chocolate cake."

"I would think you'd have had enough sweets at the party." Olivia preceded her up the stairs.

"You're just jealous that you can't have them anymore," Elsie accused.

"It's good to have a svelte figure as a ghost," Olivia said. "I noticed Drago and Oscar staring at me."

It was good to be home.